"The only way to get over your fear is to meet it."

"I'm not afraid. I just don't know what to expect," Carrie said.

"Hold on." Adam strode to the office and reemerged with his hands full.

She frowned. "Baby carrots and cut-up apples?"

"Treats." He dropped a few carrots in her hand. "Just let the horse smell them and she'll take it from there."

"I don't know."

He held out the apple pieces. When Maggie devoured them, he turned toward Carrie. "Like I said, Maggie knows what to do."

A bit tentatively, Carrie approached, holding out her hand. Adam nudged her a little closer. Maggie did the rest.

Carrie pulled her hand back. "Oh, wow. That tickles." She smiled at him and his chest constricted. "Can I try it again?"

He handed her a few more carrots. She approached the horse and laughed when Maggie took the snack.

"Before you know it, you'll be a pro," he predicted.

"I'm really not sure small-town life is for me..."

Dear Reader,

Small town or big city?

Sometimes a move is necessary for a job. Or perhaps it's simply for a change of scenery. There are always decisions to make when deciding the next steps in life. But when you throw in a chance at true love? Everything changes.

I grew up in a small town. I have fond memories of the place that formed me into the person I am today, like being able to walk down the street to my friend's house while waving to longtime neighbors along the way.

When I got older, I moved to the suburbs outside a big city. The more densely populated area had its pluses as well—better access to the theater and sporting events, along with festivals and concerts. There's an energy in a city that you can't find anywhere else.

Now I live in a great location with a little bit of both. I'm outside a major city, but far enough away where the town I live in has that small-town vibe. To me, it's the best of both worlds.

Adam Wright lived the big-city life but chose to come home to the small mountain town where he grew up. Carrie Mitchell was raised in Manhattan, only to end up on her best friend's doorstep in Golden. As Adam and Carrie are drawn closer, will the lure of new opportunities send them in different directions?

I hope you enjoy their journey.

Tara

HEARTWARMING

His Small Town Dream

——

Tara Randel

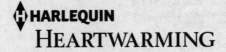

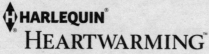

ISBN-13: 978-1-335-58464-9

His Small Town Dream

Copyright © 2022 by Tara Spicer

Recycling programs for this product may not exist in your area.

Harlequin Enterprises ULC
22 Adelaide St. West, 41st Floor
Toronto, Ontario M5H 4E3, Canada
www.Harlequin.com

Printed in U.S.A.

Tara Randel is an award-winning *USA TODAY* bestselling author. Family values, a bit of mystery and, of course, love and romance are her favorite themes, because she believes love is the greatest gift of all. Tara lives on the west coast of Florida, where gorgeous sunsets and beautiful weather inspire the creation of heartwarming stories. This is her tenth book for Harlequin Heartwarming. Visit Tara at tararandel.com. Like her on Facebook at Tara Randel Books.

Books by Tara Randel

Harlequin Heartwarming

The Golden Matchmakers Club

Stealing Her Best Friend's Heart
Her Christmastime Family

Meet Me at the Altar

Always the One
Trusting Her Heart
His Honor, Her Family
The Lawman's Secret Vow

Visit the Author Profile page
at Harlequin.com for more titles.

To my buddies in the Zone class at the gym. Thanks for your encouragement and pushing me to my limits.

CHAPTER ONE

CARRIE MITCHELL GLANCED at her watch as she headed toward the only decent coffee shop in Golden, Georgia. Living here was a far cry from the frenetic energy she'd navigated daily in Manhattan, but the town was growing on her. Not enough to keep her from her goal of returning to the corporate world in a big city, but for now, it served her purposes. Kept her busy. Gave her fresh insight that she would add to her arsenal of creative ideas.

As she crossed Main Street, Sit A Spell Coffee Shop came into view. It was nice to have *that* place, a location where she could greet her neighbors or sit at one of the outdoor bistro tables and enjoy some alone time. Sit A Spell had become her haven of sorts since arriving in Golden eight months earlier. She'd never had a special spot back home. Any shop would do as she hustled to the office. But here, the small mountain town grounded her. Made her appreciate her surroundings, something she'd lost sight of in the big city she'd grown up in.

Drawing closer to her destination, Carrie smiled as she inhaled the aroma of freshly ground coffee beans. The regular line had already formed outside. She recognized the retired judge, a group of women from the community center and… Her smile faded. Adam Wright.

Her steps slowed. He was here.

Again.

When she'd started her job at the Golden Chamber of Commerce four months ago, she'd taken to walking to work. She only lived a few blocks up Main Street, sharing an apartment with her friend Serena above Serena's stationery shop, Blue Ridge Cottage. Serena was the reason she'd landed in Golden after everything that had happened in New York. She'd needed a friendly face and a shoulder to cry on while she tried to regroup.

Initially, the walk was her way of fitting in, to interact with residents and let them get to know her. Folks had been a bit wary when the city girl rolled into town. She needed to visit with the shop owners of Golden for work, and she'd tried hard both to advocate for the business owners and to get them to accept her. She had good marketing strategies to promote

Golden, so she was finally breaking down walls. While it had taken some time to be accepted, the fact that Serena was her best friend had helped her make connections.

Adam Wright was another story.

Not that he shouldn't get coffee from the same shop as her or even that she didn't like to see him here. But his presence threw her off. Why, she didn't have a clue. He wasn't grouchy or difficult. He didn't dominate a conversation so you couldn't get a word in. In fact, he was on the quiet side. So they always made small talk. And for some reason, every time they were in each other's company, she walked away wanting more.

They'd randomly run into each other at Sit A Spell before rushing to their respective jobs, and it had soon become a ritual of sorts. It just happened that they arrived like clockwork at eight thirty, lining up behind other folks who knew this was the place to get their caffeine fix. She stood directly behind the man who made her antsy, wondering if she should say hello to let him know she was there. Instead, she pulled up an email on her phone to read over the bullet points before the meeting taking place in fifteen minutes. She sighed.

"In a hurry?" Came a deep male voice.

She glanced up, locking eyes with Adam. "I've got a meeting first thing."

He nodded but didn't say anything more.

After arriving in Golden, Carrie had first met Adam through mutual friends. He wasn't outgoing but he spent time with Serena and her group. She could count the facts she knew about him on one hand: he co-owned Deep North Adventures, a family business, volunteered in Golden activities and was highly regarded by the business community. And Carrie had sensed his walls soon after they'd started their morning chats.

Those chats were usually about light, generic topics. Town events, mutual friends, an upcoming wedding. Once, they'd had an interesting conversation about the challenges of operating a business in a small town and she was impressed by his acumen. She'd wanted to hear more, but the line moved quickly that day and their time had run out. Maybe today she'd learn more about what made Adam tick.

"I wanted to thank you," he said, turning back around.

She arched an eyebrow as she went over a mental list of reasons why that might be.

"You're welcome?"

His chuckle was warm and inviting. "For

the initiative the Chamber launched last month. I can tell it's already paying off."

"The Vacation Forum?"

"That's the one. The business owners are still buzzing about it."

She couldn't hold back her grin.

From her first day on the job, she'd taken every challenge thrown her way. Had handled each project successfully for the Chamber. A big difference from when she'd arrived devastated on Serena Stanhope's doorstep, hoping her best friend would let her stay for a while. Despite the one mark on her work history, landing the job at the Chamber had boosted her lagging confidence, and, so had advocating for the community. Her marketing experience was finally being noticed and appreciated.

And this job was important to her future outside of Golden, too. On her road back to corporate America in a big city. New York, to be exact, but after all that had happened in the last year, she wasn't about to get ahead of herself. Slow, steady, aiming for the prize.

She pulled herself from her musings. "I'm happy to hear that," she said to Adam. "My job is to make Golden a major vacation destination."

"I agree that's a good mission, to a degree."

She tried not to get her back up. "In what way is it not?" First praise, followed by a complaint? Not someone else disappointed in her.

"Golden is becoming a sought-after mountain getaway. And we want tourists, but we're also residents. Everyone helps each other, looks out for each other. To me, that's the mark of a successful community."

"So my proposal was a hit, but not a hit?"

He chuckled again. "You got the merchants together, gave us some well-thought-out strategies to increase tourism. But—"

"Please, not a but," she groaned.

"A good but," he continued. "You also took into consideration that while the business owners need tourist traffic, they also love Golden. That if we never welcomed another visitor, we still have each other. You included that vision in your presentation, creating opportunities while maintaining the small-town charm. Can't have charm without interesting people."

Genuinely grateful, she said, "You're welcome."

Adam nodded and turned when the line moved forward. She gazed at the cotton shirt stretching across his broad shoulders and basked in his thoughtful comments. Her first big marketing initiative had worked. Was it going to be smooth sailing ahead?

She glanced back at her phone to review the agenda email. There'd been a last-minute change in the schedule, which had thrown her off. She wasn't a fan of last minute, although she could scramble with short notice, but Carrie's boss was *very* last minute. In fact, Carrie'd had to improvise at the last few meetings they'd conducted with local business groups.

Adam turned around again.

"I'm looking forward to seeing what you come up with next."

She blinked. This was the most in-depth conversation they'd had yet.

"Whatever we decide in this meeting, you'll hear about it eventually."

"Then let's hope this line goes faster so you can keep that promise."

She peered around him. "What's the holdup?"

"Something about a new coffee maker. Apparently the Hopkinses haven't quite mastered it."

"I thought the way they did things before was working."

"Me, too, but progress happens whether we like it or not."

"I suppose we could always get what passes for coffee at Frieda's Bakery."

His hand flew to his heart. "Traitor."

She laughed. She didn't know Adam well, but this was the most animated she'd seen him. Most of her new friends in town were open books. She'd felt comfortable in their company right away. Adam? He was reserved, but there was something about him that caught her attention. Had from day one. She couldn't quite put her finger on it, but his reserve piqued her curiosity.

She smiled because Adam was smiling. "I'll stick with the bakery for their awesome treats and Sit A Spell for the coffee."

"Who wouldn't?"

"I can be as patient as the next person, but the clock is ticking," she announced.

"Admirable quality," he said, turning again.

They all took another step forward.

A few cars motored by, signaling the start of another busy day. The multihued snapdragons planted in bright red pots gave the sidewalk a pop of color. On the next block, she could see Serena opening the doors of her stationery shop.

Carrie had to admit, Golden was totally unlike Manhattan. There wasn't the thick traffic to contend with on this Wednesday morning, the constant honking of horns and the mass migration of pedestrians at crossroads. The sidewalks might not be shoulder to shoulder with people hustling to work or wherever else beckoned them, but the tourists who did roam Golden were pleasant, and happy to spend their dollars at the many shops and restaurants located up and down the six blocks of tree-lined Main Street. Carrie's job was to highlight Golden not only as a great vacation destination, but a potential place to open a successful business. She had a ton of ideas, and great local owners, to work with.

The North Georgia mountain town featured lots of charm to promote. Old-fashioned, cast-iron lampposts with hanging planters featured black-eyed Susans. Brightly painted buildings housed charming shops. Beyond that, a range of outdoor activities that drew the adventurous types. Beautiful sights that ran from winding forests trails, splashing waterfalls, and a blue, sparkling lake, calling to those who loved boating and fishing.

A marketing dream come true. And Carrie intended to market the heck out of Golden in order to get back to those busy streets of Manhattan. To show her father that despite a hiccup in her career, she had what it took to make it in the corporate world.

She glanced at her watch again. The line moved a step. She blew out an audible breath.

"Where's that patience?" Adam asked over his shoulder.

"Slowly being whittled away."

He spun on his heel to face her and again she couldn't help but notice that Adam was a very attractive man. With thick, russet brown hair cut short on the sides and longer on top, steel gray eyes and very tanned skin proclaiming his love for the outdoors, he cut quite a fine figure. Plus, he had a snappy intelligence she found fascinating.

Wearing a button-down shirt, pressed Dockers and a great pair of shoes, he gave off an air of roguish gentleman. Because of him she'd upped her clothing game, which had wilted after arriving in Golden. Now she was back to corporate casual, today wearing a flirty blouse, pencil skirt and heels.

From the town grapevine, she'd heard that Adam had returned to Golden a year ago to run the family business so his parents could retire and head out on the open road in the RV of their dreams. Colin, Adam's brother, led most of the outdoor tours while Adam manned the financial side of the company.

But that was the extent of what she knew. It was as if he held a part of himself back. Despite his good looks and invisible boundaries, she could imagine most single women in Golden would happily go on a date with him.

Not Carrie.

No sirree.

Not when she had the goal of getting her life back on track.

"You okay?" he asked.

A gust of wind rustled her shoulder-length hair. It was the middle of July and the temperatures had risen, even up here in the mountains. She brushed a few strands from her cheek. "Just wondering how long this line will take."

He stepped to the right and swept his arm forward, saying, "Please, go ahead of me. I'm not in a hurry."

She blinked in surprise. "Are you sure?"

"Yes."

The line moved. She took his place, wondering why her stomach did a funny little flip at his generosity. Before she knew it, she was in the shop, placing her order.

"Sorry about the holdup." Myrna Hopkins, the shop owner, couldn't disguise her flustered state. "New equipment."

"Take your time." Carrie might be in a rush, but she wouldn't add to Myrna's stress.

Soon, a cup slid over the counter in Carrie's

direction. Carrie tucked a few extra dollars in the tip jar. She'd worked as a server briefly in college. She knew how tough it could be.

When she moved away from the counter, Adam was placing his order. She held up her cup and said, "Thanks for the upgrade in line."

"You do a great job here in Golden," Adam said. "It's the least I can do."

"All these compliments. I don't know what to say."

He grinned, showing off dimples. "Keep Golden on the right road and who knows, we might find more to talk about."

"Are we becoming…friends?"

"Seems like it's about time."

Myrna handed Adam his coffee. He took it with a thanks, then they walked outside into the bright morning sun. Carrie moved to stand in the shade of a leafy tree.

"I enjoy when we start the day together," he said. "Maybe we can branch out beyond Sit A Spell."

She toyed with the cup lid. Adam didn't know much about her past. What really brought her here to Golden. Having a clean slate might be nice.

"You're really serious?"

"I am."

Hmm. Their daily interaction was one thing, but to kick it up a notch? Her prior dating life had been dismal. Any guy she got close to serious with didn't understand why she was so career-driven. Why she didn't have fun.

Maybe this wasn't a half-bad idea.

"So we could talk about improving Golden?" she asked.

"If that's what you're interested in."

She wanted to get back to the corporate world, not put down roots, but in the short term...

"Well, then, the next time I see you at Smitty's Pub, I'll be sure to come up with a riveting topic that we can discuss for longer than it takes to order a cup of coffee."

At his relieved smile, she added, "I really need to run. So we'll talk again?"

"Right."

A laugh slipped out. "You look like you're ready to walk the plank, not make a new buddy."

A pained expression crossed his face. What brought that on? Now she was more certain than ever. She had to discover what motivated Adam Wright.

"Thanks for considering my request, Carrie."

Not so much consideration as curiosity.

She tossed her hair over her shoulder. "I'm always up for a challenge."

ADAM WATCHED CARRIE hurry away. What had he been thinking to suggest they go out of their way to talk more often? It had to be his brother's nagging. Colin, and his parents, had been sensitive to his heartache when Adam first came home. But now? The gloves were off. They wanted him to start living life to the fullest, but he was more than happy to be alone.

What was a year in the grand scheme of things? Nothing, really. But getting dumped just before your wedding seemed to stick with a man, so yeah, he wasn't ready for another romance.

He pondered it as he walked to his car. Carrie reminded him of what he'd had, lost and would never go after again. Living in a big city, pursuing a career in high finance, had become his worst nightmare. He thanked his lucky stars every day that he'd come back to Golden. A place that kept him grounded. Deep North Adventures wasn't Wall Street, but it also didn't devour his energy every second of the day. In Golden, he could breathe like he never had in New York.

So, why had he been hustling to meet the

ex-New Yorker when he should be avoiding anything related to his time there? A question he had a difficult time answering, especially when greeted by Carrie's infectious smile every morning.

He hadn't told many people what had happened when he lived in New York, and he liked it that way. Only his family, who kept mum at his request. At least, he hoped they did. He wasn't so sure about his aunt Bunny, but no one brought up that disastrous period to his face. He didn't want constant prying by well-meaning townsfolk who had known him since he was a child. Guess that was part of the give-and-take in a small town. Everyone knew you, mistakes and all. Unless you moved away and kept said blunders a mystery.

He reached his luxury car, the only nod to his past life he'd kept, and drove two miles out of town to the office. He chuckled as he pictured Carrie's surprise when he'd given up his place in line. Maybe Colin had a point. He was rusty with women, for sure.

After a curve in the mountain road, he stepped off the accelerator and turned into a parking lot. Colin's truck was already there. Unusual, his younger brother beating him to work.

Savoring the bright sun on his face, Adam crossed the lot, the crunch of crushed gravel under his shoes, and opened the door to Deep North Adventures. It was eerily quiet inside. He moved down the short hallway that opened to a spacious gathering room scattered with couches, chairs and tables. His parents had always wanted the business to feel like home to their customers.

When he came back to town, Adam had added a retail section, taking advantage of folks wanting a souvenir from their time in Golden. Shirts, hoodies, hats and water bottles, featuring the store logo, to name a few of the available items. They also now had a small snack bar for those who needed a nibble before or after their outdoor trek.

There was the main counter where tourists checked in or made appointments. Down another small hallway on the opposite side of the room were two offices used by Adam and his brother. He stopped at Colin's door and rested his shoulder against the jamb.

Colin glanced up and grinned. "Hey, bro. Get your morning fix?"

"My coffee, yes."

His smile grew. "If you say so."

Ever since Colin found out Adam went to the coffee shop and ran into Carrie, he'd been pushing Adam to get out of his comfort zone.

"I say so." Adam stepped further inside. "You're here early. The first tour isn't until ten."

"Spoke to Mom last night. She and Dad are checking in on a video call this morning, so I thought I'd get here beforehand and finish up some paperwork."

His mother had also called Adam, vague but insistent that they have a family conference call at nine.

"What's up with them?"

Colin shrugged. "Maybe they want a business update."

"I send them a progress report every month."

"Then maybe they found a new place to settle down."

Definitely not. "All they've talked about for years is seeing the country. Doesn't sound right." They wanted to travel, yes, but once the traveling bug was out of their systems, they'd return to Golden.

Colin tossed a piece of paper onto the desk, which was already scattered with schedules and invoices. "Look, I'm not a mind reader. We'll know when they call."

Someone was in a mood. "Sorry to disturb you."

Colin sighed. "It's not you." He waved his hand over the desk. "It's all this."

"I told you I'd manage it."

"You have enough to do."

Actually, he didn't. Deep North Adventures ran smoothly after the systems he'd put into place. What he needed was a new project to sink his teeth into, but he knew better than to push his stubborn brother.

"If you change your mind…"

He left Colin to rub his temples as he viewed the workload piled up before him.

Adam returned to the main room, switching on lights as he went. His employees would arrive soon. Jocelyn, a mother of two elementary-school-age kids whose husband was in the military, took care of administrative work at the front desk. Brea, the magenta-haired twentysomething with a pierced eyebrow, ran the snack bar.

He walked behind the desk, placed his coffee cup on the counter and booted up the computer, pulling up the day's timetable. Three big tours today. Zip-lining, a river tubing trip for a large group and a twilight hike up to Bailey's Point with a local seniors' group. Colin would handle the first two, while Adam led the hike. He might spend most of his time in the office, but he escaped to the outdoors any chance he could. Hiking during the summer, inhaling the scents of straw pine and damp earth while walking through the dense summer foliage, was just what he needed to ease his restlessness.

He was making notes for Jocelyn when he heard Colin call his name. Upon reentering his brother's office, he saw that Colin had angled the screen of his computer with a webcam so they could both view their folks.

"Hey, Mom and Dad," Colin greeted them. "Still enjoying life on the road?"

"We have a house on wheels," his father deadpanned. "It doesn't get any better than this."

They looked good. Seeing his father's broad smile made Adam relax. His dad brushed at his thinning hair when it lifted in a breeze. His mother, her dark hair streaked with gray, smiled at them, her eyes sparkling from behind her glasses.

"I always knew you were a hot-rodder," Colin said.

"Stop," their mother cut in. "We're having the time of our lives. Is your brother there?"

"I'm here, Mom," Adam said as he took a seat beside Colin.

"Then let us get right to the point."

"No small talk?" Colin asked. "No asking about our health? If we're eating properly? Dating?"

Their mother jumped right in. "Are you dating? Who's dating?"

"Guess she doesn't care about our health," Colin joked.

"Of course I do, but the idea of one or both of you settling down is always on my mind."

"You had to bring it up," Adam muttered.

"Like we can stop her from worrying."

"I can hear you," their mother said.

"Listen to your mother," their father said as he motioned to his wife to move ahead.

Adam and Colin exchanged glances. Sandy Wright was about as even-keeled as a person could be. She'd always been the behind-the-scenes force while Beck, their father, had been the people pleaser. Their time on the road hadn't changed things.

"This is important because it affects us all," she went on to say.

"I know that. The boys don't," their dad added.

"What's going on, Mom?" Adam interrupted his parents, who'd banter on and on as if they'd forgotten the reason for setting up this call.

"Right. I might as well get to the point," Sandy said, then took an audible breath.

Adam sighed. "You already said that, Mom."

"She's working herself up, boys," their father warned, trying to lighten the mood. "Get ready."

"Beck, I swear—"

Adam put a little heat in his voice. "Mom?"

She faced her screen, squared her shoulders and blurted, "We've been approached with an offer to buy the business."

Silence filled the room as Adam's glance flew to his brother's. Colin's surprise matched his own.

"Someone wants to buy Deep North Adventures?" Adam choked out once he found his voice.

"Yes. It's an outdoor company similar to ours, based in Colorado. They want to expand and establish a presence in the East. Aiming High Sporting Goods and Adventures."

Colin whistled. That company was huge.

Immediately, Adam's mind whirled. Why now? Why Deep North Adventures? There were any number of companies in the state. He couldn't explain it, but his gut didn't like this at all.

"Can you give us a little more information?" he asked.

"Sure," his mother said. "I'm still getting over the shock of them reaching out."

"About that," Colin said. "When did they reach out?"

"A day ago. Their CEO, Mr. Fletcher, called. Seems they've been searching for a company to merge with. A company that has already made a name. He came across us and did his research, then called me to talk about it."

Odd. Why didn't Fletcher approach Adam? He ran the business while his parents were gone. And how would this guy have gotten his mother's private number? While his mom relayed the highlights of the conversation, he did his own search on his smartphone.

"The proposal is nothing to shy away from," their mother said.

When she mentioned the high number, Adam's diaphragm squeezed tight. Colin coughed, then pounded on his chest.

"What did you tell him?" Adam asked.

"Nothing, really. That I appreciated his interest. That I'd have to discuss this with the other owners of the company."

Except this wasn't usual. Or normal operating procedure. No one had asked to buy their business before. Nor had the Wrights expected anyone to come forward because they weren't considering selling.

"What do you think, Adam?" His father's booming voice filled the room.

"I don't think anything right now. I need

to know more, see numbers and what kind of deal he's proposing. A whole host of variables apply here, Dad."

"That's what I thought."

"Mom?"

She blinked, looking uncharacteristically unsure. "It is a surprise, but…"

Adam's eyes went wide at her hesitation. His mother had always loved the business she'd started from the ground up. Even if the money was substantial, he couldn't imagine what could persuade her to sell.

"I agree with you Adam," she said, her tone more pragmatic. "There is much review and discussion to be done before ever considering the offer. It's such a compliment when a major competitor acknowledges the worth you've poured into a family enterprise. And while the idea of selling our baby is—" she paused, as if searching for the right words "—exciting and sad, I can see it benefiting you boys."

Adam saw his confusion mirrored on Colin's face.

"How do you mean, Mom?"

"Colin's furniture designs are taking off. It's not just a hobby anymore."

True. What had started as a way for Colin to indulge his creative side had gotten people taking notice of the unusual furniture he hand-built and sold. He'd always been artistic, starting with whittling when he was a kid and leading up to designing his own functional pieces. Due to interest from prospective buyers, he'd taken the step to move beyond featuring his work in a few of the local stores. Adam had set him up with an online shop, taking care of the website and business details. Colin still liked to keep his hand involved in the office side of things, as evidenced by his desktop overflowing with papers, but he went to Adam when he truly needed help. Adam was always happy to lend a hand.

"Mom, yes, the furniture business is going well," Colin agreed. "But I love leading outdoor adventures. Honestly, I'd be lost without it."

She drew in a breath, as if second-guessing her own reasoning. Adam and Colin were usually her biggest supporters. Did she think that would change with a lucrative offer?

"And Adam," she went on to say, the fervor in her argument abating. "You modernized Deep North in ways I never could. I can't tell you how much I've appreciated all your improvements, but surely you want more than running a business in a small mountain town."

Did he? Since returning home he'd been happy to work for the family. He'd grown up in this place, had worked beside his parents since he was a kid and discovered his aptitude for numbers and finance. Once his dreams dissolved, he'd come home, needing connection to the family who loved him. But to start something new? Move on to... What? He hadn't put too much thought into where his life was going. Now he might have no choice.

But he didn't say anything aloud. An odd silence lingered, so unlike their usual family chitchat. Then again, the reason for the call was anything but usual.

"I know this has come completely out of the blue," Sandy said. "Why don't I send you the information Mr. Fletcher emailed to me. See what you can make of it."

Adam nodded, his mind still racing.

Colin answered for him. "We'll be on the lookout for it, Mom."

"Wonderful. Now, I'm sure you're busy—"

"We're going hiking in a few hours," their father cut in. "Old Faithful is waiting to put on a show and we didn't drive all this way to miss out."

"Take pictures," Colin said, indulging their father's new passion. When Adam didn't chime in, Colin poked him in the ribs to get his attention.

"Right. Have a good time."

"We'll talk soon," their father said, his eyes filled with empathy, then signed off.

Adam turned his focus back to the smartphone screen, reading up on the details he'd found during the discussion with his parents. He wasn't sure how much time had passed when Colin asked, "So, what do you think?"

"I'm not sure right now."

"Weird, an offer coming to Mom. We weren't even interested in selling."

The dread building in Adam grew. "Which makes me suspicious."

"My thoughts exactly."

Adam leaned back in the chair and stared at his brother. "We need more information than what Mom will send us."

"Agreed."

He gave Colin a penetrating gaze. "Be totally honest. Would selling be okay with you? In light of your other interests?"

Colin rested his elbows on the desk. "I don't know. I'm trying to process the entire call."

Adam nodded. "Mom's right, though. Your furniture business is taking off."

"It is, although I have mixed feelings about the growth. But to sell this place? I can't even fathom."

Adam was of the same mind. He'd made a career out of analyzing business opportunities, had bought and sold more companies than he could recall, but it had never been personal. Until now.

The side door opened and closed. It was one of their employees. Adam rose and returned the laptop to Colin's desk. "We keep this between us for now," he said.

Colin nodded.

His mind still spinning, he walked out front. Jocelyn sent him a cheery "Good morning."

"You, too," he replied, grabbing the cup of coffee he'd left behind when his parents called. He took a swig and grimaced. Cold.

Catching his expression, she said, "I'll make a pot," then moved to the snack area.

Adam went to the sink and poured out the dregs before tossing the cup away. He moved past the floor-to-ceiling windows spanning the front of the building, noticing a few cars driving by. Locals off to work, most likely. Once behind the counter, he stared blindly at the computer screen.

He wondered how Carrie's meeting was going. Not that he was particularly fascinated with the inner workings of the local Chamber of Commerce. No, more to take his mind off the pressing question that wouldn't leave him alone. A question that had been niggling at him since he moved back to Golden.

If he didn't have Deep North to manage, what would he do?

CHAPTER TWO

CARRIE HAD FIVE minutes to spare until the meeting started. She dashed into the Chamber of Commerce building and to her shadowy office—only a tiny window, thank you very much—and retrieved the file with her notes, and her phone so she could quickly prepare. Taking a moment to breathe, she had a final sip of coffee—thinking of Adam's generosity as she did—then smoothed her skirt, tossed her hair over her shoulder and sauntered to the large, sunny room like a calm and composed professional.

Lindsey Fuller, the financial director, sat at the long, dark maple table, spreadsheets fanned out around her. One finger twined the wisps of her short, white-blond pixie cut.

"How long have you been here?" Carrie asked.

Lindsey's head jerked up. "A few hours. When I got Shelia's email, it sent me scrambling, so I came in early. I had intended to finish a report for Carter this morning, so I wanted to get a head start."

Carter Tremaine ran the executive board of the Golden Chamber of Commerce. He and his wife, Lissy Ann, worked tirelessly to magnify Golden's image as the vacation town to visit in the picturesque Georgia mountains.

Carrie set down her folder. As the manager of business development and marketing, she also had a busy day planned. As usual, Shelia had complicated her schedule. But she wasn't about to complain. She had a job she liked and another experience to add to her résumé once she returned to corporate life.

Carrie picked up her phone to read the email. "There are four bullet points that don't really say a thing."

Shuffling through her papers, Lindsey found the one she was searching for. "Number one: end of summer festival." She glanced at Carrie. "Doesn't she realize it's mid-July? How can we plan anything in such a short time?"

Carrie took a seat opposite Lindsey. "It'll be tricky, but I suppose we could pull it off in the six weeks until school starts again." It was a big ask in a short time period.

Her eyes moved to the next point. "Number two: increase visibility." Carrie set down the phone and blew out a breath. "Visibility of what?"

"Good question." Lindsey grimaced. "I don't know about you, but I didn't take shorthand in business school."

Carrie chuckled.

"Number three: up sales revenue," Lindsey read. She met Carrie's gaze. "For local businesses? We already work on that year round."

"And four: time off." Carrie rubbed her forehead. "Whose time off?"

"Shelia did mention she wanted to travel up north. New Hampshire, I think. Something about a lake." Lindsey made some notes. "I'm surprised she didn't talk to you about that since you used to live in the northeast."

"I'm not that familiar with New Hampshire, but I did have some friends who vacationed there." Carrie brushed her hair behind her ear, loosening her dangly earring from the strands. "But this memo? It's too vague to brainstorm ideas."

"Hopefully Shelia can share more details in the meeting."

Carrie glanced at the wall clock. The operations director was running late. Again. In the past couple of months, Shelia had been fifteen to thirty minutes late two out of three days of the week. Clearly there was something going on, personal or job-related. Carrie wasn't privy to the reason, but it created a low-grade tension in the office.

"Do you think Shelia is all right?" Carrie asked. "She's been distracted lately. It's not like her."

"Not that I've heard, but her husband did retire at the beginning of the year. Maybe they're having to readjust their lifestyle."

"I suppose."

The strain in the office reminded Carrie of the days before she'd been fired from Craigerson and Company. The senior executives had been planning to boot her out and she hadn't suspected a thing. Not until she learned about a client's lies when they complained about her handling of their account. Then, to make matters worse, she discovered a coworker, who happened to be the executives' favorite, had stolen ideas she'd been working on for a different high-profile client. She'd been blindsided when the firm sent her packing. She'd argued her case, showed them proof of her work, but to no avail. At the time, she'd been working on both projects, plus taking additional work the senior executive handed her. Had she missed the signs because she'd overextended herself?

The situation hurt as much today as it had

then. But she was determined to stop second-guessing herself, no matter what it took.

Carrie stood, needing an activity to take her mind off the past. "Since Shelia's running late, I'm going to the break room." She walked to the door, then paused. "Can I get you anything?"

"I'm good," Lindsey answered, focusing on numbers that would have made Carrie's eyes swim.

On the way, the office phone rang. "I'll get it," Carrie yelled, then ducked into the nearest room. Shelia's office. The boss was wary of anyone in her work space, but usually the three of them answered the phone nearest to them.

"Golden Chamber of Commerce."

"Do y'all deliver welcome baskets to new residents?" a voice asked.

"No, I'm afraid not. We work with local businesses."

"Okay, but if I ordered a basket, could you deliver it?"

Carrie took the phone from her ear, held it out to stare at the receiver, then returned to the call.

"I'm afraid not. Perhaps you could call one of the local restaurants, or a church, to help you."

"I thought all y'all's job was to help the people in Golden?"

The question stumped Carrie. "If you'd leave your name, I can look into—"

"Never mind. I was just tryin' to be nice." The caller hung up.

"Good day to you, too," she muttered, then placed the handset in the cradle.

As she did, she noticed printouts with pictures of lakes on the desk. Looked like Shelia really was hoping to take a vacation. Not wanting to be nosy, Carrie left the room. She couldn't help wondering how much vacation time Shelia was entitled to. She'd taken two weeks off right after Carrie started working here, then another week barely a month ago.

Carrie chastised herself. Just because she didn't take vacations didn't mean others couldn't. She'd worked long hours to prove her worth in the corporate world. The idea of taking personal days had been foreign to her—a page out of her father's playbook—until she'd shown up in Golden with free time on her hands. Even while she'd been deciding next steps, she'd worked part-time in her best friend's store.

"Not everyone is a workaholic," she told the empty break room. She found a bagel and returned to the meeting room.

"Do you take vacations?" she asked Lindsey when she returned, taking her seat.

Looking up, her coworker blinked. "At least once or twice a year with long weekends thrown in. I'm of the opinion that you have to get away to recharge."

"Hmm."

"You don't agree?"

"It's not that. I've just never taken time off."

Lindsey's light brows rose over dark blue eyes. "Ever?"

Breaking off a piece of the bagel, Carrie said, "I can't think of a time."

"That's just…sad."

Carrie tried not to be offended. "Not really. I'm committed."

"You can be committed and still have a life."

That just sounded wrong.

Her father's example had been quite the contrary and she'd always followed in his footsteps. Not that her efforts were applauded.

"What about when you were a kid?" Lindsey asked.

Carrie swallowed her bite of bagel. Her chest felt hollow when she replied, "Nothing much. My dad was always at the office. I guess I learned my work ethic from him."

That, and absorbed his criticism.

When her mother had walked out on them, he'd become hard-hearted. More exacting. Carrie hadn't understood the adult dynamics: all she knew was that her mother was gone. So she shadowed her father, striving for a measure of his attention.

When she landed her first job, she'd asked for his advice. He'd said, "Work your way up the ranks. That's the only route to make it in business. Failure is not an option."

She didn't want to admit that she worked as hard as she did in order to gain his approval. Trent Mitchell applied the same expectations at home as he did in the office. That made the whole misunderstanding at her firm worse in his eyes.

Lindsey didn't seem convinced. "Didn't you take family trips? We always hooked up the camper and went on adventures."

What would that look like? Carrie broke off another chunk of bagel but dropped it on the napkin she'd brought to catch crumbs. "My folks got divorced when I was in fifth grade, so no trips, camper or otherwise."

"I'm sorry."

Carrie waved a hand. If only shaking off the lingering hurt was that easy. "It's okay."

"Still, none of your employers insisted you take time off?"

They hadn't. Instead they'd been impressed by her loyalty. Her steadfastness. Her sense of duty.

Until they so easily believed the lies and fired her.

"I took some time off when I got here. Can't say I liked it much."

Lindsey laughed. "And why not?"

"Too much time to think." And dwell on the disappointment etched on her father's face? Not when she was already upset with herself. No, coming to Golden had been a much-needed reprieve, but dreams of returning to New York kept her awake at night. She couldn't go forward until she went back. That was what she told herself when she'd signed the six-month contract to work at the Chamber, giving her time to revamp her résumé and carefully decide her next move.

"Well, you picked the perfect place to settle down. I don't think there's anywhere as beautiful as Golden."

Carrie had to agree.

At first, she hadn't cared about her surroundings, holing up in her friend Serena's apartment. But once Serena coaxed Carrie outside, she'd been intrigued by the small town's charm. She got it, why people settled here. There was a peace she hadn't found anywhere else.

But that peace would have to end at some point. She needed to show her father, and herself, that what happened at her last job was an anomaly. Sure, things had gotten away from her, but she deserved a place in a large company where she could make the most of her marketing skills. If she put her mind to it, she could be as aggressive as the next person.

"If you don't want to get away, you should take a tour with Deep North Adventures," Lindsey suggested. "They have all kinds of outdoor excursions."

"That's a good idea." So far she'd only hiked to Bailey's Point with Serena, huffing and puffing the entire way, and that was to carry her friend's art supplies.

"I would have thought you'd have gone on a day trip with them before now."

Carrie wrinkled her brow. "Really? Why?"

Lindsey stared at her like she was dense. "Because you hang out with Adam."

"I wouldn't say we hang out," she countered, more firmly than warranted. Standing in line to get coffee was a far cry from hanging out.

"I see you two at Sit A Spell every morning when I drive into work."

"We both like coffee," Carrie informed her coworker. Goodness, the claims about the small-town rumor mill were true.

"That's about the height of our socializing. I mean, yes, I do see him from time to time at town events. He's in Serena and Logan's group of friends, so I've been to different functions the same time as him. Waved at him at a wedding we both attended. We run into each other at Smitty's, but never on a hike, or whatever."

When she finished her explanation, she frowned. She saw him more than she thought. And now he'd asked her to spend even more time with him.

Lindsey grinned. "Deep North offers more than whatever. You could zip-line—"

"No way." She cringed at the idea.

"Okay, then how about you go out on the lake?"

Carrie's eyes narrowed in thought. "I suppose that could be fun. My dad and I used to sail when I was young."

Of course he'd turned it into a means to impress his business associates, so Carrie had made herself useful in the hope of earning one of his rare words of appreciation. Just his saying, "Great job, Carrie," would have meant everything to her.

"Nothing like a few hours out on the water to wash your blues away," Lindsey said.

The memories of the times when it was only Carrie and her dad still remained. The boat slicing through the water, the spray from the waves on her cheeks, the wind in her hair. Her father's smile, as if he was really present in the moment. As if he finally loved her.

The snapshot in her mind had faded over time, but never completely went away. How she'd cherished those rare moments with her father until reality intruded.

So, why did she try so hard? Maybe because he was the parent who had stuck around. She owed him.

Lindsey's voice shattered the sad memory. "Ask Adam. I'm sure he'll take you. He's a pretty avid outdoorsman."

That always surprised Carrie. He seemed like he'd be more comfortable in a boardroom than in the woods. Even though he was mum on the topic, she'd heard he'd left that world. But it hadn't left him. They may not be the best of friends, sharing intimate details of their lives, but she'd worked with enough executives to recognize the signs.

"I'll have to ask him," she said, hoping to let it go at that.

A beat passed.

"He is single, you know."

It was all Carrie could do not to roll her eyes. "I'm aware."

Her friends, Serena and Heidi, tried to set her up on a regular basis. She, in turn, reminded them she didn't want to date. It might open her up to rejection, of not feeling good enough, of not being successful no matter how much of herself she poured into a relationship. All the things she had escaped from. Not knowing all that, the girls just grinned at her, sharing the secret smile between two women in love with incredible men. Both were in loving, committed relationships and didn't understand Carrie's reluctance to try her hand at romance.

Still, a day in the wild with Adam? Not the worst idea.

The front door opened and closed. Moments later Shelia marched into the room. Short and on the plump side, with brown hair dyed to within an inch of its life, the fifty-something dropped her tote bag on the table. Her brown eyes flashed. She was late and riled up.

"You got my email?" she barked.

"Yes," Carrie and Lindsey said.

"Good." Shelia withdrew a stack of papers and tossed them on the table. They slid the length, almost falling off the edge. Carrie reached out to grab them.

"I had a meeting with Carter Tremaine last night."

Carrie's mouth opened in surprise. "There was a board meeting?"

"No, he stopped in after you two left. That's why I sent the email."

Carrie pushed the papers back to Shelia. "I think we need a little more context."

Shelia dropped down into a chair and rubbed her forehead like she was fighting a headache.

"Carter wants an end-of-summer spectacular."

Carrie blinked. "We're in the midst of the Summer Gold Celebration now. The merchants have promoted the heck out of it and we've seen a significant increase in tourist traffic."

"Because of that, he wants something to cap it off. Said a big to-do was missing when they ended the celebration last summer." Shelia huffed.

Trying to remain calm, Carrie asked, "Did he mention what he had in mind?"

"He said to ask you to handle it since you're the marketing department."

Tight, but she could do it. She'd been on short deadlines before. "Okay. First I'll need to come up with a concept."

"You have until four today."

Her stomach dipped. "Come again?"

"Carter was clear."

Carrie was good, but was she that good? Especially since she'd only lived here a short time. She was still trying to fit into the community. She didn't know all the history or what kinds of celebrations were popular.

"I'll get on it right away," she told her boss.

Shelia nodded. "Let's hit the other points."

Next up: visibility. It turned out Shelia meant an initiative to get local businesses and civic organizations to work together to increase tourism. Shelia narrowed in on Carrie again.

"Carter mentioned the proposal you suggested for the print campaign. *Discover Golden!* I believe you called it? He thought it might be too much at the time, but has given the go-ahead now. I'll need a report on the details."

Carrie nodded.

One of her first projects for the Chamber had been coming up with an idea to feature local merchants in an ad sweep geared toward major cities, highlighting the advantages of relocating to a vacation town, promoted by the business owners who had taken the gamble and found success in a smaller market. After she put hours into the proposal, Carter had been on the fence. Seemed that fence had come down.

While Shelia and Lindsey discussed finances, Carrie tuned out, doodling ideas on a notepad.

Now that *Discover Golden!* was a go, she thought about talking to Adam. He'd opened the door, hadn't he? Since he'd come back to run the family company, he had relationships with most of the store and restaurant owners in Golden. From the little they'd talked about his previous experience, Carrie gleaned that Adam had a keen insight into the community. She was impressed with his understanding of small business needs and how that could help Golden as a whole.

But going to him for advice felt like something a couple would do, like chatting about their day after long hours at work or bouncing ideas off each other. She wasn't exactly sure how to label their relationship, except for their morning routine. Did that constitute a relationship? And why was she trying to hash out her circumstances with Adam when she had two projects to start?

"And finally…"

Looking up, Carrie gulped at the sheepish expression crossing Shelia's face. "I may be taking some time off."

Carrie and Lindsey exchanged glances across the table.

"I know it's sudden. I'll give you the details when I have the dates nailed down."

At the don't-question-me tone of her voice, Carrie bit the inside of her cheek.

Shelia collected her things and breezed out of the room.

"Okay, then," Carrie muttered.

Lindsey smiled. "That wasn't as bad as I thought it would be."

"Are you kidding?" Carrie's voice rose. "We have to come up with a summer splash."

"No. *You* have to come up with a summer splash."

Her stomach cramped like it always did when she contemplated failure. "Any off-the-cuff ideas?"

Lindsey thought for a moment. "This is kind of hokey, but there's a traveling Wild West show scheduled for the end of August. They've come to Golden once or twice. Maybe they could help."

"Wild West? Like a rodeo?"

"A scaled-down version."

What did she know about rodeos? Zero.

Lindsey gathered her spreadsheets. "You're good at what you do, Carrie. I'm sure you'll figure out something spectacular."

After Lindsey left the room, Carrie sat in the silence, staring at the wall. Deep inside a small voice was whispering that pulling off this summer splash was her chance to show the movers and shakers in New York that despite the events that had led to her firing, she still had good ideas and ways to implement them. In turn, she would prove to herself that she had what it took to regain her place in the corporate world. Could she do it in the short time she had to prepare?

Shaking her head, she gathered her papers, placed them in her folder and went to Lindsey's office. "I need to think. I'm going to the park for a while."

Lindsey waved, then turned to her computer screen.

With a deep sigh, Carrie walked past Shelia's closed door and stopped by her own office to fetch the thick idea binder she'd started compiling during college. Armed with it, and a pen and notepad, she left the Chamber and made her way across town to the park, hoping, no, needing, a spark of inspiration.

If she couldn't make a splash in Golden, what chance did she have again in New York?

"I SAW THEM together again."

All eyes of the Golden Matchmakers Club converged on Bunny Wright as she joined them for their weekly meeting in Gayle Ann Masterson's kitchen. They'd been trying to decide which lucky couple would be their next target, er, project. So far they'd successfully found the perfect match for Gayle Ann's youngest grandson with a woman he'd been best friends with for years. They'd also assisted another member, Wanda Sue Harper, in finding her daughter the man of her dreams. Two for two. Gayle Ann had been waiting for Bunny to make her pitch for some time now. It seemed today was the day.

"Do tell," Gayle Ann said. As founding member along with Alveda Richardson, she took the lead during their meetings. Social gatherings were one thing, but matchmaking was serious business.

"Any time I drive through town early in the morning, Adam and Carrie are in line at the coffee shop." Bunny's green eyes were bright with excitement. "At first I thought it was a coincidence, but now I'm sure it's fate."

Alveda, her thinning gray hair pulled back in a neat bun, shook her head. "Fate, huh?"

"Yes." Bunny was beginning to warm up to her story. "I know Adam had his heart broken…" Her hand flew to cover her mouth. "You didn't hear that from me," she mumbled.

"Bunny, most everyone knows Adam's fiancée broke things off with him right before the big day. We choose to honor the fact that he doesn't want to talk about it." Alveda's nod was resolute.

Bunny lowered her hand.

Gayle Ann had let it be known around town that Adam's private life was his alone. No one needed reminders of painful memories. Since her reputation for toughness and fairness was known far and wide, especially around Golden, folks respected her request.

"Right. Anyway, I've seen him talking to Carrie…" Bunny scrunched her brow. "Talking is a big deal, since he insists on keeping to himself mostly." She shook her head and carried on. "I promised Sandy and Beck that I'd keep an eye on my nephews. If anyone needs a nudge to reengage in a social life, it's Adam."

Alveda chuckled. "I believe they mentioned

you should make sure Adam and Colin are handling Deep North properly while they're gone. Not that you should be plotting romance for them."

"Whatever. I made a promise and I mean to carry through."

"That's all good and well," said Judge Harrison Carmichael. Harry was the only man in the group. He'd uncovered the matchmakers' scheme early on when Gayle Ann was working behind the scenes to match her grandson, and had announced he wanted in. Apparently golf had lost its luster. He enjoyed both conspiring and spending time with Gayle Ann much more than hitting a ball across a well-maintained fairway. "If he put in any effort, he'd be very popular among the ladies."

"And how would you know that?" Gayle Ann asked.

He winked at her. "I have my sources."

Gayle Ann brushed off her fluttery reaction to the wink. Ever since Christmas, when Harry had given her a delicate bracelet with a shimmery snowflake charm attached, she'd been acting like a teenager. Her tummy went haywire when the handsome man with thick silver hair and mustache set his dark gaze on her. It was obvious he wanted more than friendship, but Gayle Ann was torn. They were both widowed. Both retired. Both looking for new adventures. That made them a perfect match, right? She more than liked Harry, but as a suitor?

Not wanting to dwell on her personal conundrum when she should be focusing on the young lovebirds they would be matching, she motioned for Bunny to continue.

"The more I noticed, the more I got suspicious. So I asked Myrna at Sit A Spell to give me the 411 whenever she spotted them in line."

Alveda chuckled again. "We've got spies now?"

Gayle Ann tapped her chin. "We really should make Myrna a member of our little group."

Bunny continued, "They started off with short conversations, but recently, Myrna's noticed that Adam's been very gentlemanly toward Carrie. Just this morning he stepped aside so that she could move ahead of him in line."

Alveda frowned. "And that's a big deal?"

"Since his broken engagement? Yes. This is the most interest he's shown in a woman since he returned home."

They all nodded.

Gayle Ann tugged at the hem of her jacket.

She always dressed well for these meetings, from her finely styled hair right down to one of her power suits, to show how seriously she took the proceedings. Never let it be said Gayle Ann Masterson didn't give her all when interfering in other people's lives. She opened the Golden Matchmakers Club official notebook she brought to each meeting, where she added notes for the membership and on each individual romance.

"Pros?" she asked the group.

"They must genuinely like each other," Wanda Sue pointed out.

"They both have a flair for business," Harry added.

"Adam does come across as lonely," Alveda said before taking a bite of her homemade apple pie.

"Cons?" Gayle Ann asked.

"He was badly burned by love," Bunny said. "Is he ready to trust again? It's one of the reasons I hesitated to bring him up for consideration."

Wanda Sue drummed her fingers on the table. "And Carrie is a big-city girl. Would she be happy in a small town like Golden in the long run?"

"To be honest, I'm surprised Adam came home after getting his heart broken." Bunny said. "He was so prominent at his Wall Street firm. Despite the circumstances, we never thought we'd see his shadow in little old Golden after he left."

Gayle Ann spoke next. "They've both had careers in the corporate world. I get the feeling that Carrie still wants to go that route, but love has a way of showing us what we *think* we want and revealing what we really *need*.

"It's been true in the young couples we've been able to bring together so far. Sure, there were obstacles, but what great love story doesn't have a blip or two?"

When no one responded, Gayle Ann confided, "I've had time to chat with Carrie when she fills in part-time at Blue Ridge Cottage. You know Serena needs the extra time to plan her wedding to my oldest grandson. I get the impression that Carrie thinks she has something to prove, that she needs to return to her old life to make a name for herself. Why, I don't know, but the way she talks about Golden, and how hard she works for the merchants here through the Chamber of Commerce, make me wonder how easy it will be for her to leave one day."

"I don't see Adam leaving town again," Bunny said as she pulled over a plate of freshly sliced pie.

Harry cleared his throat. "May I?"

Gayle Ann nodded.

"If I recall, the mission of this club is to encourage the young adults in Golden to get together and stay, so the town will grow and prosper. The fact is that Golden is making a splash as a vacation destination. And cozy small towns are becoming trendy. We've seen an uptick of folks moving here in the past two years, for sure. Our downtown is inviting, not to mention the abundant outdoor activities in this area. Who better to put their skills to work here in Golden than Carrie and Adam? She is a marketing whiz, and he certainly has the right touch when it comes to finance." He paused, then wrapped up his case. "So the broader question is, do they work for each other?"

All eyes moved to Bunny.

She put down her fork. "I never thought his fiancée was the right woman for him. Carrie, on the other hand, has that big-city appeal, but in a down-to-earth way. There's a sweetness that Adam responds to, and I think she could be the one to bring him out of his shell.

"I've noticed that her eyes sparkle when she's with him. And he smiles in her company more than he ever has, even before he left to strike out on his own. There's something missing from both of their lives, and as I've observed them together, I sense a real affection that they might not have paid attention to. Because of that, I believe they hold the key to each other's happiness." She held up her hand. "I know it'll take convincing, but I also know we can do it. As a team. Because let's face it, together, we rock."

Wanda Sue clasped her hands over her heart. Harry smiled. Even skeptical Alveda looked intrigued.

"Well, then," Gayle Ann said, touched by Bunny's words. "I nominate Carrie and Adam as our next couple-to-be. Let the matchmaking begin."

CHAPTER THREE

AFTER THE CALL with his parents, Adam needed to get out of the office and expend some energy. Cooped up inside while handling daily affairs would only make him more antsy. Running usually cleared his mind. Today, he wasn't sure how he felt about his mother's news, so getting fresh air was the only remedy for his mood.

After changing into a T-shirt, shorts and running shoes he kept in his office, he made his way to the main room, nearly colliding with Brea as she arrived for work. She heaved a cloth bag onto the snack bar counter and sniffed the air, then sent an impressive scowl Adam's way.

"Someone's been in my space."

"Jocelyn made a pot before you got here."

She pulled a plastic bag of oranges from her satchel. "Just because I stopped at the farmers market like I do every morning?"

If there was one thing Brea took seriously, it was keeping fresh fruit on hand for their customers. She also prepared healthy snacks. For all her bluster, she had a heart of gold.

"Which we appreciate, but it's been a tough morning and Jocelyn was just helping out."

Brea's moment of outrage was the only concession she'd allow concerning the snack bar breach.

Chuckling under his breath, Adam listened to Brea now muttering about no one respecting her boundaries. Once he made sure Jocelyn had things under control, he hit the road.

The late-morning sun beat on the asphalt as he navigated the quiet streets of Golden. He found a steady rhythm, the pounding of his feet vibrating in his ears. Along the route, he waved to longtime neighbors, knowing he was fortunate to live in such a wonderful town. But what if his family decided to sell Deep North Adventures? Would Adam stay here, trying to determine what to do next? He hated that this second-guessing was a necessity, but until a decision was made, he had to consider all options.

He picked up the pace.

Thankfully, he'd started investing at a young age and had a diverse and substantial financial portfolio. He had a knack for it and had made himself, and his family, each a tidy sum. But what about their employees?

Did this new offer include a guarantee of employment for Jocelyn and Brea? Would they be laid off in the aftermath?

Adam hated the idea of putting them at risk. Jocelyn needed the job to make ends meet, and no matter how cranky Brea pretended to be, she was like family. He had to look out for them.

Twenty minutes of hard running brought him to the town center. He slowed his pace, stopping outside Kelloggs' Five and Dime, his hands on his hips as he bent at the waist, slowing his breathing. After nodding to a few folks, he strolled inside for a bottle of water and placed it on the checkout counter.

"Adam," Mr. Kellogg greeted him. "I was going to give you a call to thank you for that upgrade for my computer software. I'm amazed at how behind the times I'd become."

"My pleasure," he said, tossing a few bills on the counter. "I'm always available to help."

"Word is getting around, you know, after you updated the system at Frieda's Bakery and Tessa's clothing store. You might be in demand."

Adam chuckled. Helping out the merchants in Golden was his way of giving back. He did it because he enjoyed it, not because he needed any additional income.

"I still have a few questions," Mr. Kellogg said, "but you're out for a run. Can we get together later?"

"Sounds good."

"Hope you don't mind, but I gave the owner of the Mountain Spa Center your number. She's thinking about expanding her operation and needs a sounding board."

"Assisting businesses so they run more efficiently is one of my pet projects."

"Good, 'cause most of us old-timers need a push to modernize. I balked initially, but after you explained my new system, I can't believe I waited so long."

"Then you're good advertising for me, not that I'm actively taking on clients."

"Maybe you should. More and more folks are coming to the area to escape big-city life. You would be busy, here in Golden, and the surrounding towns."

Would he? It wasn't an idea he'd considered. Made sense, he supposed, but right now, Deep North Adventures was his top priority. Until then, lending an ear to small business owners would be a side project.

Adam picked up the water bottle and stepped outside. He took a long drink, then his gaze fell on a person walking down the sidewalk opposite him. Carrie, a somber expression on her pretty face. As a concerned citizen, it was his duty to find out what was wrong.

At least that was the excuse he was going with.

By the time he crossed Main, Carrie had walked under the stone arch leading into Gold Dust Park. Was she playing hooky? Seemed out of character for the workaholic he thought she might be, but then, today had kind of rocked him off his axis. He'd actually gone with his brother's urging to be more social and suggested to Carrie that they get together more. What had sounded like a wild idea at the time might not be so outrageous after all.

He turned the corner just as she took a seat on a bench located under a leafy oak limb. Fishing through her purse, she came up with a pen and tapped it on a closed binder. As he drew closer, he noticed how the sun lit her lustrous honey-blond hair, the waves already lightened by the summer sun. A thought occurred to him: she should be lounging on an exotic beach somewhere, not on a simple wooden bench working so much. He had no clue if she liked the beach, although her skin always had a pretty glow. Maybe she preferred to stay out of direct sunlight? He shook off those thoughts and stopped in front of her.

She'd been staring off into the distance, but she blinked and focused on him. Her eyebrows angled over topaz-colored eyes, not in a good way.

"Are you following me?"

"No." He held up his half-full water bottle. "I was at Kelloggs' and when I came out, I saw you. Worried that there must be a major catastrophe at the Chamber if Miss Work Ethic was off to the park midmorning on a business day."

Carrie took in his running clothes. "I could say the same about you."

"I'm employed at an outdoor adventure company. Being outdoors is kind of the point."

"Then how come you don't seem to be enjoying nature today?"

He frowned. Was it that obvious he was distracted?

"You're thinking too hard," she accused.

"Back at you."

The color of her eyes, not to mention the interest shining there, got to him every time. Carrie was a beautiful woman. Smart. The real deal. A woman he'd admitted he would like to get to know better if he wasn't guarding his heart.

Getting serious once had been a disaster.

Did he want to ruin the tentative friendship he had with Carrie by rushing things?

She went all formal on him. "I will grudgingly agree that since coming to Golden, it's been nice to have the option to come to the park and think. In New York, I paced my office when I needed to brainstorm." She met his gaze and scrunched her pert nose. "Plus, my current office has a tiny window."

Adam mock shuddered. "Horrible."

"It is. Especially on a beautiful day like today."

Adam grinned. "Glad to see you're taking advantage of the Golden lifestyle without totally ditching work."

"As if I could."

He nodded to the bench and she scooted over.

"Trouble?" he asked as he took a seat.

"No. Just Shelia and Carter springing a project on me last minute." She paused. "Make that two projects."

"Sounds like Carter."

"Doesn't he realize he can't just give me a job at any old time and expect answers before thinking it through?"

"What does he want now?"

She waved her hand in the air. "What he always wants—exposure for Golden." She twisted to face him. "I get it, but he's been at the office a lot. Surely he has other important business to do?"

"Maybe he and Lissy Ann are on the outs. There was a weird vibe between them the last time I saw them together."

"That would explain why he's been looking over our shoulders." She pressed her lips together, then said, "I'm sorry for them. I like Lissy Ann, even if she's pushy when it comes to recruiting volunteers for town events. Maybe she's just parroting Carter? Or trying to save their marriage?"

Confusion crossed Carrie's face. "I know he's into finance, but what does Carter do specifically? For a job, I mean, besides being the head of the Chamber of Commerce. It's never been clear to me."

"Manages the family fortune. They made it big in timber around the turn of the century, but now they mainly make investments."

"Explains Lissy Ann's amazing wardrobe. Tessa's clothing store has a great selection to choose from, but Lissy Ann's designer clothes are a step beyond Golden."

"You've got an eye for fashion?"

"Hard not to, living and shopping in Manhattan."

He nodded. As much as he tried to put

the time he'd spent in the city behind him, he found it difficult. Especially since Carrie had arrived in Golden. She didn't always talk about her past, except for a few hints here and there and a mention about the disastrous end of a job, but she had an air about her that he'd come to associate with someone who loved bigger places. And yet, paradoxically, Carrie also seemed to like Golden's small-town atmosphere.

"All I know is that the Tremaine trouble is giving me trouble."

"It can't be that bad."

The sparkle in her eyes turned sly. "Oh, it won't be."

He didn't miss the determination in her voice. Had to admit, he liked it. She didn't back down, a trait he could relate to. Or used to relate to, anyway.

She looked out at the park again. "So you had to get out of the office, too?"

"Didn't have to. Chose to."

"Care to tell me why?" she asked as she focused on him again.

"Because you're so forthcoming?"

Carrie threw up one hand. "Hey, you're the one who suggested we talk more."

She was right. Her interest wasn't feigned—he could hear the genuine curiosity in her tone.

"It's a nice day and I needed to think," he finally answered. It was the truth. The bombshell news this morning was forefront in his mind. "How about you? What do you do when you need to get a fresh take on things?"

A smile curved her lips. "I used to window-shop."

Flashes of how much his ex lived to shop snapped through his brain and he quickly put a lid on them. Now that he'd had time to analyze the relationship, he wondered why he and Rachel had thought marriage was a good idea. Still, he couldn't deny how much being jilted had hurt.

Adam had admitted up front that he would forever carry being a small-town guy in his bones. But Rachel? The closest she came to nature was driving by Central Park while seated in the back of a hired car. She was urban through and through. How had he expected them to coexist? He supposed that was when he'd been caught up in the hype. His career had skyrocketed and he'd been a popular name in financial circles. He'd been the go-to guy in her father's firm. Everything he'd hoped for when he arrived in New York in pursuit of his dreams.

From the first time he met Rachel, they'd gotten along. They had the same circle of friends, and they both liked to explore the city. At her family's urging, it had seemed natural to date, to get engaged... Until she'd shockingly ended things. Rachel had always battled confidence issues, so at first he'd thought she was just overwhelmed by the Harrington family pressuring them to have a large wedding. But then she'd opted for the luxury honeymoon in the south of France, without the ceremony, and it became clear their relationship was over. He found out officially when she sent him an "it's not you, it's me" breakup text only hours before the wedding.

He'd had questions. Been embarrassed by the looks aimed at him at the office. The chilly change in the partners' attitudes. How could she dump him with no explanation? Then it occurred to him that she might have just been using him all along.

That hurt more.

Suddenly the high-end, fast-paced lifestyle he'd cultivated was less appealing, and after a quick trip home to visit his folks, he'd decided to leave it all behind. Hadn't regretted his decision since.

Carrie's voice intruded on his memories.

"I'd walk for blocks," she was saying. "Staring into shop windows. I didn't need to buy anything—I guess it was the exercise that cleared my mind. You know, that scientific theory about a body in motion? But I took pleasure in viewing the window dressings—getting a glimpse of the current styles, caught up in the hustle of people on their way to…"

She lifted her hands in the air and wiggled her fingers as her sentence trailed off. He couldn't help but notice how slender they were, how she gestured when she was searching for the right words. He found it endearing.

"…wherever they were going. By the time I returned to the office, I had an inkling of how I would tackle a project."

He kicked his legs out and crossed his ankles. "I used to stare out my window. My office was on the thirty-first floor, so I'd gaze over the city, past all the buildings until I focused only on the sky, imagining I was back in Golden."

"No wonder you came home. It is lovely here."

"Definitely needed a change."

They both fell silent. Was he glad she didn't ask for details? Maybe a small part of him, oddly, felt let down that she didn't press the issue. He found himself wanting to open up to Carrie, as strange as that might be. He couldn't deny the confession slowly dissolving on his tongue... Words he'd been ready to speak for the first time, and to a relative stranger, of all people.

No, talking about getting dumped was not on his to-do list today.

A group of mothers and small children entered the park, sounds of laughter and parental warnings as they ran for the playground pulling Adam firmly into the present.

"Guess I should get going," he said. "I've already been gone for too long."

Carrie sighed. "Me, too. Maybe I'll pop into Blue Ridge Cottage and bug Serena. It's almost lunchtime."

As she stood, her binder slipped from her lap. She tried to catch it, but her purse toppled over at the same time. Adam reached out, catching the binder before it hit the ground. When he handed it over, their fingers brushed and he couldn't deny the spark.

"Thanks," she gasped. "If my binder exploded, that would have been a disaster."

He shook off the intensity of the physical reaction and asked, "What have you got in there? It's pretty heavy."

"Every idea I've ever had since I started my career."

He raised an eyebrow. "Every idea?"

At his response, she almost looked embarrassed. "Pretty much. I jot down any little detail that comes to mind, then expand on the ideas later. You never know when something you've already fleshed out comes in handy."

"Talk about commitment."

She shrugged. "It's a good way to stay ahead."

"Ahead of what?"

"Just ahead. Advancing." A fleeting sadness filled her eyes, gone as quick as a blink. "In marketing, the one with the best pitch gets the best clients."

"And you want to be the best?"

"Of course. Who wouldn't?"

"Then why did you leave your job?"

She turned away, but he noticed the flush creeping up her neck. She'd never mentioned why she'd chosen to settle here in Golden. But then, she was like him in that department, keeping her personal life personal. But she clearly loved what she did, if the binder was any indication. So, what had happened?

"Goofing-off time is over," she said as she clutched the binder to her chest.

He doubted she'd goofed off a day in her life.

Carrie glanced at him. Their gazes met and held. He sensed lots of secrets, sure she'd never reveal a one. Again, that made them more alike than he'd suspected.

Shouting from the children pulled her attention away, which made him feel...adrift.

"Thanks for the talk," she said, rising from the bench.

"Anytime," he answered.

She nodded, then headed in the direction of the stone arch.

He jogged in the opposite direction, his mind returning to the future of Deep North Adventures. Only then did he realize Carrie hadn't mentioned what the project was that had her scrambling for ideas. Nor had he brought up the possible acquisition of the family business.

Seems they were both experts at holding back.

As Carrie made her way through the park, she mulled over her morning. Adam had proved to be a well-timed distraction from her fruitless brainstorming about the end-of-summer celebration.

While it was nice to talk to him, it also unnerved her. They'd spoken more in one day than all the rest of her time here.

It would have been nice to tell him about the debacle at her last job and how it had affected her, but she didn't want to admit to losing her employment. How embarrassing would that be? Here she was, touting her marketing skills after losing her previous job. No, she didn't want to see the disappointment in Adam's eyes any more than she had when she looked in the mirror.

Easing out a breath, she shook off the unwelcome sensation. She had no intention of connecting with anyone in Golden whom she'd regret leaving when she moved back to NYC.

The sounds of the children playing dimmed as she headed away. She would have liked to linger, but duty called.

In Manhattan, she'd purposely avoided the parks. When she was a child, her mother had always made each outing a special event, so the park lost its appeal when she left. In Carrie's adolescent dreams, she'd hoped her mother might change her mind. Return home. And they'd all go back to being a happy family. Wishing those dreams to come true, Carrie had begged the nanny to take her to Central Park every day. She'd only been ten at the time, thinking this mission would fix her family.

The park wasn't far from home. They'd pass the Metropolitan Museum of Art, then follow the path to the terrace by the lake. This had been her mother's favorite spot to visit, so Carrie and the nanny would sit and wait. But each day, there was no sign of her mother. After a few weeks, the nanny insisted that Carrie was hurting herself by expecting her mother to show up, only to be heartbroken each time. But at least Carrie had tried.

After her firing, she was still trying. Looked like she'd keep trying in hopes of getting her old life back. If she did nothing, she'd get nothing.

She wasn't up for failure again.

But oddly enough, here in Golden, she could breathe. Focus on what was important without being pulled in twenty different directions. Watching the kids playing while smiling moms hovered nearby didn't hurt as much as it once did.

Eventually, her mom had gotten in touch with Carrie and they spoke maybe one or twice a year now. She missed her mother but had decided a long time ago that it was her mom's loss not to know much about her or be in her life more.

She'd almost reached the door to Blue Ridge Cottage when Gayle Ann Masterson stepped out, her eyes lighting up when she glimpsed Carrie. The woman was a dynamo. She loved Golden and all who lived here.

Rushing over to hold the door open, Carrie greeted her. "Hey, Mrs. M."

"Good morning, my dear." The older woman frowned. "Or is it afternoon?"

"Not quite, but close."

They stepped away from the store entrance and moved out onto the sidewalk.

"I lose track of time when I'm with Serena. That girl needs to act on some of her wedding plans before any more time goes by."

"Tell me about it. We were up into the wee hours with her endless lists. I had to drag myself out of bed this morning."

"So she's not taking your advice, either?"

"No. I keep telling her that she and Logan could get married by a justice of the peace in the middle of the woods and he'd be more than happy. She has to make some concrete decisions soon, and Logan will support her no matter what."

Mrs. M. sighed. "He has shown great patience."

"Which I also reminded her of. Still, Serena thinks every little detail needs to be perfect. I guess I don't blame her. Getting married is a huge life moment."

Mrs. M. tipped her head and sent Carrie a

considering glance. "Have you ever thought about marriage?"

She took a moment before answering. "In the abstract. I'm sure it's great for some people."

"But not for you?"

"I'm not saying never. More like not right now." She grimaced. "Besides, you need to be seeing someone to move in that direction."

"So you're happily single?" Mrs. M. asked as she adjusted her purse over her arm.

"I'm too busy to date."

"Big project at work?"

She narrowed her eyes at the older woman. "What have you heard?"

"Carter has ideas. Something about a summer splash?"

Carrie shouldn't be surprised by the woman's knowledge, but she was. "How do you know these things?"

"I have my ear to the ground," Mrs. M. said.

"Clearly." Carrie shook her head. "Actually, it's two projects, not one."

Mrs. M. shot her a questioning glance.

"One is covered, but Carter expects details for the other by four this afternoon."

"Oh my."

"He hasn't given me much to go on, but expects results."

"What have you come up with so far?" She paused. "For either project."

"I already had the first one sketched out. It's a print campaign to better publicize our merchants in order to draw interest to Golden. Carter had put that on the back burner but wants to revive it now."

Mrs. M. sent her a grin. "Sounds like he appreciates your hard work."

Carrie shrugged. "Usually. That's why I'm not surprised he brought up the concept again."

"Have you reached out to the merchants?"

"That'll be on my agenda for tomorrow."

Mrs. M. paused. "Did I just see Adam Wright running through town?"

That was random. "Yes," she replied in a wary tone.

"He was big on Wall Street. Why not feature him first in the print ad? You can talk about him coming back to Golden. How the big-city lure couldn't compete with the satisfaction of small-town life in Golden."

Sure, Carrie had heard that Adam used to work for a successful financial firm, but Wall Street? Why hadn't he said anything when she mentioned Manhattan?

"That's a thought."

And a mystery to solve at another time.

Right now she had to move ahead. Mrs. M.'s angle was smart. He was a perfect candidate for the focus of this campaign.

Carrie snapped her fingers. "And I can make sure travel outlets in major cities get access to the ad, enticing potential business owners to visit our small town."

"It could work."

"It will more than work," Carrie said, her mind racing now. "But that doesn't help me with plans for the splashy end-of-summer event Carter requested today."

The blare of a car horn made Carrie pivot toward the street. A sedan was following a slow-moving truck pulling an enclosed horse trailer. In faded, scratched lettering on the side of the trailer, Carrie read Wild West Rodeo Show. Mrs. M. waved at the driver of the truck while the impatient person in the car honked again to no avail. The truck inched on and there was nowhere for the sedan to pass.

Turning back to the conversation, Mrs. M. asked, "Where were we?"

"Summer celebration ideas." Carrie said, feeling the weight of her assignment. "I could come up with a bunch of different scenarios, but they would be generic. Every event this town holds has a purpose—to bring attention to Golden. I realize that I haven't lived here long enough to be steeped in your history. So, what would be unique to Golden? What would draw tourists? What is something a person on vacation couldn't find anywhere but in Golden?"

"Hmm. I see you've been thinking hard."

Carrie pointed to the disappearing trailer. "You know them?"

"Why yes, I've known Brando and his family for years now."

"So it's some kind of Western show? Like a rodeo?"

"A hybrid, with different events, but yes. They're scheduled to perform here at the end of the summer. It's a popular draw with the locals." Mrs. M. stared down the street as if following the trailer's progress. "But I have it on good authority that this will be the last show."

"Lindsey mentioned them. Since Carter gave me very little time to get this splash together, the Western show might solve my problems." She tugged on her bottom lip with her teeth.

"Why not get behind the show, give them a big boost on the way out and draw tourists at the same time?" Mrs. M. suggested. "And, Adam has ties to the show. You can merge both projects together."

"He does?" She couldn't imagine the usually well-dressed Adam Wright involved with a rodeo. What would he do? Ride a bronco? Rope a calf? No, that didn't fit Adam's image.

"I'm afraid you'll have to press him for details."

Which Carrie would. Gleefully.

"Has this chat helped?" Mrs. M. asked.

"You need to work for the Chamber of Commerce," Carrie informed her.

Mrs. M. chuckled. "No. I simply believe in the vision of Golden. And like you said, I know the history here. You would have hit upon the idea eventually, I'm sure."

It felt nice for someone to have faith in her.

As she pushed that thought aside, the old excitement kicked in. "Sounds like I have a lot of planning to do."

Mrs. M. beamed. "And I'm off to the grocery store. Alveda forgot an ingredient for the feast she's making tonight, and since I'm out, she asked me to pick it up. After my son's cardiac scare, she's been cooking heart-healthy meals." Mrs. M. glanced down the block with longing. "That's why I have to sneak out to Frieda's Bakery every once in a while."

Shocked, Carrie protested. "But Alveda makes the best pies."

"She does, but she's been cutting back of late."

Carrie leaned close and said in a low voice, "Your secret is safe with me."

"I appreciate that." She patted Carrie's arm. "Now, time to get back to the office. If I were you I'd talk to Adam tonight before a better offer comes his way."

From whom? "Right. I'll do that, after work. And thanks again. I owe you."

At the mysterious way Mrs. M. smiled, Carrie wondered if she'd spoken too quickly.

With a quick wave, she hurried down the sidewalk, forgoing a visit to see her best friend while thinking about Adam as her first local model. He had the looks, no doubt. And the way he held himself, with such confidence and dignity, he was sure to be a perfect spokesman for *Discover Golden!*

She smiled as she picked up the pace. Yep, Adam was the perfect candidate to draw attention to Golden. To move forward as quickly as possible to reclaim her life. But the question was, would he go along with her plan?

She'd have to convince him.

CHAPTER FOUR

THE LATE-AFTERNOON SUN hung low in the clear blue sky, casting a golden glow over the lush green mountainside. When Carrie left Manhattan, she'd wondered if she would miss the noise, the tall buildings and the constant rush. To her surprise, the laid-back atmosphere of the small town appealed to her. Who knew she liked the country? The beautiful views, with more trees than the eye could see, tumbling waterfalls and the rushing river on the outskirts of town, had given her a different perspective on life. Instead of forcing life to change her way, she was slowly becoming a part of the fabric of Golden. Truth be told, it wasn't so bad. Yes, she still planned on going back to New York, but while she was in Golden, she'd enjoy her time here. Take deep breaths. Slow down a bit.

Gravel crunched under her tires as Carrie entered the Deep North Adventures lot. Shortly after six now, there was only one car visible. Adam's black luxury sedan. Yes, she recognized the car he drove, not that she was paying attention or anything.

After talking to Mrs. M. earlier in the day, she'd gone back to the office and laid out a *very* preliminary idea for the summer splash. Linking the Wild West Rodeo Show together with the end-of-summer spectacular solved many of her problems. One, she didn't have to come up with a new concept. And two, since the show was already scheduled, she didn't have to find entertainment in the short turnaround time. She'd spoken on the phone with Ty Pendergrass, who ran the show with his father. He confirmed that this was the last performance, and he was on board with tying it into a larger town event. She had more to prepare, but it was enough to meet her four o'clock deadline.

Carter had arrived right on time, curious about her concept. "What've you got for me?"

When she explained her idea, he hadn't seemed thrilled. "I was expecting something bigger."

"I've only had hours to work on it," she reminded him pointedly. "It's a start, anyway."

"Your experience speaks for itself, so I'll let you run with it."

After he left her office to speak to Shelia, Carrie pored over the *Discover Golden!*

campaign. She added a few more notes now that she was going to approach Adam about becoming the spokesperson. Convincing clients was her bread and butter, so she had no doubt Adam would be smiling into a camera lens in no time.

Her camera, actually.

She shivered at the thought. The man was magazine cover material. His dark hair and gray eyes were compelling, his cheekbones high, his skin tanned. He might be a financial genius, but he clearly loved the outdoors. Would that translate to a print campaign? She'd soon find out.

When he focused on something or someone, he held your attention. Carrie knew from experience, when one of his keen, penetrating looks made her skin tingle. Okay, more than once. And what was she going to do about it?

She shook off the meandering thoughts. She didn't have time for romance. She had goals to meet, none of which was catching Adam's eye. Maybe once she'd gotten that corner office and knew her career was secure? And let her dad know it? Not that that was a lot to ask.

And by then, Adam will have moved on.

The idea made her chest tight.

Time to get to work.

With the stock pictures she'd printed out and a short sales pitch tucked away in her leather briefcase, she strode to the building. She faltered when she reached for the door handle. Where had the sudden case of nerves come from? Probably the fact that Adam had been a high-flyer on Wall Street and never mentioned it. She'd snooped online to find out more about him, discovering he'd bought and sold multimillion-dollar businesses.

Or could the hesitation be that the attraction simmering deep down between them was slowly making its way to the surface? Adam was extremely handsome, but it was the confident way he carried himself that appealed to Carrie. He was reserved, yes, but he smiled a lot when they were together. Was that because of her? The idea caused a host of butterflies to take flight in her stomach.

She hadn't been looking for romance, but had it found her?

She was pretty sure that Adam would be nothing less than professional when she made her pitch. But still, would he be the tough and clever negotiator she'd read about? Would she become more intrigued by the man whose smiles made her day?

Shaking off the unusual apprehension, Carrie forged ahead, chin held high. If she didn't believe in herself, who would?

Escaping the summer heat of the day, Carrie made sure to keep her steps sharp as she crossed the main, open area. She slowed as Adam glanced over the counter from where he was staring at a computer screen. His full eyebrows rose, but that was all the reaction he displayed at her showing up so late in the day. As she drew closer, she noticed he'd changed from his usual office attire and into a tight T-shirt that showcased his broad shoulders and wide chest. He stood up to greet her and she saw the old, faded jeans, too. Apparently he carried off either casual and professional clothing to perfection.

She stopped to slow her breathing. Oh yeah, he was exactly the right man for this campaign.

"Carrie. Is anything wrong?"

Time to tamp down her reaction to the man. "No." She glanced around. "Nice place."

Adam's eyes moved over the room. "We like the family feeling."

"Must be nice working with your parents."

"It has its moments." He paused. "You ever work with your family?"

She struggled to keep the sadness from her voice. "I could never work with my dad."

"Too different?"

"Something like that." She needed to move on from that topic. "I wanted to talk to you. Can you spare a few minutes?"

"Sure." He leaned over and tapped some keys, then straightened, giving her his full attention. A strange awareness skittered from her head to her toes.

Clearing her throat, she placed her briefcase on the counter and zipped it open. Adam watched, curiosity shining in his intelligent gaze. In her mind, she silently clicked off the steps for a successful presentation. Marketing 101. Reference past discussions, short elevator pitch, highlight benefits, include pertinent data and tell a story.

"Do you remember today when we ran into each other in the park?" she started.

"How could I forget? I nearly dislocated my shoulder when I lifted your idea binder. That thing weighs a ton."

She felt her cheeks heat. Why did people think keeping every single one of her ideas was overkill? "It's not *that* heavy."

"Close enough."

She let his comment slide. "Anyway, I'm here representing the Chamber. We're about to start a new campaign to draw business to Golden and I'd like you to be the spokesperson for *Discover Golden!*"

One eyebrow lifted. "Spokesperson?"

"Yes. Highlighting our merchants is a great way to publicize the perks of setting up shop in Golden. You're successful, and you've got credibility with the business community. I've heard through the grapevine that you talk to owners when they need advice."

"And that's important? Credibility?"

"Of course. Adam, you define the benefits of hard work and success. And this campaign will help all the merchants of Golden."

He studied her for a moment, then crossed his arms over his chest. "What does it involve?"

She blinked as his muscles bunched at the movement, then removed a page from the briefcase. In her prep for this pitch, she'd found some stock pictures of men dressed in power suits, posing before various famous buildings in major cities, as a visual aid. She slid the paper in his direction.

"I thought we could set up a photo shoot and get pictures of you at different locations in and around Golden. Then I'll write copy about the lure and benefits of small-town life for the intended audience."

"Which is?"

"Big-city financial centers. Other Chambers sharing our information."

Uncrossing his arms, he dragged the paper

toward him with one finger. He went silent for a long moment, then met her gaze.

"Why do you think I'd make a difference?"

"Your prior financial success on Wall Street. How you transitioned so well to Golden."

He didn't respond, but his eyes grew chilly. Or was Carrie imagining the flicker?

"I see."

She was losing him. Move to step two. "We'll tell a story. Make Golden the main character."

He tapped his finger on the paper. Was he considering her pitch?

"I have data to back up the validity of the campaign. The Chamber of Commerce will foot the bill, of course, reimbursing you for your time." She gave him a once-over. "You'd have to dress more professionally."

He peered down at his clothes. "This is professional. I'm leading a twilight tour soon."

"Sorry. I just mean, you know, a suit."

The corner of his lips tipped up. "No one wears a suit in Golden."

"Then whatever passes for business casual."

Good grief. Had she managed to mess this up?

He turned his attention back to the paper. What did that mean? Had she insulted him? For the millionth time she wondered why she hadn't stayed in New York where she knew her clientele.

Finally, he met her gaze again.

"You don't need to pay me."

Then he needed to hear the benefit.

"This is also prime exposure for Deep North Adventures. We'll make sure to have the name of your company prominently displayed in the campaign."

The tension in the room wore on her shoulders.

His voice was all-business when he asked, "How involved are you in the process?"

"I'll be at the shoot, of course."

"Do I get any input into the ad copy?"

"If you'd like to. I'm good at my job, Adam, but I understand your concern."

He nodded. "What about the other merchants?"

"Come again?"

"How will you incorporate them into the advertising?"

"I thought we'd see how the initial photo shoot pans out, then perhaps add other locals in the future."

"They would be thrilled to be a part of your campaign."

"What about you?" she asked, nearly holding her breath.

"I'm still thinking."

The mad negotiating skills she'd read about?

She couldn't read his gaze when he asked, "And if I turn down your project?"

Disappointment washed over her. "I suppose I'll reach out to someone else."

"Is Carter involved?"

"He gives the go-ahead for a promotion, but he usually leaves us to do our jobs."

"Usually?"

She clasped her hands together on the counter. "Do you have a problem with Carter?"

"Yes."

His firm tone surprised her. "Oh."

"But that's not your concern."

Maybe not, but she sure wanted to know their history.

"Will this eat up a lot of my time?"

"Half a day, no more" she rushed to assure him. "We'll take the pictures downtown and here at your building."

He walked out from behind the counter and stopped before her. "Do you really feel this will attract people to Golden?"

She dug down deep for her most confident tone. "I do."

His gaze moved to the big picture window at the front of the building. Cars zipped by, most likely folks heading home after a day's work or tourists driving to dinner.

"And you will be there?" he asked again as he turned back to her.

His steady gaze met hers and her stomach did flip-flops.

"Yes. I'm very involved with my campaigns."

A slow smile curved his lips, making her twitchy.

She unclasped her hands and let them fall to her sides. Every time she was with him, she became more aware of how handsome he was. Would that be a problem if they worked together? Not that dating had ever been a consideration. But what if he asked? She couldn't deny her curiosity.

Her thoughts were cut off when Adam's head jerked back to the window at the sound of squealing tires. She stepped closer to see what had happened. A green minivan careened into the parking lot, coming to an abrupt halt.

"Oh no," Adam said on a low breath. "Aunt Bunny is driving again."

She glanced over her shoulder at him.

"And that's a bad thing?"

He strode to the door. "She should have had her license revoked years ago."

They went outside to find four older women

and a man alight from the car, dressed in casual clothing. One woman reached into the vehicle and backpacks went flying onto the gravel. They seemed to be talking over each other until another woman held up her hand to rein them in.

Carrie gaped. "Is that Mrs. M.? Wearing leggings?"

"I'm afraid so."

She turned to him. "Adam, what's going on?"

"My six-thirty Twilight Hikers."

She blinked at him.

"To paraphrase my aunt, they aren't ready for the grave yet. They need to be one with nature. And they are in the twilight of their lives."

"So they…hike?"

"Indeed, they do."

She watched as the group began slipping on the backpacks.

"They're pretty seasoned," he said.

"I'm just…"

He grinned at her. "Surprised?"

"More like impressed."

He chuckled.

Carrie took a step toward the building. "I'll let you get to it." She walked inside, wishing their conversation hadn't been interrupted.

Gathering up her materials, she left the concept pages for Adam to look over later.

When he came back inside, she said, "You can give me your decision another time."

"I've made up my mind."

Delight whooshed through her.

"But I have a caveat."

Oh dear.

"Caveat?" she echoed.

With a twinkle in his eyes he said, "I'll agree if you join us for the hike."

ADAM HELD BACK a grin at the shock on Carrie's face. Catching her off guard had its perks. Her cheeks turned bright pink and her mouth moved until she finally blurted out, "Hike?"

"Yes. With the group." He pointed to the seniors who were filing into the gathering area.

She moved closer and said in a low voice, "Tonight?"

He leaned closer, too, inhaling the light scent of sunshine and coconut in her hair, which evoked memories of summer. "Do you have other plans?"

"Well, no."

"Then you can join us." He pointed to her heels. "You'll need different footwear."

She shook off her surprise, took in his sturdy hiking boots and frowned. "I have sneakers in my car. Will that work?"

If she had to ask, she had no idea what she was in for.

"That'll work for last minute. The longer you live here, you'll learn to keep the right gear on hand."

"Which would mean I plan on doing more outdoorsy activities, and I'm not sure that's in my wheelhouse."

"C'mon. Everyone loves nature."

"Coming from the guy who owns an outdoor adventure company."

"No sweat. I'll have you giving me a run for my money in no time."

"No sweat? Really? Seems like a big claim because I've hiked before and I wasn't exactly dry afterward."

He chuckled. "Okay, maybe a little. But it's for a good cause. Your cause."

She didn't look convinced.

"It won't be a taxing hike, I promise."

Why was he pushing her? Suddenly it became important that she join him. He wanted to see what Carrie was made of, outside of her usual domain. She'd been competent in her pitch; could she show that same confidence out of her element? He thought so, but was curious to see it for himself.

"Oh, well, if you promise…"

The words hung between them for a drawn-out moment before his aunt joined them.

"What's the holdup?" Aunt Bunny asked.

Adam pointed at Carrie's shoes. "Great for the office, bad on trail inclines."

Aunt Bunny nodded. "Carrie, honey, if you're going to join us, you'll need a better pair of shoes."

Mrs. M. ambled over. "You're joining us? What fun."

"The jury is out on that, Mrs. M."

"Did I hear someone mention a jury?" Judge Harry Carmichael added his two cents.

Aunt Bunny poked Adam in the side. "You must have something that'll work. You can't risk Carrie getting hurt."

Carrie sent him a pleading glance. "I could always go home."

"No," came a resounding chorus.

Adam shrugged as if her joining them was a foregone conclusion. "They'll never let you leave now."

She seemed to mull it over, then said, "Fine. Let me get my sneakers."

He held out his arm to stop her. "I have a better idea."

She raised a brow.

He took her hand and led her to the wall displaying different hiking boots. "We'll find you a good pair. On the house."

"Adam, you don't have to supply my boots."

"I insist. This was my idea."

He scanned the wall and removed a pair. "What do you think?"

"I think I have no idea."

He chuckled. "Shoe size?"

"Eight."

"Stay here."

He jogged to a storage room and found a box with her size, along with a pair of sturdy socks. When he returned, the seniors had circled Carrie as if to keep her from bolting.

"Don't worry," Alveda assured her. "Adam will keep you safe."

"He knows the trails like the back of his hand," Wanda Sue joined in.

He knelt down beside Carrie. "Foot."

She lifted her leg and he slipped off her heel, forcing himself not to enjoy the tingling response from the silky skin under his fingertips. Not wanting to seem overly familiar, he reluctantly let go and pulled the boot from the box, loosened the laces and…

"I can do it," she said, her voice tight. She

grabbed the socks and tugged them on, followed by the boots, before standing.

"Well?" Mrs. M. asked.

She made a few passes across the room, testing the comfort of the boots. "Actually it's a pretty snug fit."

Aunt Bunny clapped her hands. "Then we're good to go. To the bus, people."

"Wait." Carrie considered her skirt and blouse. "I can't wear these clothes."

His aunt glanced at him, eyebrows angled. Adam knew another suggestion was coming his way.

Carrie spoke before his aunt. "I have some workout clothes in my car. It'll just take a minute to change."

With that she disappeared. Adam faced the group. "I believe you scared her off."

Mrs. M. waved a hand. "She's made of stronger stuff and can certainly hold her own."

"Besides," Aunt Bunny added, "don't you always say adversity builds character?"

"Indeed." The judge grinned, his mustache shaking. "Why do you think we took you up on your challenge to stay healthy?"

"And we needed another activity to round out our schedules," Wanda Sue added.

Adam glanced over the group. They did have a good point.

Carrie came back in, disappeared into the restroom and returned shortly. She was dressed in a fitted tank top and shorts, along with the boots, a tote bag draped over her shoulder.

"Where should I put my things?" Carrie asked as the seniors headed to the door.

"I'll lock everything in my office."

Ten minutes later he had the group in the passenger van they used to transport guests to different outdoor venues. Tonight they were headed to Bailey's Point. The group's excited chatter filled the van during the trip. Carrie was quiet until he pulled into the parking lot.

"I've been here," she told him as she leaned forward to gaze out the windshield. "With Serena."

"One of the places she likes to sketch?"

"Yes. For her, climbing to the first look-out is fun."

"For you?"

"I kept hoping for an escalator."

He chuckled. "No such luck."

They exited the van as the seniors started toward the trailhead, chatting and enjoying each other's company.

"That's quite a group," Carrie commented.

"They've known each other for a long time. Mrs. M. and Alveda go way back to when Alveda first started cooking for the Mastersons. Aunt Bunny and Wanda Sue joined their little squad not long after." He watched the folks ahead of them. "I'm not sure when the judge joined their merry band."

"It must be nice. To have friends you've known for so long."

He glanced at her profile. "What about you and Serena?"

"College roommates. We're close but don't have the longevity yet."

"And that's important to you?"

"I… I suppose I find the loyalty refreshing."

Adam secured his backpack and they moved from the parking lot to the red dirt path scattered with leaves. Forest overgrowth crowded the way as they stayed a short distance behind the others. The temperature dipped a few degrees, cooling the evening air. The sun dappled between branches, creating shadows as the leaves rustled from small animals scurrying through the trees.

"Didn't you have friends in New York?" he asked, wanting to uncover more about the lovely woman at his side.

"More like acquaintances. I'd sometimes

go out with coworkers at the end of the day for dinner and made a few friends from spin class, but Serena is the only one I'm tight with. Heidi Welch, too, now that we've worked together at Serena's store and gotten to know each other better."

He paused as they stepped carefully over a large rock smack in the middle of the path.

"How about you?" she asked.

"I guess my brother is my closest friend, although Logan and Reid Masterson are high on the list. Jamey Johnson, too."

"Jamey's a sweetheart."

Something resembling jealousy stirred in Adam's chest. He kept his tone light when he said, "Sweetheart, huh?"

"For a big guy, he's mush in the right hands."

"Your hands?"

She sent him a sidelong glance. "We're just friends. Wedding buddies."

That fact didn't make him feel any better.

"What about Carter?" she asked, navigating a turn in the path.

"Let's just say we have a past. Not a good one."

She went silent. Guess he'd need to tread lightly since Carter was her boss.

"So there's no special guy in your life?" he asked.

"No. I don't have time for dating. You?"

"Happily single." *With a miserable track record.* He wasn't about to reveal his baggage on this pleasant stroll up the mountainside.

"Don't we make a pair," he eventually said.

She shrugged. "Guess we're too career-minded."

For once in his life, he didn't like the notion of putting business first. Work had been a pleasure, then an escape for him. Now? With the purchase of the Deep North up in the air, along with his future, what would his third act be?

They passed the first lookout and continued climbing. The incline became steep for a quarter mile, then flattened out. He could hear Carrie's labored breathing as she grabbed hold of his arm for support. He stopped, shrugged off his backpack and reached inside to remove a water bottle.

"Drink," he said as he handed it over. He enjoyed the rush when their fingers brushed.

"Thanks." She opened it and gulped a mouthful, then wiped her lips with the back of her hand. "No wonder you're the fearless leader. I didn't think to bring any water."

"That's why I get the big bucks."

She took a few more sips and nodded. "Of course. What was I thinking?"

"Also, I've been trained in search and rescue, so I'm always prepared."

"So I can wander off the trail and you'll find me?"

"I think I'd always be able to find you."

Under the last rays of the sun, her face colored. "I'm good. We can continue."

They took a few steps and he chuckled. "Spin class?"

Her lips curved downward. "It's been a while. I definitely need to work out more if I'm having a hard time breathing after this short walk."

Once the trail leveled off, he led her to the second, higher lookout. The sun cast a mellow haze over Golden Lake. The water sparkled. From here he could just make out a motorboat creating a wide wake.

"Wow, I've never been up this far," Carrie gushed. "The view is breathtaking. The lake from this vantage point is huge."

He smiled at her, appreciating her positive outlook. "Yeah, it's pretty impressive up here."

"I can see a boat. It reminds me of when I used to sail."

"You like to be on the water?"

"Used to." She sighed. "I had no idea the panorama from this height."

"Wait. I thought you came up here with Serena?"

"To the first lookout. I think she took pity on me. While she found bliss in the surroundings, I crabbed about not having any bars on my phone." She sent him a wry glance. "Pitiful, I know."

Adam stared at the view before him. He'd sworn when he came back to Golden he'd never take this place for granted again. He'd almost lost a part of himself in New York, and Golden had been a much-needed balm when he returned home.

"I get what it's like to be driven. I also know the downside. We all need a place like this to ground us. Reminds you why you're alive."

Carrie stared out at the vista before her. "I never believed there was a downside in working hard. Reaching goals. My dad raised me to find ways around roadblocks. Manage my problems until I came up with a solution. But when I left New York? I was at my lowest. Coming to Golden helped me realize I could get it all back if I refocused."

A sliver of unease snaked through him. "Get it all back?"

"A job with a major corporation."

She bit her lower lip. In the setting sun,

the gesture made it hard for him to breathe. The highlights in her hair shone as the sun angled lower in the sky. So vulnerable, but at the same time, so determined.

"I lost my job before I came here. It wasn't pretty and I don't like to dwell on it, but I want to try again. Prove myself. Get that corner office everyone talks about."

He'd had that corner office. "Not if it comes at too high a cost."

Her serious gaze met his. "Is that what happened to you?"

Questions were reflected in her eyes. He'd opened the door, now how go through it?

"I don't like to dwell on the past, either. But unlike you, I don't want, or need, to prove myself to the people I left behind."

"Not everyone has that luxury," she said, her voice tight.

Carrie moved away and Adam wanted to kick himself. Obviously he'd struck a nerve.

"Sorry. I didn't mean to upset you."

She ran her fingers through her hair, leaving a delightful tangle in the wake. "I get touchy about my career. I know I shouldn't, but there it is."

And here all he'd wanted was to enjoy a hike with the woman who had stolen his attention at a time when he'd thought he'd guard his heart forever.

"How about no more career talk tonight?"

She shot him a wry grin. "I'd say yes, but I need to be sure you're really okay with the *Discover Golden!* campaign."

As much as he should pass on the project, he didn't want to let Carrie down. Or the people of Golden. Her proposal was sound, she'd really thought the idea through and he could see it working. Being a spokesperson wasn't his dream job, but if he got to spend more time with Carrie, it would be worth it.

"I get that I approached you about this out of the blue," she said. "But not only will you help the merchants in Golden, it'll be a way to promote Deep North Adventures."

There was that, although until he had more details about the unexpected buyer, he didn't know if any promotion was necessary.

"You came through on your end by joining me tonight, so yes, I'll be your spokesperson."

Her face lit up and he felt like he'd just given her a precious gift.

"You won't regret it."

"Just make sure my brother doesn't get wind of the photo shoot. He'll rally the gang and make my life miserable."

"Your secret is safe with me. No joking interlopers while we work."

Her shining eyes met his and his chest went tight. How he wished he could confide his frustrations. They had more in common than he'd realized, but while she seemed to have a plan for her future, his was murky. Could she be a sounding board? A business ally?

Until she went back to her old life, apparently. Was it smart to imagine a relationship with her?

His gaze dropped to her lips. The questions faded away and all he wanted to do was kiss her. It had been building for a while, but here, with the leaves rustling and the sky growing darker, and knowing stars would soon dot the inky night, he wanted more from her than just business. He wanted the things he'd never had with Rachel. A deep love. A true partnership.

He wanted a second chance. The idea crept up on him and knocked the wind out of his sails.

Carrie, of course, was unaware of the direction of his thoughts, and her voice reflected her excitement. "So we'll meet tomorrow. Around ten? We can start at the coffee shop."

He shook off his revelation. For the first time since his disaster of an engagement, he wanted a relationship. Carrie wanted work.

Could he risk his barely mended heart over a woman who might leave?

"I'll get my day covered."

"Thanks, Adam. This means the world to me." She went up on tiptoe and brushed her lips over his cheek. He froze, holding his breath. Their gazes held and before he could give in to his impulse and kiss her properly, his aunt shouted.

"Let's go, Adam. You know how fast it can get dark in the woods."

Carrie shook her shoulders as if she too realized what almost happened. Then she hurried over to the group and started an in-depth conversation with the hikers. He took up the rear, uncertain about tomorrow and his close proximity to Carrie, yet hoping the hours flew by until they met again.

CHAPTER FIVE

THE NEXT MORNING, Adam noticed a woman hovering by the stone arch leading into the town park. From his vantage point he could make out a wide-brimmed floppy hat and large sunglasses. The woman resembled a celebrity on the run.

The back of his neck prickled.

"Take a look," Carrie said, holding out the camera so he could scroll through the thumbnails of the photos she'd taken.

"I like the natural beauty in the background. What about you?"

He nodded, his gaze moving back to the woman who still stood sentinel. Why was she bothering him?

A cell phone ring brought him back to the reason he was in the park, sweltering under the intense sun while in a suit and tie, all because he couldn't resist Carrie and her project.

"That's me. I'll just be a minute."

While Carrie took the call, Adam stuffed his hands in his trouser pockets and paced.

When he glanced back toward the strange woman, she was marching his way, her sandals wobbly in the thick grass. His heart sank. He knew that determined stride.

Halfway to him, the woman pulled off her sunglasses and her gaze collided with Adam's, who now had a laser focus on her.

"Some things haven't changed," she said in a cheery tone when she stopped before him. "Still dressed to make a deal and pacing in the meantime."

"Rachel."

"Adam." She wiggled her fingers in a wave. "Hi."

With a poker face, despite the turmoil churning inside, he asked, "What are you doing here?"

"Funny thing…" A nervous laugh escaped her. "I'm sort of on the run, which, now that I say it out loud, sounds ridiculous for a put-together thirty-year-old woman, but sadly, it's the case."

He placed hands on his hips. She must have recognized that stance, because she cringed.

"Okay, not so funny. I…um…was in the neighborhood."

"Golden is hardly your neighborhood."

"Fine. I came to see you. I need your help."

He didn't speak until he could trust that his voice canceled out all emotion.

"You're kidding me, right?"

She held up a hand with pretty, manicured nails. "You have every right to be terse with me. I know I hurt you. At the time I wasn't thinking straight and made everything so much worse, but now I'm in a predicament."

"What now?"

Her shoulders stiffened at his tone. Yes, it was harsh, but really, she was here asking him for help after running out on their wedding?

"This was a bad idea."

She turned on her heel, ready to run, again, when Adam called out to her.

"Rachel, stop."

She paused as Adam came around to face her. He took a steady breath. "What are you doing here? Really?"

She blinked back what looked like tears. "I realize you're the last man on earth I should ask for help," she blurted. "My parents are pressuring me to get my life together. They're still angry with me for canceling the wedding."

"So you decided to come to Golden?"

"You talked up this place so much and

came back here to live. I thought it might be a good place to stay for a while."

This could not be happening.

"I thought maybe we could talk. Make up and try again?" Her voice wavered.

"After you broke up with me in a text?"

"Not my finest moment," she muttered.

"And left me with the fallout when you took off?"

"I'm sorry. I panicked."

He shook his head. "You've got to be kidding me."

"Sadly, no." She adjusted the bag on her arm and pouted. "I have no place else to go."

The tension between them crackled.

"You're busy. I can come back—"

"Stop."

She tilted her head as if waiting for him to say more.

He blew out a breath. "I can't believe you're actually standing here, asking for another chance."

"We had something good, Adam. Until I messed it up."

"Did we? Because your actions proved otherwise. Made me question just how firm our commitment was."

"You remember the pressure."

"I do. And I tried to make it easier for you."

"Which I appreciated, but you know my parents. They never listen to me."

"I wished you'd come to me instead of running away."

"Even you were caught up in the hype, Adam. Don't you remember? How you wanted to impress your clients?"

He flinched. "And now you expect me to pretend nothing happened? I was hurt and confused, and you skipped the ceremony and went directly on to the honeymoon. I assume you enjoyed it." He brushed a hand though his hair. "Why would I consider your request now after you broke up with me?"

"Because you're a good guy?" she asked with a wry grin.

He dropped his chin and shook his head. They were not going to solve anything right now, not when his emotions would get the better of him. He needed time to sort this out.

"Where are you staying?" he finally asked.

"A place called the Nugget Bed and Breakfast."

"For how long?"

"Um, I'm not really sure. I'm on a budget."

"I'll make arrangements for you to remain there until we straighten this out."

"Adam, you have no idea how much this means to me. If we can try again…"

The hurt he couldn't deny sounded harsh when he said, "There is no *we*, Rachel."

A beat passed. "Still, I can't thank you enough."

"I need to get back to work. We'll talk later."

"Of course." Rachel started backing away. "Later."

Trying to compartmentalize the shock of seeing his ex-fiancée, Adam returned to Carrie, who had finished her call and was concentrating on the camera. If Rachel honestly thought they'd get back together, she was wrong. He had to nip whatever plan she was scheming in the bud.

"Hey. I wondered where you went." Carrie glanced over his shoulder. "Friend of yours?"

"I'm not sure how to answer that."

Her bright smile made him flinch. "It wasn't a tough question."

He rubbed two fingers over his temple where an ache was building. Rachel was in town. Why now, when he was finally ready to test the waters and see if his heart could trust again? He knew he'd have to get answers at some point, but the shock and anger consuming him made his thinking fuzzy.

"How about we get back to the project at

hand," he said, a bit more briskly than intended.

"Are you sure?"

He leveled his tone. "Positive."

Slowly, she scrolled through the rest of the thumbnails for him to see. They'd started the morning outside of the coffee shop, rather symbolic, before moving to the steps of the city hall, then taking random pictures outside of different shops on Main Street before ending up at Gold Dust Park. She stopped on a picture of Adam striding up Main Street, the shops at his back. "Do you like the lighting in this frame?"

"I do, but I'm not smiling."

"You look deep in thought."

"I don't think that's what you're going for."

"Maybe, but it's an interesting angle." She pulled the camera closer to inspect her work. "If we could go back and reshoot, you could lift your head this time. Have your eyes meet the camera, as if you know the secret to being successful in Golden."

"Being successful has a look?"

She grinned. "Don't play coy. I imagine you've worked with enough powerful people to recognize that expression."

"True. But I also know the merchants here in town. Their smiles say it all."

"Point taken. But you're going to be the initial print campaign. Look successful and when I photograph more locals later, we can capture the joy of living and doing business in Golden."

"I'll defer to your expertise."

Her hand covered her chest. "Be still, my heart."

Despite his shock over Rachel, he smiled.

He hated that he'd have to tell Carrie about Rachel. Not because he had anything to hide; he seldom talked about that period of his life. But he and Carrie had just begun spending time together. Were in that stage of learning about each other. He wasn't sure how Carrie would feel about him not broaching the subject of Rachel right off the bat. Yes, they'd admitted that they both held back by not revealing parts of themselves. For good reason. He'd planned to lay it all out, but the time hadn't been right yet.

And now it's less convenient with Rachel here.

It wasn't like he'd spent enough time with Carrie to bring up the non-wedding. How did he introduce that into a conversation?

I know we have this whole work thing in common, but have you ever been stood up at the altar?

No, he'd hoped to be smooth about it, but now…

He glanced at Carrie as she reviewed the pictures. As usual, she'd dressed professionally, in a bright pink sleeveless blouse and navy skirt. Tall heels. She'd pulled her hair back, but a few strands escaped and curled around her cheeks.

Did she sense their attraction, too? Was he enough to keep her interested in staying in Golden? Yes, he was getting ahead of himself, but once he made a decision, he acted on it. Right now, getting to know Carrie better was on the top of his list. Even if Rachel's arrival had thrown him a curve ball.

Carrie loaded up her supplies into a cloth bag and they walked through the park to return to Main Street.

Not ready for the conversation that was going to get real personal, real fast, he said, "I'm guessing Carter isn't generous with his advertising budget. No professional photographer?"

"First of all, thanks for your faith in my skills, and second, you're right. I can hire a photographer, but who knows what I'll get. At least if I'm the one taking the pictures, I control the narrative."

"Did you take the photos for other clients

at your old company?" Despite the surprise visit, he was committed to moving forward with the getting-to-know-Carrie plan.

"When I could. We worked with professional artists who usually took care of the creative content, but after receiving a few less than stellar proofs, I bought a camera and started practicing on my free time."

He smiled. "Not much of a high achiever, are you?"

She shrugged. "I prefer to think that I'm particular. Exacting."

"And when things don't go your way?"

"I regroup."

Like she would when he revealed his relationship with Rachel? Maybe Carrie wouldn't care and he was blowing this out of proportion, but still, he hesitated. "From what I've seen, you have a keen eye."

She sent him a saucy smile. "Then no more questioning my decisions?"

He actually chuckled at her amused expression. "I wouldn't go that far."

They arrived at the vicinity of the shot Carrie wanted to recreate.

"Go down about twenty feet, then start my way. And remember, I want to capture success."

He did as he was asked, trying to broadcast

"successful." It wasn't a feature you could just adopt: either you had it or you didn't. He'd worked with enough high-profile executives to know the difference. Should he smile? Scowl? Glance at his watch like he was a busy man?

"Now," she called out to him.

Starting with an easy walk, he remembered those days in the New York office. Imagined he was working on an acquisition. How his mind would crunch the numbers. Consider the gains or losses. It all came back to him like second nature, which should have bothered him. Instead, he realized his mind had always functioned this way, whether in New York or in Golden.

"Great," Carrie said, snapping away as he moved. Before he knew it, he'd reached her.

She scanned though the pictures. "Adam, these are perfect." She looked up at him. "I swear, you could be a model."

"No thanks." He shuddered. "Leave me in the background."

"Except for *Discover Golden!*"

"Deal."

She lowered the camera. "I think we've gotten plenty for me to start with. Thanks again."

"Save your thanks until I okay the picture choices. You promised me input."

"I did."

"And visibility for Deep North."

She snapped her fingers. "We need a few shots in front of your building. Maybe get the seniors to join you."

He imagined the chaos posing with his aunt and her friends would bring. "Although I told you not to let anyone in on our project today, how about adding Colin and some of the guys instead? They're all successful in one way or another."

"Ooh, better idea. You're good at this."

"So we're finished for the day?"

"You're free!"

He paused, then said, "How about lunch? My treat."

She blinked at him. "Um, okay. Where to?"

Thrilled she'd accepted his invitation, he thought about the choices in town. "Smitty's Pub?"

"Sure. We can walk from here."

At lunch, he'd tell her about why he left New York. Hope she took it in stride as she seemed to with everything else.

They headed north in the direction of the pub, which catered to the locals of Golden.

Antsy now, he asked, "How long will it take for you to finish this project?"

"Hopefully not long. But I have the summer splash to oversee, so I'll be doing both at the same time."

"Multitasking?"

"Seems like I'm always running but I can handle the time crunch."

"If there's anything I can do to help, just ask."

"Thanks. Mrs. M. gave me an idea I'm working on. I'll let you know."

They reached the rustic log-cabin-style building. Smoke trailed from the chimney in the back, the scent of hickory growing stronger the closer they came.

Carrie touched her stomach. "I forgot to eat breakfast. I'm starved."

He held the heavy wooden door open for her, leading her into the pub, which was filled with tables of varying sizes, mismatched chairs and a long bar. Country music streamed from the speakers. The lunch crowd was already here, if the rowdy greetings were any indication.

"There's a table," he pointed, letting his free hand rest on the small of her back as he directed her. They got settled as Jamey Johnson, the owner, came to the table with menus.

"Must be a special occasion if you two left the office for lunch."

"Could be we were craving your cooking," Carrie countered.

Jamey bowed with a flourish, which should have been ridiculous for a man his size but came off as graceful.

"How about two specials," Adam said. He'd seen the board outside with the item listed: barbecue beef with a savory sauce on a brioche bun and a side of homemade potato salad. His mouth was already watering.

"Hey." Carrie took the menu. "Maybe I want to consider my options first."

"Yeah, Adam," Jamey teased. "Carrie has a mind if her own."

Didn't he know it.

She sent Adam an I-told-you-so glance, then handed the menu back to Jamey. "Two specials and iced teas."

Jamey winked at her. "Good choice."

She pointed a finger at Adam. "Don't say a word."

"Never."

She chuckled.

He tried not to let the easy camaraderie between Carrie and Jamey bother him. The two had teased and challenged each other since day one, but Adam noticed that as much as they liked each other, they'd never dated. Still, he didn't want to be *that* guy, the jealous one.

"Hey," Carrie said, nodding toward the door. "That's the woman from the park. Who is she?"

The ache in his temples started banging again. Knowing whom he'd see, he looked over his shoulder anyway, confirming his hunch. It was time to reveal the secret he'd been holding back.

"My ex-fiancée."

CARRIE'S MOUTH DROPPED OPEN. Had he said ex-fiancée? "Come again?"

"Sorry I didn't tell you earlier. I'm still wrapping my mind around her showing up out of the blue."

She had so many questions, but started with, "How long has it been since you've seen her?"

"Over a year."

Carrie followed the progress of the dressy woman who practically glided from the door to the bar where she took a seat on a stool and fanned out her skirt. She flipped her brunette hair over her shoulders in a careless manner.

"Should we invite her over?" Carrie asked,

at a loss over etiquette involving a man she was very interested in and his ex.

"No," came Adam's adamant reply.

Carrie shook off her momentary surprise. "Things didn't end well?"

"If you call her sending me a text a few hours before the wedding to cancel not ending well."

Oh dear. And she thought leaving New York because she'd been fired was humiliating. Seemed they both had good reasons for making their exit from the city.

"Why is she here?"

"She claims she wants to get back together."

Carrie's stomach pitched. She glanced at the beautiful woman and her spirits sank.

"It's not going to happen," Adam assured her.

But she knew things could happen out of one's control. Her mother leaving. Her father reacting by becoming rigid. Losing a job at a company she'd trusted to have her back.

The woman at the bar turned their way, with a calculated expression on her face. Apparently, she hadn't gotten the memo.

"I... I don't know what to say."

"It feels like a lifetime ago. I didn't mention it because I don't want to dredge up the past."

She understood. Then suddenly realized this must be why he was so closed off. Carefully, she placed her hand over his, trying to go for compassion instead of pity.

"Is she the reason you left New York?"

"Partly." He frowned. "Mostly."

Jamey returned with their drinks. He caught sight of her hand on Adam's and raised an eyebrow. She shot him a glare and his expression went neutral.

"Food should be out in a minute," he said, then turned to another table.

The lull in conversation was uncomfortable. She and Adam had finally begun to talk about all sorts of topics. Their doubts were disappearing. They were becoming real friends. More, maybe? But what did she say in this moment?

He spoke for her. "Please don't make this awkward."

"Okay." She glanced at the ball game playing on the TV above the bar. "Um, the Braves. Think they'll go far this summer?"

He grinned. "You follow baseball?"

"No, but every guy I've met in Golden loves it."

"We all played in high school."

"Yes, I've heard the stories." She tapped a finger against her lip. "I should try to get one of the players to come up here and endorse Golden. Wouldn't that be a hoot?"

"And cause a riot?" He sat back and crossed his arms over his chest. "I never pegged you as a troublemaker."

"There's a first time for everything."

"Then I want a front-row seat."

His words warmed her heart. She'd always followed the straight and narrow to impress her dad, but maybe a tiny walk on the wild side with this man might be just what she needed. This summer could be more fun than she'd imagined.

Adam pressed his lips together, then said, "Thanks."

She rose an inquiring eyebrow.

"For making lunch...normal."

Their eyes met and held. Her stomach whooshed and her heart raced. In the short time they'd decided to be in each other's company, her interest in the man had skyrocketed. By his steady gaze, she thought—hoped—he felt the same way. Yes, she had goals, but was getting involved with Adam one of them?

It should be.

She had to agree with her inner voice. Even if a relationship muddied the waters. Pulled her in two different directions.

Was she up for that?

The sound of a chair being dragged over the floor broke the spell. They both jumped as the woman joined their table.

"I'm sure Adam mentioned me," the woman said. She held out her hand. "Rachel Harrington."

After a brief pause, Carrie shook the woman's hand. "Carrie Mitchell."

"Are you a…friend of Adam's?" the woman asked, her eyes on Adam.

"Rachel." Adam's tone issued a warning.

"Any friend of yours is a friend of mine," she said, forcing a hurt expression.

"Business associates," Carrie answered when Rachel returned her gaze.

She thought she heard Adam groan but when she glanced his way, his face was expressionless.

"Adam's putting me up in a cute little B and B while I visit," Rachel added, leaning her elbow on the table and dropping her chin in her upraised palm. Could she be any more adoring?

Adam met her gaze. "Until she decides where she's off to next."

Rachel patted his arm. "You're so funny. I'm not going anywhere."

"We'll discuss that later."

Before the tension level reached the danger

zone, Jamey returned to deposit two plates on the table.

"I didn't know anyone was joining you." He nodded at Rachel. "What can I get you?"

Rachel examined their plates, inhaled and winked at Jamey. "I'll have what they're having."

"Be right back."

Rachel took Adam's napkin and placed it over her dress. "So, tell me all about Golden."

Carrie's appetite fled, along with her desire to make small talk with a woman who clearly wanted her ex back.

And since she was hanging around town? Should Carrie step back and let him deal with this problem?

Normally Carrie would be on her way to figuring out a solution to this woman suddenly showing up, but her lightning-fast thinking escaped her. This was personal, not professional. Did she keep this newfound relationship with Adam from advancing any further? Focus only on a high-stakes career, which would mean leaving Golden?

Just like after she'd been fired, Carrie was stumped. Needed time to sort out her emotions.

One thing she did know for sure: the remainder of this lunch was destined to be a disaster.

CHAPTER SIX

"You're late."

Carrie looked up from the document she was reading on her smartphone and caught a glimpse of Adam. She'd had a restless night, rehashing the uncomfortable lunch yesterday with him and Rachel. Coffee from Sit A Spell was a necessity right now.

She wasn't sure how she felt about Rachel. Carrie and Adam weren't a couple; he hadn't been obliged to confess that he'd once been engaged. But if Rachel hadn't come to Golden and forced the issue, would he have ever told Carrie about her?

Not that he owed her anything. After all, Carrie had made it plain that she intended to return to New York at some point. But the times they'd spent together, had been…fun. Easy. Had made her imagine what a life not ruled by work could be like. Was that why the other woman, and Adam's connection to her, bothered Carrie so much?

She straightened her shoulders. "I didn't

realize I needed to check in with you every morning."

She took in his usual preppy outfit she'd convinced herself she didn't like. Today he wore a gray polo shirt, black jeans and a great pair of shoes.

He is definitely your type.

He flashed her a wide smile, dimples in full view. This man was dangerous. "I can set my watch by your punctuality."

She should really overlook those dimples. Though she tried not to be any more attracted than she already was, she failed. If anything, he was more handsome in the morning light. Why did she have to become interested in the man just when his ex appeared in Golden?

Talk about timing.

And were they really not going to talk about the ex-fiancée situation?

She kept her voice level when she spoke. "Sorry to mess up your schedule. I'm reviewing notes." In a few hours she had a meeting with the owners of the Wild West Rodeo Show and needed to get up to speed about their operation.

"More ideas for your binder?"

"For the summer splash," she said, pocketing her phone. "And why does it matter to you if I'm punctual or not? Until recently, this was the only time we ran into each other."

Adam rocked back on the heels of his shiny shoes, but didn't move from his position in front of one of the iron bistro tables placed outside courtesy of the coffee shop. If she were a more suspicious person, she'd wonder what he was up to. Especially after his reluctant admission of his ex.

Yesterday, the atmosphere at the lunch table had been tense, with Adam trying to act as if Rachel leaving was a foregone conclusion, while the other woman chatted away about people they knew in New York, and how she was excited to see where Adam lived. That had made Carrie wonder why Rachel had never been to Golden when they were engaged.

Despite the brave front, Carrie had caught an uncertainty in Rachel's eyes. Adam was not playing her game.

She swallowed a sigh. When all was said and done, Carrie had no idea where her own fascination with Adam was going.

"It matters because I've found myself waking up in the morning with a smile on my face, knowing I'm going to see you here bright and early to start the day."

She hadn't expected that answer, and darn if it didn't zing right to her heart.

Adam, so easygoing and considerate, looked at her expectantly. She felt frustration and a tingle of something else, both of which she tried to ignore. Meeting Rachel had changed the dynamics of their morning routine. For her, at least.

On the heels of that thought came another. Maybe he'd been so hurt he didn't want to dwell on the past. She could commiserate, but the situation still didn't put her on solid ground.

"The topic of your punctuality is just what I need to get a reaction out of you," he continued, unaware of the thoughts bombarding her brain.

"Please," she muttered, even though it had worked. "I'm not overly late, so you'll just have to go about your day like normal."

His forehead wrinkled. "That doesn't sound like fun."

"Sorry, don't have anything in my bag of tricks to entertain you this morning. All I need is my Friday morning coffee and I'll be on my way."

He tilted his head. "What's wrong?"

"You can ask me that after introducing me

to your ex yesterday? A woman I had no clue about?"

He winced. "The operative word here is *ex*. Sorry for the surprise. Trust me, it came as a shock to me, too. I didn't think she'd ever show up here."

"Fine. Honestly, I have too much on my plate to worry about your drama."

"There is no drama. Rachel and I have been over for a long time. I have no intention of playing into whatever scheme she's cooking up."

She almost laughed. Whether he wanted to admit it or not, his beautiful ex was in town and drama would ensue. So no, it wasn't over.

She moved to step around him but he blocked her way.

"Adam, what gives?"

His face turned serious. "I'm afraid I'm the bearer of bad news."

Her chest went tight as she waited for the worst. Had something happened to his aunt? His brother?

He jerked his head toward the building behind him. "The coffee machine is down. Myrna came out to tell us just before you showed up."

She blinked at him, at a loss for words.

"No coffee," he emphasized.

Carrie sputtered in disbelief. "I thought they got a new machine?"

He shrugged.

For a split second, she thought she might cry. After the never-ending night, she'd been desperate for coffee to get her through her morning.

"But I'll have to drink the office coffee." She shuddered. Then glanced at her watch. "Maybe I have a few minutes to run home and make my own."

"No need."

She stared at him, wondering what he was up to. Those steel gray eyes held all kinds of secrets, but at this moment, they mostly shone with contained mirth.

"Adam?" she pushed out between clenched teeth.

With a flourish, he stepped away from the bistro table. "I snagged the last two cups."

Her jaw dropped. "You've been hiding those the entire time?"

With a pleased smile on his face, he said, "That's why they call me a man of mystery."

"No one calls you that, but I'm grateful." She paused. "Wait, one of those is for me, right?"

"You may have crushed my dreams of being a mystery man, but I'm not cruel." He handed her a cup. "One for each of us."

She reached out, then paused before taking it. "What if I wanted iced tea today?"

"Like you had to read the menu after I ordered the lunch special for both of us yesterday?" One dark eyebrow rose. "Have you ever had anything but hot coffee in the morning?"

"It is summer and it is exceedingly warm." She pretended to think about it, then wiggled her fingers in a gimme motion. "Never mind. Hand it over."

"One coffee with a packet of sweetener and a splash of creamer."

She couldn't squash the little thrill that he'd paid attention to her usual order, even if she was miffed with him.

After taking a sip and swallowing, she sighed. Heaven. "How about we replace man of mystery with do-gooder?"

"That doesn't have the same flair, but I guess it's apt."

Which left her wondering what other secrets he had hidden, because the one about his ex was a whopper.

She took another sip, the cobwebs in her mind clearing. "The machine is really broken?"

"No. I was just getting a rise out of you. Although, no one would want a repeat of Delroy's reaction from the other day. Especially moms who were freaking out over their children hearing his choice of words."

She chuckled, imagining a scandalized mama covering a small child's ears with her hands. "I'm glad there's no new emergency."

Golden had its fair share of characters. The longer she lived here, the more they grew on her.

"Gave me an excuse to buy you a cup of coffee."

They'd only taken a few steps in the direction of the sidewalk when Adam said, "I owe you an explanation."

"No, you don't."

"I was going to tell you about Rachel, but how would I start that conversation? We've only recently started spending time together and the canceled wedding is not a topic one discusses right away when getting to know another person.

"Bringing up the past is painful. I was between a rock and a hard place, Carrie, and I'm sorry for not being up-front with you."

Now she couldn't be mad at him. He'd just answered all her questions.

"I'll admit, I was caught off guard."

"Me, too. When Rachel approached me in the park, I wanted to tell you and get it over with so we could move on, but I wasn't sure how."

She glanced at his sincere expression. "You really don't want to get back together?"

"No. She needs something from me, I can tell. I just don't know what it is. And despite all that happened, I don't want to leave her in the lurch."

Which made him a wonderful man. His ex had hurt him, yet he was willing to help her. How did Carrie get so lucky to have garnered his attention?

"So, are we good?"

She didn't know for sure, never having been in this kind of situation. Should she be concerned that he'd be around his ex? Possibly fighting any rekindled feelings? If she were smart, she'd be on her guard, despite his assurances. But the hesitation in his tone made her heart go all gooey. This was an awkward situation, mostly for him.

Instead of voicing any of that, she answered, "Yes. We're good."

Relief crossed his handsome face.

They resumed their walk in the direction of the Chamber.

"Busy this morning?" he asked, regarding her with inquisitive eyes that read too much. How did he manage to make her so restless when he was merely standing there, being polite and inquiring about her day after just explaining his sticky personal situation?

"I have to visit the Pendergrass farm and see about recruiting their show for the summer splash."

His eyes lit up. "That's a great idea. Ty and Brando are good people."

"I already talked to Ty over the phone, but we have a few things to address before moving forward."

"I'm sure it'll all work out."

She hoped so, too, so she kept her fingers crossed.

"Working at the Chamber must be so different than your career up north."

"It is, but honestly, I've learned a lot. Maybe because there's no competition in the office. We each have a specific job and we do it but come together for the greater good."

"Unlike the cutthroat world you came from?"

She forcefully pushed away those memories.

"Different, yes, but not any less challenging. You know yourself how important it is to keep Golden in the spotlight."

"Deep North Adventures has always had loyal return customers and new folks who love the outdoors, but yeah, the Chamber's push to get Golden on the map has given us a bump in revenue. Your newest campaign will certainly bring us more visibility."

A bump? Their business was a top producer in town. "Please, it's unlike you to be modest."

His smile was genuine. "We've been fortunate."

That was putting it mildly.

"Well, fortunate or not, we all need to work together. So this project Carter has given me will be advantageous to everyone."

"Good ol' altruistic Carter."

"You do realize you're going to have to tell me the reason for your animosity one day."

"Let's just say that when we were in high school, Carter was all about Carter. At all costs. Things didn't end well between us."

Hmm. What did Carter's actions have to do with Adam?

"I have to admit, I'm surprised by his real investment in the future of Golden. I just haven't deciphered why," he said.

"Not everyone has an ulterior motive."

One of his dark eyebrows rose. Was he only thinking about Carter, or Rachel, too?

"Really? You're not giving him any credit?"

He laughed. "Oh, I give him credit. Doesn't mean I trust him."

"Sounds like history rearing its ugly head."

He went serious again. "Perhaps. But I can be big enough to put it behind me, as long as Carter behaves."

"Behaving or not, he's done a good job so far."

Adam smiled, a small crack in his facade. "You have to say that. He's on the board of directors."

"Carter is still gung ho about getting the news of Golden out to the world, but he's been a little short with the staff." She chuckled. "All three of us."

"But I give credit where credit is due," she continued. "And yes, I was fortunate enough to get the job at the Chamber. It doesn't mean I wear rose-colored glasses. I realize Carter is all about Carter."

"Good, I don't want him bamboozling you."

She reared her head back. "Does anybody really use that word?"

"Men of mystery do."

She laughed. He might tease her, challenge her and give as good as he took, but he was also fun. She hadn't allowed herself to have any fun before moving to Golden. A point she needed to seriously consider while plotting her New York reboot.

She pointed a finger at him. "Just don't interfere with Chamber of Commerce projects and we'll be fine."

He placed a hand on his chest and pulled a pained expression. "I would never."

"Remember that."

A wry smile twisted his lips.

Her phone dinged. She didn't have to look at it to know she was going to be late if she didn't get a move on.

"As usual, it's been a pleasure. Now, I have important things to do."

His smile kicked up a notch, making her wish she could call in to work sick—something she'd *never* considered before—and spend the day with him.

"I wouldn't expect anything less."

ADAM GRINNED AS Carrie sashayed down the sidewalk. He loved her sass, the way she tossed her hair over her shoulder, the way her topaz eyes sparkled, either in humor or frustration, whenever they sparred. And spar they did. He'd be a liar if he said he didn't anticipate their daily banter.

Yeah, he knew Rachel had thrown her for a loop. All he could do was tell her the truth and hope Carrie understood. She'd left upbeat, so things couldn't be that bad, could they?

He strode to his car and headed to Deep

North Adventures. His mother had texted him this morning, informing him that she was waiting for documents concerning the potential sale. She'd insisted that Adam be copied in all correspondence from now on as the company contact, so he would have a better idea of where they stood soon with the CEO of Aiming High Sporting Goods and Adventures.

As soon as he entered the building, Brea stopped him in his tracks.

"You promised that the snack bar was my domain."

By her expression, whatever had happened wasn't good. "It is."

"Then tell her."

Brea pointed across the room at Rachel, who was leaning against the counter and talking to Jocelyn like they were long-lost friends. Rachel had always had the ability to make small talk with anyone. It took more to draw Adam out of his shell, and when they'd been together her gregarious nature had helped ease him into new social situations. Back then he'd been charmed by it, but that was a lifetime ago.

"What now?" he muttered under his breath.

"Now you set guidelines," said the girl with the magenta-colored hair.

He didn't need his employee to tell him what he needed to do. He knew Rachel, and this was not going to be easy.

Jocelyn looked up when he crossed the room. Her eyes went wide, and she turned her attention to the computer. Rachel, dressed in a sleeveless lace top and matching skirt, swung around. She shot him a practiced smile when she saw him. Yeah, she was going to be a problem and he needed to expedite her exit from town.

She'd always known how to dress. Knew how to use it to her advantage. With her hazel eyes and wavy brown hair, she was stunning. No man with a pulse could deny that. But while once he'd seen her beauty as part of the entire package, now all he felt was mistrust. No amount of cajoling was going to change his mind. They were done and she needed to accept it.

"Adam. I love your company's headquarters. You never told me it was so…homey."

She seemed honestly captivated. Back in New York, Rachel had been accustomed to Adam or her father's plush offices. Top-of-the-line furnishings, subtle decorating, thick carpet the heels of his shoes sank into. The million-dollar view. This humble gathering place for clients was a far cry from Manhattan.

"Rachel, what are you doing here so early?"

"I'm here in Golden, so I wanted to see what you were up to." She looked over the shelves of merchandise. "I'm impressed."

"You would have known what to expect if you'd ever come here with me while we were engaged."

Her cheeks went bright red and she tipped her head down.

He regretted his tone immediately.

"Sorry. That was uncalled for."

She lifted her head. "No, you're right. I never bothered to see where you came from. What your life had been like."

They stood in uncomfortable silence.

Rachel spoke up first. "Um, business is doing well?"

"Yes."

"Jocelyn tells me you have tours booked all day."

"Summer is our busy time."

She nodded. Her gaze moved across the room. "I love that you offer food for your clients. There's nothing that brings people together more than good food."

He narrowed his eyes. She liked to cook, the one thing she could do quite well.

"I was just telling Brea that I can give her some healthy options if she's interested."

Adam's eyes went wide. Rachel had given Brea a suggestion about her beloved snack bar? No wonder Brea was ticked.

"Brea is in charge and I trust her. Now, if you'll excuse me, we've got clients arriving soon."

"I'll just be a minute. I've been trying to have a conversation with you and you've ignored me since I arrived."

"Rachel—"

Colin appeared at the counter. "Adam, you need to come to my office."

Grateful for a reprieve because, really, he didn't know what to do with Rachel hanging around, he nodded.

"Excuse me."

"I'll be out here waiting," came her singsong reply.

Yep, there was no doubt she was going to be a problem.

As soon as he was in the office, Colin shut the door.

"Bro, what is going on?"

"I'm not entirely sure. Rachel showed up unannounced."

"She's got some nerve."

"She wants to get back together."

Colin's jaw dropped. "So, what, you're

gonna let her hang around while you figure it out?"

"Figure it out being the key point."

Colin shrugged one shoulder. "Your funeral, man."

"It's not that dire."

"What about Carrie? You two just started your…thing."

"Carrie is up to speed, so there will be no funeral."

"If you say so. Have you read Mom's email?"

"Not yet, you?"

"More like skimmed. I know you'll have a better handle on the particulars after you examine the proposal."

"I'm going to my office."

His brother reached behind the desk for a backpack. "I have a hiking trip in thirty minutes, then need to stop at my shop. The search and rescue last night put me behind."

"I was going to join you when the call went out, but Chief Maloney said you and the others had it under control."

"We did. You can catch the next emergency."

"I will." He headed to the door. "We'll regroup later after I make heads or tail of this offer."

Adam went to his office and for the next hour, pored over the contents of the email.

Rigby Fletcher, CEO of Aiming High, had sent over a detailed report. Adam had researched as much as he could already, but now he had more relevant information about the company that consisted of ten stores, all located out West.

Profit and loss statements. Projected sales. Details explaining why he wanted Deep North. The purchase offer was well above market price. So, why did Adam still have that nagging sensation that something was off? Why did Fletcher want to acquire their small business? Expansion alone might be a good enough reason, but why did he insist on dealing with Adam's mother?

Ultimately it was a family vote, but he knew they would wait for his guidance. He had to be impartial, even if he didn't know where to go next if they sold.

He leaned back in his chair and clasped his hands behind his head.

His parents had retired, wanting to travel. Colin had a side business that could become a full-time business if he had more hours to devote to his craft. Maybe his family was ready to move on.

Are you?

The question that had hounded him ever since their mother had told them about the

unexpected offer. He didn't like feeling this…
untethered. He hadn't felt like this since Rachel left him and he had to decide if he would stay at the New York firm or come home.

Numbers always grounded him, but in this case, after reading the Fletcher report and considering his future, he felt aimless.

Enough. He tidied his desk and stood, stretching his arms over his head before going out front to check on things. He opened the door and made his way down the hallway, raised voices meeting his ears.

"How can you show your face here?"

"Adam and I are working things out."

"There is nothing to work out. You made sure of it."

He strode into the gathering area to see his aunt and Rachel in a face-off.

"I know you don't like what happened—"

"Like has nothing to do with it. You humiliated my nephew. Broke his—"

"Aunt Bunny."

His aunt spun around midsentence, her face red, tears glistening in her eyes.

"Adam, what are you thinking?"

He walked over and placed his arm around the older woman's shoulders. "Everything is okay," he assured her.

"Why now?"

Adam shot Rachel a glance. "That's a fair question."

Despair flashed across Rachel's pretty face. She tangled her fingers together, not the first glimpse of doubt he'd noticed since she arrived. Yeah, there was more going on under the surface than she was divulging.

"I… This is complicated."

"Well, you can just take your complications and go home," Aunt Bunny said, her body shaking. "Adam deserves better."

He put some steel into his tone. "Aunt Bunny."

Rachel blinked away the hurt and turned to drag her purse from the counter. When she faced him again, features composed, she said in a firm tone, "We need to talk, Adam."

"I have to work."

"Fine. I'll see you later." She started to walk away, then stopped. "I understand your anger," she told Aunt Bunny. "I deserve it."

Rachel's heels clicked as she crossed the room. As soon as she was out the door, Aunt Bunny whirled on him.

"Are you really going to humor her?"

He dropped his head back and started at the ceiling.

Why?

As the question hung in the air, he tried

for reassurance. "Give me some time, Aunt Bunny. Let me help Rachel and she'll be on her way."

"You're sure about that?"

He wasn't sure about anything, but he was positive that Rachel was not his future. Could that role belong to Carrie? To answer that question, he'd have to let go of the old wounds that had made his heart less willing to trust again.

CHAPTER SEVEN

AT NOON, THE MEMBERS of the Golden Match-makers Club, minus one, sat around a picnic table in Gold Dust Park waiting to start the emergency meeting. The heat was sticky, but the group enjoyed iced tea and finger sandwiches courtesy of Alveda.

Bunny Wright appeared under the arch, scanned the park to locate her friends, then hurried over.

"We've got trouble," she announced as she sat down, concern etched in the lines on her face.

"It's bad," Wanda Sue piped in.

"You know about this?" Alveda asked.

"Yes. I'm the one who urged Bunny to call the meeting."

Gayle Ann held up her hand. "What's going on?"

Bunny swallowed a few times before saying, "Adam's ex-fiancée is here."

"In Golden?" Gayle Ann gaped.

"Yes. Making waves. I ran into her at Deep

North Adventures. I'm telling you, she has her eye on gettin' Adam in her clutches again."

Alveda pushed out a breath. "You know you tend to exaggerate, right? It can't be that bad."

"He's putting her up at the bed-and-breakfast."

The group went still.

"You're positive?" Gayle Ann asked, not liking the current situation. If anyone had asked her, she'd swear Adam would never reunite with the woman who had destroyed his confidence.

"We all know Adam wasn't quite like himself when he returned from New York," she continued. "Yes, he was always more on the quiet side, but when he came home…it was like he'd locked his heart and soul away."

"That's the best description," Bunny said with a nod of her head. "He's still smart when it comes to finances, but falling in love? I don't know if he'd risk getting burned another time."

"We all agree that around Carrie, he's more like himself. It makes sense that if he did fall in love, it would be with a woman like her."

But what if Gayle Ann was wrong? Adam had always been hard to read. And Carrie, was she up to the task of breaking down his walls?

"Start from the beginning," Gayle Ann instructed.

Bunny told them how she'd gone to see her nephews and found Rachel hanging around the business.

"We had words," Bunny finished.

"Oh boy," Alveda muttered.

"She insists that Adam is helping her and he confirmed it. If he's not careful, she'll lure him into her selfish plans."

Harry took a sip from his tall glass and laid it on the table. "Adam is a grown man. I'm sure he sees what is going on."

"Does he?" A helpless frown wrinkled Bunny's brow. "Rachel is beautiful and charming, a dangerous combination for a guy who weighs the odds before making decisions. She knows that about him and is playing on his good graces."

"Or," Alveda added, "maybe Rachel truly regrets driving Adam away. Who would show up out of the blue unless her intentions were to make things right?"

"That's assuming she wants closure." Bunny frowned. "I'm not so sure."

"You're also biased," Wanda Sue said.

Gayle Ann rested her elbows on the wood table and clasped her hands. "Could Rachel have ulterior motives? You didn't show up to see the man you left at the altar unless there was a compelling reason."

"Do you have any idea what Adam is helping her with?"

Bunny frowned. "No. They're both tight-lipped about it."

The group went quiet again.

"I think we knew going forward that this would be a challenging match," Wanda Sue said, wiping the condensation from her glass. "Adam has always kept his emotions hidden, even when he was growing up. Yes, he was hurt, but he is also a very compassionate man. Do we really know if he would give his ex a second chance?"

"I remember how devastated he was when he returned to Golden." Alveda poked one finger against the table. "He needs a project to keep his mind busy. Rachel could be that project, which will affect our mission."

"Or Carrie could steal his attention," Gayle Ann countered. "They both thrive on discovering solutions to problems. So we throw roadblocks in their way. They'll come together for the greater good and discover they love each other."

"What did you have in mind?" Harry asked, his mustache quivering as he grinned. "I recognize that cat-got-the-canary gleam in your eyes." Alveda cut in before Gayle Ann could speak.

The members kept their focus on Gayle Ann.

"I might have unintentionally set the ball in motion," she said.

Harry smiled at her. "Do you do anything unintentionally?"

"Not usually, but I was speaking to Carrie the other day, sort of picking her brain to see what she was up to. Sent her in the direction of the Pendergrass rodeo show."

"But they're fixin' to close up," Wanda Sue countered, her brow wrinkled in confusion.

"Originally I mentioned it because Adam has a tie to the show. And it was a good option to her work dilemma. But now that I think about it, because the show has limited resources, Carrie will do what she does best—problem-solve. And Adam will be there to support his friends with the show's final hurrah."

Bunny didn't look convinced. "How can you be sure about Adam?"

"I'll call Brando after our meeting. Maybe he can get the boys back together for the final show. I'll pitch it as a nostalgic touch for Golden. At this point, he'll take all the help he can get."

Understanding dawned in Bunny's eyes. "So Carrie is there to find out about the show and Adam rides in like a knight in shining armor—"

Alveda snorted.

"Okay, a financial whiz who knows how to hit a bull's eye."

"Better," Alveda teased. "Especially when Carrie learns about his role in the show."

"My point," Gayle Ann continued, "is that we maneuver Adam and Carrie together whenever possible by whatever means necessary. Now, our secondary assignment is making sure Rachel doesn't play on Adam's heartstrings. She may have a good reason for seeking him out, but we need to buffer whenever possible. What do you think?"

"That you have a sneaky mind?" Alveda said with awe. "We knew that already."

Gayle Ann shot her friend a scowl. "It's not like I use my powers for evil."

Wanda Sue grinned. "No, you have a very developed sense of honor. Why do you think we joined up with you?"

"Because our young people need our leadership," Alveda said.

"Precisely." Gayle Ann couldn't agree more.

Alveda pushed her glass away from her. "I have to say, I feel rather bad making Rachel the villain here." She held up her hand when Bunny sputtered. "Yes, she didn't handle the breakup in the best way. But do we really know why she ended things with Adam?"

Bunny frowned. "Adam never said."

"Right, because that's how he rolls." Alveda's forehead crinkled. "I agree that Adam and Carrie have a shot, but what about Rachel? Can we delve into the reason why she's here? Maybe lead her in a different direction?"

"You're a lot more charitable than I am," Bunny groused.

Alveda's eyebrows rose. "Whatever we decide, Bunny should stay away from her."

"It is worth considering." Gayle Ann picked up her pen to jot the idea in the club notebook. She knew where Alveda was coming from, how losing love in the past had shaped the woman's life, making her an ally with a soft side for the underdog.

Right on cue, Alveda said, "No one says we can't assist another in finding true love."

"We've never done two matches at one time…" Gayle Ann trailed off, contemplating the idea.

Bunny crossed her arms over her chest. "I don't much like the idea, but if it directs Rachel's scheming elsewhere, I'm all for it."

"Then leave it to me," Alveda said.

Bunny, her mouth set in a mulish line, nodded.

"There is one problem," Harry reminded them.

All eyes turned to him.

"In the end, what if Carrie decides to return to New York or some other city?" He turned to Gayle Ann. "We can't control everything."

"That's true, but sometimes you have to believe in the greater good."

"Which I do," Bunny interjected. "We may have a double purpose in this matching commitment now, but we are up to the task."

Gayle Ann straightened her shoulders. "So we continue as planned, with a few modifications?"

Every head nodded in agreement.

"Then let's get to work."

As the group broke up, Harry lingered while Gayle Ann collected her pen and notebook.

"Something you wanted to say, Harry?"

"I noticed you've given leeway to Alveda. Care to explain?"

If there was one thing Gayle Ann would not do, it was reveal a past Alveda had overcome. Even to a man Gayle Ann was sweet on. "No. But believe me when I say that she's the perfect person to root out Rachel's motivations."

"Then I'll take your word for it."

Her lips twitched. "Good to know."

"Now." He held out his arm so she could link her own through his. They strolled the park in a leisurely manner. "There's the matter of you and I."

Gayle Ann glanced down at the beautiful bracelet Harry had given her and her heart picked up a beat. "What did you have in mind?"

"How about we use the summer splash as a sort of announcement that we are a couple."

"Are we?"

His bushy eyebrows angled. "I thought so. Was I wrong?"

"No." Gayle Ann hated to admit the next part. "I haven't told my family. Or Alveda."

Harry stopped walking. "Do you think they'll have reservations?"

"I can't see why."

He tilted his head. "Then what is the problem?"

"I… This is so unexpected at our age."

"I don't see why age makes a difference. You are an attractive, vital woman and I've wanted to make my move for a while now."

She chuckled. "Make your move?"

"Show you how I feel." He lifted her hand so they could both see the bracelet. "Who knows how much more time we have on this earth? Why not enjoy it with a special someone?"

"You do have a point."

"We spend a lot of time and energy matching young couples. Why can't we have our own happy ending? Lead by our own example."

Gayle Ann wanted to be happy with Harry. She'd been a widow for many years and never thought she'd encounter romance again. And to have it now in her twilight years? She should be rejoicing, not second-guessing.

"I'm not trying to pressure you, Gayle Ann."

His words put her uncertainties at ease and made her heart race.

"How about we focus on this match? In the meantime, I'll think it over."

He patted her hand with his. "I'm going to hold you to it."

CARRIE GLANCED DOWN at the line items she'd crossed off her list. Her prospects for the summer splash, which still needed an official name, were slowly vanishing.

"So, besides the horses, you have no livestock?"

"Two cows. Five goats. We kept them for the farm." Ty Pendergrass grimaced. His sable-brown hair needed a trim and his clothes were dusty. "Since we've cut back dramatically, we mainly feature horse events. This is why Golden is our last show. Due to financial constraints, we had to sell most of the cattle that were used in the more popular rodeo acts."

This was not what she'd expected when she drove out to Crestview Farm this morning, banking on the rodeo to be a crowd pleaser. When she'd arrived at the Chamber earlier in the day, she'd been greeted with the news that Shelia was going to be late. Instead of preparing for this meeting and putting the finishing touches on the *Discover Golden!* promo, Carrie had to run interference with other business owners who hadn't been happy with the director's no-show.

It was midafternoon by the time she'd been able to escape the office. As she stood talking to Ty, she wished she'd changed into cooler clothing. The air was thick and hot, but an occasional breeze lifted her hair from her damp forehead. The earthy scent of animals, hay and dust tickled her nose. Not unpleasant, but a world away from the scents she remembered from city life.

"So, what does the show entail now?" Carrie stared down at her notes. "Your website lists roping and riding."

"Sorry, we haven't updated our site. We've been focused on moving the entire operation here to Golden and getting ready to open the farm as an entirely new enterprise." He lifted his wide-brimmed hat and brushed a hand through his thick hair. "We'll continue the horse acts. I do the stunt riding, my sister is a competitive jumper and my nephew entertains the crowd with goat tying. We still wear period costumes to give the folks some flavor."

This was nowhere near the summer spectacular Carrie had in mind.

Ty frowned. "I guess I should have been more up-front when you called, but you sounded excited, and to be honest, we'd like our final show to go out with a bang."

A horse whinnied in the distance. Carrie rolled her shoulders, thinking through the current dilemma. She didn't know much about horses, although she'd had friends who rode when she was growing up. The idea of a rodeo had been her entire hook, but with no calf roping or bull riding, she was limited in what she could publicize.

"Back in its heyday, this farm featured equestrian shows," Ty went on to say. "Since buying the property, we've already fixed up the training arena, stables and paddock. The former owners hosted our rodeo here, so the folks in Golden are familiar with the setup."

"That's one thing in our favor." Carrie scanned her surroundings.

The farm was beautiful but run-down. The outside of the stable had been recently painted and the fences around the event arena were in the process of being repaired. She had no desire to step inside the stable and check its condition. Horses made her nervous.

"What are your plans for the farm?" she asked.

"We're going to offer horseback riding excursions for tourists and lessons to locals."

"Sounds like your entire family is experienced."

"You don't spend years riding for other people's entertainment without it being in your blood."

But was it enough? "Any other acts you can incorporate?"

"No. The other performers moved on when we streamlined the show."

She clasped the notebook to her chest and breathed deeply. "Okay, so it'll be a pared-down version, but I can work with that. What do we need to do from here?"

"We've already gotten the word out about our grand finale. If you can get the news out through your channels, it'll help."

"That I can do."

In the distance she saw a tall boy herding goats into a pen. "Is that your nephew?"

Ty glanced in the direction of her focus. "Colton, yes. He tends to the goats, as well as performing the goat-tying event."

Goats were smaller animals. Maybe there was a way to use them to her advantage.

"Any way we can make the goat-tying act interactive?"

"Liability-wise, probably not, but I like the train of thought."

"What about some kind of animal show-case? Is there a local 4-H group?"

"As a matter of fact, there's a chapter in Golden. Plus, there's a 4-H camp about five miles out of town located on the lake."

"Since it's summer, there would be kids at the camp?"

"Most likely."

She tapped the pen against her lower lip as her mind raced.

Ty slipped his fingers into his jeans front pockets. "What're you thinking?"

"That I call the camp. Get some of the kids on loan to promote the program. The local kids might have livestock they can bring here, maybe as a kind of petting zoo?"

"Now, that is interaction on a manageable level."

"Kids always love to be around animals and it's a great way to promote the 4-H program."

Ty grinned. "All in all, good for Golden."

"That's the plan."

She jotted down her ideas, organizations to call and notes on how to blend these new ideas together.

They discussed details for thirty minutes. Ty gave her a tour of the facilities, where they would park cars and other logistics, giving Carrie the big picture. They ended back at the stable. She was ready to get back to her office to brainstorm when a red truck slowly made its way down the driveway leading to the parking lot. To her surprise, Adam hopped out, followed by Jamey climbing out of the extra cab and Colin from behind the wheel.

She turned to Ty. "Looks like you have visitors."

He smiled. "More like good friends. I called

them to help me get rid of some outdated machinery in the barn."

She crinkled her forehead. Adam? She couldn't picture it in his business casual clothing. Colin and Jamey, on the other hand, were dressed to work in a barn in jeans and T-shirts. The three joked around with the ease of a longtime relationship.

Adam's lips curved into a welcome smile when he finally noticed Carrie, which made her pulse pick up. So far her day had been one problem after another, but seeing Adam filled her with peace and excitement at the same time. She corralled her racing heart as he headed directly for her. No time to wipe the dust from her pants, straighten her blouse or fix her hair, which was currently pulled back in a ponytail.

"Carrie. I didn't know you'd still be here."

"I needed to go over logistics with Ty."

"Lucky you," Colin quipped as he joined his brother. "We're the hired help."

Jamey pulled up the rear. "More like the heavy lifters."

"You wish," Ty said, but the relief on his face telegraphed his gratitude at their arrival.

"You did call for assistance," Jamey reminded him.

"For a good cause." Ty glanced at Carrie. "I used to perform with these guys."

"Perform?"

"They were part of the rodeo for a few summers."

Her mouth fell open.

"Not the reaction we'd expect," Jamey joked.

"At the height of our rodeo popularity, we needed extra hands during the busy summer months. Jamey's dad and mine were old friends, so he got them involved," Ty explained.

She held up a hand, still processing this interesting news. "Hold on. You were all in the show?"

"Guilty," Colin said.

"What did you guys do, exactly?"

"Cowboy mounted shooting," Colin said, his grin widening at Carrie's shock.

Jamey chuckled. "Rodeo clown. You need to be fast on your feet or have a bull stomp you. Also kept the performers fed."

"Archery," Adam said with a twinkle in his eyes.

Carrie rubbed her forehead. "How?"

"Jamey's dad traveled to state fairs as an advisor," Adam explained. "He recruited us to go with him during summer break and we signed up with the Wild West Rodeo Show."

"They quit coming after high school, but we remained friends. It's part of the reason my family bought the farm here," Ty expanded.

Carrie's surprise slowly turned into curiosity. "So you guys all worked together?"

"We did," Adam confirmed, "We were a pretty solid team at the time."

"The ladies appreciated our horsemanship," Colin said with a wink.

"Speaking of skills," Ty said. "I found some sports equipment in the barn you might be interested in." He tipped his hat at Carrie and led Colin and Jamey away. Adam stayed behind.

"You looked shocked," he said.

"I am, although I shouldn't be. Mrs. M. mentioned that you had ties to the show. She just didn't elaborate."

Adam had a way of surprising her that both delighted and intrigued her. She liked the dichotomy.

"Where did you learn archery?"

"We own a sports adventure business, remember?"

"As if I could forget."

He chuckled. "When Jamey talked us into

going with him on the road, we focused on our different strengths. I was on the archery team in high school."

"How does that fit into a rodeo?"

"With the stunts. Ty and I had a routine where he would ride, holding up a giant hoop, and I'd shoot arrows through at a prearranged target. Turns out the sport depends on a lot of precision and concentration."

"Which made you a natural?"

"It did."

"Why am I not surprised?"

He nodded to the paddock where a lovely chestnut-colored horse came to greet them. Adam reached out to stroke the animal, waving Carrie over. "I also took care of grooming the horses after the show."

Carrie stayed put. "I'm not very good with animals," she informed him. "We didn't have any pets when I was growing up."

"There's nothing to be afraid of." Adam ran his hand along the length of the animal's side. "Just talk to them. Maggie here is a sweetie."

Not wanting to act like a coward, she inched closer. "Don't tell me you're an accomplished rider, too?"

"Not accomplished, but I have a degree of comfort." He glanced her way. "So, how are the preparations going?"

"I'm afraid that what I have to work with might not be enough. I thought it was a complete rodeo. Now I discover they're just really a horse show."

"What's wrong with that? People enjoy equestrian events."

When the horse shook her head and snuffled, Carrie waited for it to hurt Adam, but he continued stroking.

"True. But it's not as big a showstopper as I'd hoped."

"What more do you need?"

She mentioned her idea about the 4-H organization getting involved. "I'll have to see if we can work it out."

"See? You're already making it bigger."

"I wish I had another draw." She sighed. "Something the locals will be talking about for months after."

"This is Golden. They're always talking about something."

"True, but…" Her eyes lit up. She pointed a finger at him. "You, Jamey and Colin."

"What about us?"

"Resurrect your acts. It's not strictly a rodeo now, so we can go in whatever direction we want."

He placed a hand on his broad chest. "You want us to be involved?"

"Why not?" The more she talked about it, the more she warmed up to the idea. "The fact that we have hometown boys performing will make it a huge hit."

"That was a long time ago."

"You're backing out?" she challenged, sure he couldn't resist her goading.

His eyes narrowed. "I didn't agree to anything."

"Yet."

"It's been years, Carrie."

"You can practice. The show isn't for another five weeks."

He chuckled. "It's not that easy."

"So make it easy. I'm going to promote Golden and by extension, Deep North Adventures. Can't you pitch in and do this one last thing for Ty's family?"

"You do realize that I'm already helping you by being a part of your *Discover Golden!* promotion."

"Yes, but we can always do more."

He glanced at the horse, not appearing the least bit convinced.

"Maybe performing in the act is like riding a bike. You never forget."

"And when do you expect us to practice? We all have jobs."

"If you agree, I'm sure Ty can work around

your schedules in order to refresh the acts with you." She reached out to squeeze his arm. "Please consider it."

"You'll have to get the others on board."

She waved her hand like it was already done. "Piece of cake."

He stared at her for a long time, then closed his eyes for a beat. When he met her gaze again, she tried not to melt at the warmth there.

"Since you asked so nicely."

She jumped up and down. "You won't regret this." Her ankle twisted as she landed wrong on her high heel, and she reached out to grab hold of Adam so she wouldn't fall. He pulled her into his arms.

"Whoa, there."

"I suppose I should wear more sensible shoes when I come out here."

"Sound thinking."

She glanced at him, hoping he didn't notice her pounding heart. If he did, he didn't react. Instead, he held her gaze with an intent expression that made her breath lodge in her throat. His gray eyes flashed and still she held on.

She should move away. She would. In a moment. Right now the feel of his arms around her, how he only had eyes for her, made her pulse race. How did he have this hold over her? Yes, he was good-looking and nice and smart, but it seemed like this mutual attraction had suddenly jumped to the next level. Like neither of them expected it and didn't quite know what to do about it.

Voices in the distance broke the spell.

"This will work, Adam," she said, stepping back to smooth her blouse. Was she talking about the show or what was blossoming between them?

"Trust me, I'll make sure of that."

Her face heated at his vow, but she took his agreement as a win.

She collected her composure just as the men rejoined them. Had they seen her in Adam's embrace? Colin raised an eyebrow at his brother, but no one said a word.

"I have an idea," Carrie said, hoping to draw their attention away from what they might or might not have witnessed.

"What's up?" Jamey asked, amusement shining in his eyes.

Yeah, they'd seen.

"What do you guys think about dusting off your act for the show? It'll be a draw and help out Ty."

Ty removed his hat. "My dad mentioned

the idea but I didn't give it much thought." He glanced over at his friends. "But maybe…"

Colin and Jamey exchanged glances, then looked at Adam.

"I already said yes if you guys are in."

Jamey shrugged. "We can't very well let Carrie down by saying no."

"How about letting me down?" Ty teased.

"You'll survive," Colin said.

"So," she asked, holding her breath as she awaited their reply.

"You up for this?" Colin asked Ty.

"Actually, I think it would be a blast."

Colin met Carrie's gaze. "Then I guess we've got you covered."

Relief poured through her. "Thank you."

"Don't thank us yet. We need to discover if we still have our moves," Jamey said.

"I have faith in all of you." She purposely didn't meet Adam's gaze. She was on over-load with that man as it was. "So we'll set up a practice schedule for you."

The men nodded.

"We need to get back," Colin said, tugging his truck keys from his pocket. "I have a zip-line excursion in an hour."

"Yep, got a dinner crowd showing up soon." Jamey clapped Ty on the shoulder. "They won't like the chef missing."

"Thanks for stopping by," Ty told them.

"I'll be back with the truck to help you haul off that machinery," Colin told him. "Next time I'll get my brother to actually help."

Adam made a production of looking around. "I don't see anything that needs hauling."

"No, you were otherwise distracted."

Carrie willed herself not to blush.

As the men walked to the truck, Adam lingered.

"Looks like you owe me this time."

She swallowed hard. "Looks like I do."

A roguish grin tugged at his lip and his dimples appeared. "Good, because I plan on collecting."

As he walked away, Carrie hugged her notebook to her chest, happy to have gotten the direction of the non-rodeo back on track. With everyone's help, the splash would be spectacular.

Her gaze moved to Adam, catching his salute as he got into the truck.

As long as she wasn't distracted.

CHAPTER EIGHT

A WEEK LATER, Carrie wandered into the cozy living room she shared with Serena, before starting her Friday. The sun streamed through large windows framed by sheer panels, casting a glow over the wood floors. From the first day she'd arrived in Golden, she'd fallen in love with the homey apartment Serena had created above Blue Ridge Cottage.

She went directly to the kitchen of dark wood counters and white cabinets to pour herself a cup of coffee, then turned, to notice her friends Serena and Heidi camped out on the navy couch, wearing matching smiles.

Carrie stopped short and narrowed her eyes.

"What's up with you guys?"

"Why don't you tell us?" Serena asked, flicking her black hair over her shoulder, her probing blue eyes twinkling.

Carrie recognized her friend's amusement and didn't like it. She dropped into an oversize armchair, smoothing the green shorts she'd paired with a light sleeveless shirt, ready to be outdoors for most of the day. What she wasn't ready for was the upcoming conversation. By the matching expressions on the women's faces, they were going to ask about Adam. What did she tell them when she hadn't figured it out for herself?

Heidi, all grins, snuggled deeper into the cushion. Great. They were in for the long haul.

"I'm headed to Crestview Farm this morning," Carrie informed them.

Heidi's forehead wrinkled in concern. "On a weekday?"

"It's for work. I need to check in on the summer splash preparations."

Serena sipped from a mug. "Hmm."

"We talked to Lindsey," Heidi confided. "She said you're super pumped about this project. It's all you talk about at the office."

"It's finally coming together. The kids I met at the 4-H camp are amazing. They're so knowledgeable about animals and so much fun to be around. They're very excited about the splash." Carrie paused. "Speaking of the splash, I need a name for the event so I can start printing material and get the word out. It'll be at the end of the Summer Gold Celebration, so what do you guys think about

Golden Summer Spectacular? Golden Glory Days. Golden Summertime Smash?" She wrinkled her nose. "Too much gold?"

The room went quiet as they all ran ideas over in their heads.

"You said it's less a rodeo and more a collection of outdoor acts," Heidi said.

"Carter wants a catchy name in case we do it again next year."

"How about Eureka Games?" Heidi suggested. "It has a fun ring to it."

"You can't go wrong with Heidi's idea." Serena took a sip from her mug, then said, "If the event is a success and we hold it every year, you can build on the game premise."

Carrie ran the name over her tongue. *Eureka Games.* Yes, it would work.

"Good. One thing to cross off my list."

"Are you going to the office at all?" Serena asked.

"At some point. Why?"

"Just wondering what Lindsey will have to tell us after you leave, that's all."

Carrie narrowed her eyes. "What has Lindsey been saying?"

"Only that you've been singing the praises of one Adam Wright."

She really didn't want to go down this road. Yes, she more than liked Adam. Yes, she'd talked him into assisting in her projects. And yes, they were enjoying each other's company, but she still put the job first.

"It's strictly business-related."

Serena chuckled. "And we know you're all about your career."

Carrie blew out a frustrated breath. "Okay, you two, stop with the innuendos and just come out with it."

"Adam," they said at the same time.

She placed her mug on the coffee table. "What do you want to know?"

Serena sent her an amused glance. "When this started, because you've been mum on the topic."

"There's nothing much to tell. We bump into each other in the coffee line most mornings and started talking. I asked him to help with the *Discover Golden!* campaign. Then, when I realized the rodeo show wasn't really a rodeo, I talked him, Colin and Jamey into reviving their acts."

"According the Mrs. M., you went hiking with Adam."

"With the seniors, too!"

Heidi sent a smirk to Serena. "She does seem a bit defensive."

"Because she doesn't have a good reply," Serena said.

"I'm right here," Carrie protested.

Serena's knowing expression made her twitchy.

"It had to happen sometime."

Carrie decided to play dumb. "What had to happen?"

Serena held up her mug in Carrie's direction. "That you would find a man who caught your attention."

"Yes," Heidi piped in. "Life isn't all about work."

Carrie gaped at her friend. "It was until you started dating Reid."

"So I can speak from experience. I thought I was living life, but really it wasn't until we got together that I started truly enjoying myself. There's a difference."

Carrie rolled her eyes. "I get it. You two are happy with your significant others."

Serena's humor turned serious. "Do you see Adam as a possible boyfriend?"

"I might have. Before his ex showed up in town."

Heidi grimaced. "Yeah, we heard that, too."

"From what I've seen," Serena added, "Adam has no intention of getting back with her. So you can't let that stand in your way."

"I'm working hard so I can earn my way back to a job in New York."

"Are you still going to be stubborn about that? You don't need to update your résumé—you're a part of Golden now," Serena insisted.

For all her talk about getting her résumé in order, Carrie couldn't remember the last time she'd looked at it. Because she was so busy?

Serena's expression changed. "Wait. You haven't spoken to your father, have you?"

"No."

If anyone knew just how much the past had a hold on Carrie, it was Serena. There was no doubt that the idea of disappointing her father again was a strong motivator to do a good job and return to her old life so he would be proud of her. He'd been the only parent she had growing up. The one constant she could depend on, criticism and all. Plus, she'd already learned a lot, like applying her skills to unique situations and for different audience sizes, whether it was rural or urban, that would add to her arsenal when she got that job with a big company. It felt good to build on her experience. Leaving her last job the way she had had been a blow, but she was slowly regaining her confidence. She hadn't totally lost her creative edge.

Still, Carrie pondered Serena's words. She really was starting to feel like a part of this small town. Liked that she'd been able to leave her mark here so far. If she hung in for a few more months, would it make it difficult to leave Golden? For what she considered the big time? She worried she was simply hiding, afraid of what her father might think if she didn't meet his expectations.

On the heels of that came the daunting revelation that since she'd joined forces with Adam, she hadn't thought about her father much. Or the circumstances leading to her coming to Golden. She'd settled into her job, had made real friends. Maybe being so career-minded—if it meant giving up other aspects of life—wasn't all it was cracked up to be. So, why was proving herself still so important?

She held up her hand when it looked like Heidi was going to jump on the stay-in-Golden bandwagon. "It's still a real possibility, but I can't think about it until after the summer ends."

Her friends exchanged glances but wisely withheld their opinions.

"How about this?" Serena said after a few moments. "Why not enjoy your time with Adam? No pressure. I can see you two being good together in so many ways, so be open-minded."

Oh, Carrie was indeed relishing her time with Adam. That was the problem. She found herself craving a touch of his fingers or the shiver of delight when she saw the banked heat in his eyes. From time to time, she thought about ditching work for a few hours so he could introduce her to a new hiking trail in the woods. Did she risk having her heart broken over a man she wasn't sure could give of himself completely?

Carrie didn't want to fall for Adam, only to be rejected for Rachel. She wasn't sure she could survive that kind of hit.

A romantic relationship was not like a business deal. In the latter scenario, she made contingencies, perfected her well-researched pitch and delivered for the client. Nothing personal. But love? She'd seen it go bad with her own parents. It could be messy, hurtful and darn right exhausting if it went wrong. She decided to voice her concerns to her friends.

"I'm not saying this will happen, but what if Adam and I get involved and he decides he wants to get back with his ex?"

"You have a lot to offer," Serena told her.

"And the two of you think alike," Heidi added. "It's all about the bottom line. Well, if you decide the bottom line is that everyone needs love, including you, my friend."

She silently agreed. No point saying the words, *Yes, I more than like Adam* out loud, then have her world blow up when she thought everything was going so well. Just like it happened in the New York office.

Carrie rose, grabbing her mug to carry to the kitchen.

"I'm grateful that both of you are watching out for me, but I'm a big girl. You know I'm going to put one hundred percent into my job. And if that means working with Adam, fine, but it doesn't translate into dating or whatever."

Serena smirked. "That's code for you haven't figured it out yet."

That was the trouble with having a best friend. She knew Carrie's tells. But Carrie did like someone having her back.

She'd never had close friends when she was younger. After her mother took off, she hadn't wanted to get close to anyone, afraid to be hurt when they left. As she got older, she concentrated on excelling at work, never cultivating her social circle. Looking at Serena and Heidi, she realized that she'd missed out, but was fortunate to have found these women and valued them in her life.

Unable to help herself, Carrie went to the couch and hugged Serena. "I do love you, even when you're interfering."

"I know."

Heidi pulled an offended expression.

With a laugh, Carrie hugged her, too. "Before Reid, you never would have let me hug you."

Heidi shrugged, but Carrie didn't miss the pleasure on her face. "What can I say? Love changes a person."

"You should try it." Serena winked at her. "Now, I need to get ready. The store opens in fifteen minutes."

"I'll get down there and be ready for my shift," Heidi said.

Shaking her head, Carrie gathered up her tote bag loaded with her supplies for the day and left the apartment. She jogged down the wooden staircase behind the building, wearing flats as Adam had suggested. She'd taken two steps out of the alley onto Main Street when she noticed Mrs. M. and Alveda loitering by Blue Ridge Cottage.

"The store doesn't open for a while yet," she told the ladies as she joined them. "Serena is still getting dressed."

"We know, dear. I have some wedding ideas I want to run past her, so I'm excited. And early."

Alveda smiled at Carrie. "It's nice to have the chance to chat with you."

"How is the job going?" Mrs. M. asked.

"Great. As you suggested, I talked to Adam and he agreed to be the spokesperson for *Discover Golden!*, so I'm putting in the hours to complete that project."

"I'm pleased to hear that."

"I also called Ty Pendergrass about the rodeo like you mentioned. We're teaming up."

"I heard something to that effect. In fact, I understand Adam is involved with that project as well?"

Carrie held back a grin. Mrs. M. knew full well that she'd not only contacted Ty, but that Adam and the others had signed on.

Moving past the mention of Adam, and her conflicting emotions for him, Carrie said, "We've had to tweak the concept, but I think the new direction will suit Golden."

"Brando hated to give up the show," Alveda said with a tsk. "But it was time. We aren't young forever."

Mrs. M. nodded solemnly in agreement. "But the show will be in good shape with you overseeing."

"I'm not the overseer, per se, but I am working closely to make sure I match the promotion to the acts we've lined up."

"You'll be checking all the stunts so that everything goes off without a hitch, though, right? It's your responsibility to keep an eye on the process." Alveda smiled.

"I'm sure Ty has it covered." Carrie frowned.

Mrs. M. tapped gently on Carrie's arm. "I know you haven't been in Golden long, but since you're semi in charge, it's important to keep those involved with the show in line.

"Technically this might be the last Wild West Rodeo Show, but Brando can't help himself. He'll try to make it bigger than it should be and who knows what can happen."

"It's the entertainer in him," Alveda said.

"So I'm supposed to rein him in?"

"Exactly. And the only way you can do that is to confirm all the activities are safe and will go off without a hitch."

No one had mentioned Brando's tendency to overdo things. Immediately her mind leaped to safety measures and crowd control.

"I'll check into it," she assured the ladies.

"We knew you would. You are a true asset to Golden."

Carrie smothered a cringe at Mrs. M.'s praise. Yes, she wanted this day to be a success, wanted to make a name for Golden. But she also wanted to return to her old life. Her guilt rose. Carrie heard the voice of her father urging her to work harder with no distractions in order to take on the world; but she also envisioned Adam, smiling with a heat that made her toes curl. She was happy to make this small town a tourist destination in order to benefit the merchants. Could she have both?

"Well, I'd better get to the farm and see what's going on."

"Have a wonderful day, my dear," Mrs. M. said the same moment Alveda pointed to the shop door as Serena unlocked it.

The women had given her a lot to think about.

Before long she pulled her car into a parking spot beside the stable. Expecting to see Ty, she was surprised, and a little nervous after her conversation with her friends, to see Adam strolling her way.

"To what do I owe the pleasure?" she asked as she exited the car, hiding the shiver of awareness that showed up on a regular basis now. His thick hair was windblown, his face tan from the sun and he'd dressed today in rugged, outdoor clothing.

"Ty had a meeting he couldn't miss, so he called around to find someone to fill in while he's gone."

"And you were the lucky one?"

"Everyone else was busy."

She reached in her tote for her sunglasses.

"I find it hard to believe you didn't have your nose in a ledger."

He shrugged. "Maybe the numbers can take care of themselves for a while."

She doubted it, then wondered why he looked away when he made that claim. "You okay?"

"Sure. Why wouldn't I be?"

"Because it's been brought to my attention that I live to work. I'm sure the same can be said of you."

He smiled. "I got the impression we had the same outlook. But when the numbers don't need you…"

"So there is a problem?" she pressed.

He shook his head. "I'm not sure, so for right now, why don't we concentrate on why we're standing in the hot summer sun getting *your* summer splash under control."

She slipped on her glasses. "Eureka Games. And are you saying it's out of control?"

"Like the name. Catchy."

"No dodging. Is everything under control?"

"Yes," he assured her. "We're still figuring out logistics. The show will be streamlined, but we've carved out time to practice. Brando is still determining how the acts will play out."

"Then it's a good thing I'm here. In my capacity as promoter, I need to make sure all the stunts will be safe."

"Meaning?"

"I need to go over each act."

He raised an eyebrow. "That's a tall order. You don't trust Ty?"

"Of course I do, but Mrs. M. and Alveda told me it was important I kept a firm handle on the show. Especially Brando."

"As in?"

"Making sure we have security protocols."

He pointed to the stable. "Ty will go over our acts with you when he gets back, but I can vouch for the safety. They've been doing this for years. He wouldn't put his family or the animals in danger, no matter how much they want this farewell show to be a success."

"Have you been practicing?"

"Pulled out my bow last weekend and went to a target range. I was a bit rusty, but as the week progressed, I got up to speed in no time."

"And Colin?"

"Same. He goes to the range often, so it's just a matter of getting his seating on a horse."

"Jamey?"

"Since we don't need a rodeo clown, he's going to stick with helping with the horses."

"What about a pen for the smaller animals the 4-H kids are bringing?"

"As we speak, Colin is building one to keep the animals safe, as well as a fenced area to allow visitors to pet the goats." He pointed to the arena nearby. "Ty thought placing the pen between the parking lot and the arena would create a streamlined flow of traffic."

Good. It was all coming together.

"Then things are going smoothly?" she asked.

"Yes." His eyes glittered with humor. "Were you convinced they wouldn't?"

"This is just me, making sure it all goes as planned."

"Why do I think this has something more to do with your last job?"

This man was way too perceptive. And like Adam, she didn't want to talk about it. "Because you're too smart for your own good."

He shot her a grin that made her insides go topsy-turvy.

"You know you can talk to me, right?" Adam teased. He didn't want to scare Carrie away from a more serious conversation, but wanted the skinny on everything about her.

"I know. I choose not to."

He'd gotten her back up.

"Because?"

She narrowed an eye at him. "You don't give up, do you?"

"No."

She huffed out a laugh. "I told you, I thought things were going swimmingly with my job at Craigerson and Company. My clients liked me. The bosses were happy with my work. Unbeknownst to me, trouble was brewing. The office was very competitive. Cutthroat at times. I let my guard down. I can't do that again."

"What really happened, Carrie?"

She paused, as if finding the right words.

"One day I was finishing a promotion for a client, the next my boss called me into her office to tell me the client was unhappy, and another colleague was working with the company rep going forward. A colleague who had gone behind my back and ruined my integrity. I'd been so sure I had everything under control that I missed the signs of someone undermining me. Needless to say, the company wrongly backed my colleague, and I was eventually told to leave. So I ran to Golden with my tail tucked between my legs to get over the shock and disappointment."

And the hurt. He read it in her eyes.

He'd been there.

"It's hard to come back from something

like that, Carrie. Finding out you'd been used, recovering from the secrets that deeply affected you makes you rethink every step of your life. I wished I'd been there for you."

"Thanks." Her face softened. "Does it beat your non-wedding?"

"Not quite, but I'm sure the impact was just as life-altering."

"On that we can agree." She shrugged. "So I'm a perfectionist who wants to make sure this show goes off without a hitch."

"Noted." He rubbed his hands together, wanting nothing more than to spend the day with her. "Let's get to it."

He took her around the stable to the arena to show her the targets he'd set up earlier. There were four for Colin's act, large boards with blue and red bull's-eyes. "These are placed in different sections of the arena. We can remove them quickly and put out the crossrails for the jumping act."

"What about the archery part? Where do you aim?"

"Away from the audience. I have my back to the stands while Ty gallops by."

"It's like a well-oiled machine."

"The show might be closing down, but Ty and his family have done this for so long that they can sniff out problems before they happen."

She sent him a sideways glance. "Sorry about going on about safety."

"I don't blame you for being concerned, especially since Mrs. M. brought it up. This is your first go-around."

He led her to the stable, noticing her pause.

"C'mon. The horses are locked in their stalls."

She moved until they heard a whinny and a loud huff of breath.

"The only way to get over your fear is to meet it."

He brought her to Maggie, hoping Carrie would remember the animal.

She pushed her sunglasses on top of her head as she started walking again. "I'm not afraid. I just don't know what to expect."

"Hold on." He strode to the office and re-emerged with his hands full. When he got closer, he let her take a peek.

"Baby carrots and cut-up apples?"

"Treats."

He dropped a few carrots in her hand. "Just let the horse smell them and she'll take it from there."

"I don't know."

He held out the apple pieces for the horse.

When Maggie devoured them, he turned to-ward Carrie. "Like I said, Maggie knows what to do."

A bit tentatively, Carrie approached, hold-ing out her hand. Adam stood close, hoping to give her some confidence. Maggie did the rest.

Carrie pulled her hand back. "Oh, wow, that tickles."

"Not so bad, huh?"

She smiled at him and his chest constricted.

"Can I try it again?"

He handed her a few more carrots. Again, she approached the horse and laughed when Maggie took the snack.

"Before you know it, you'll be a pro," he predicted.

Carrie stepped closer to the stall door, peering over as the horse turned around.

"Since you're going to be with horses at the events, it's a good idea to be comfortable around them."

She glanced over her shoulder. "That makes sense." Her brow puckered. "I'm really not a chicken, you know."

"You've proven yourself."

She blinked, as if his words surprised her, then moved to face him.

"Thank you."

The gratitude in her eyes did surprise him. His pulse kicked up a notch when she leaned in to brush a soft kiss over his lips. Her perfume held him hostage, a scent he'd only ever noticed on her. The fragrance, and the woman, would always make him think of summer. Before he realized what she was doing, she'd stepped back, acting a little shy.

"What did I do to deserve that?"

She shrugged. "You urged me to try, not believing I'd fail."

"That's because I don't think you'll fail."

"It's a big deal."

He wasn't sure why, but he'd take the compliment.

They continued walking through the long stable, passing stalls, the feed storage, tack room, office and finally the grooming area. He stopped to show her the assorted brushes he would use to groom the horses after the show.

"You'd be surprised how much dirt and mud gets in their hair. It takes a lot of work to get the grunge off the coat and make it shiny again."

She lifted a soft brush that was nearby. Ran her fingers over the bristles. "Do you think I could watch sometime?"

"Sure. Come to a practice and we'll do it together."

She beamed at him.

"Maybe you'll want riding lessons."

She held up a hand. "Slow down. Baby steps here." But she didn't look opposed.

The more he got to know Carrie, the more he was charmed by her. She had that effect on people. Her sunny personality was infectious, and she was so determined to bring Golden to the forefront of the vacation market. No wonder the locals loved her.

She'd even admitted to being nervous around large animals but hadn't shied away from feeding Maggie. This city girl had no idea what went into taking care of horses, let alone the show events, but when she put her mind to it, she gave her all.

She jumped into projects with the certainty that they would be a success. Despite being fired, under what sounded like less than friendly circumstances, she hadn't lost her enthusiasm for pulling out all the stops for a client. Would she be like that in a relationship?

That short kiss had nearly knocked him off his feet. What would it be like to kiss her again and have her return the gesture? With each minute spent with Carrie, he wanted the answers to these questions more and more.

Before he had a chance to tell her so, Colin texted to say he needed Adam's help.

"Duty calling?" she asked.

"Afraid so."

Since Carrie had been told she needed to be on safely patrol, Adam invited her along, happy when she strolled by his side.

"What do you need?" Adam called as they approached Colin, who was hammering a nail into a block of wood.

His brother looked up, seemed to be surprised to see Carrie in tow, and called back, "Two hands."

Adam went to hold up the pen door while Colin screwed in the hinges. When he was finished, Colin pointed to a stack of bales. "Now that you're here, you can spread the straw. I need to get back to Deep North for a tour."

He took off, sending a teasing grin at Adam as he walked by. Carrie turned to go .

Adam cleared his throat. "Excuse me. Where do you think you're going?"

She stopped. "To… I'm not sure."

He pointed toward the pen. "Then you've just been recruited to spread straw."

She blinked, like he'd spoken in a different language. Taking pity on her, he walked to the first bale and pulled out a pocketknife to snip the wire binding. He shook the bale and found a pitchfork, handing the tool to Carrie.

"Here you go. I'll get the bales loose, you transfer."

"Just spread it on the ground?"

"That's the idea."

She slipped her sunglasses down and worked until all the straw covered the ground in the pen like carpeting. By the time they finished, strands of hair had escaped Carrie's ponytail, her cheeks were a bright red from exertion and her clothes were rumpled. He'd never enjoyed a sight more.

She ran the back of one hand over her forehead and leaned on the tool with the other. "Is that it?"

"For now."

"There's more?"

"I think you pulled your weight today."

Her smile sent reverberations to his toes. "You did, too. It was enlightening, seeing this side of Adam Wright."

"As opposed to?"

"You slaying the financial world."

He raised an eyebrow.

"I looked you up on the internet."

"Wonderful."

"And not once was professional archer in any bio."

"For a reason."

She laughed, a sound that burrowed clean through to his soul. Rachel had never affected him like this. Sure, they'd gotten along. But his feelings for Carrie went deeper than anything with Rachel. She was uncovering his heart when he'd been determined to keep it buried.

"My dad runs in that same financial world as you did."

This was a surprise. "Maybe I know him."

"Trent Mitchell."

"Don't know him personally but I believe the owner of the firm I worked for is friends with him."

"Probably. He moves in pretty important circles."

"And you didn't?"

"Oh no, I'm not in the same echelon as my dad."

There was something in her tone. Pain, maybe? He remembered the conversation they'd had at Deep North when she'd only mentioned her relationship with her father. He totally respected her privacy but found that he really wanted her to confide in him.

"Your mom?"

"Left when I was a kid."

"I'm sorry. That couldn't have been easy."

She lifted one shoulder in a practiced shrug. "It happens."

Not to everyone.

His parents were as much in love today as when they'd met in college. Their example of what a loving, mutually respectful marriage could be got under his skin sometimes. Adam had hoped for that once. Wanted what his folks had. Was it too late?

They were both quiet on the walk back to the stable. He went to the office and returned with two cold bottles of water.

"Thanks," she said, opening the top and swallowing the contents like her life depended on it. He followed her example, and soon they were staring at each other.

She ran a hand over her hair. "I must look like a total wreck."

He couldn't drag his eyes from her. "I think you're beautiful."

Carrie ducked her head, but he didn't miss the pleased smile on her lips. "In case you couldn't tell, I'm extremely out of my element."

"You did fine." He swallowed. "Hard work shouldn't matter whether it's in an office or a petting arena."

"I agree."

A horse huffed. In the distance he heard a

car door slam. He hated to ruin the mood but needed to give Carrie an update.

"I talked to Rachel last night."

She froze.

"The reason I'm telling you is because today was special. I think you're special. And I don't want Rachel's presence in town to come between us."

Carrie shifted. "How much longer is she here for?"

"She was going to head home today." He took her elbow and moved her to a shady spot.

"Did you ever find out why she wanted to see you?"

"Her parents weren't happy with how she ended our relationship. She got this crazy idea that if I went back to New York with her, all would be okay."

"Why would it matter after all this time? Doesn't she have a job? Or work with some charities?"

"No. She's had a hard time finding a career that sticks."

Carrie peeled the bottle label. "She seemed kind of…adrift."

"That's a good description."

"In my experience, people who don't have

an anchor refuse to let go of the one object that will keep them from floating away."

Adam hadn't thought of Rachel's actions in those terms.

Carrie read his face, then said, "Whatever you decide is up to you."

"I'd like it to be up to us."

She gazed up at him, her lips parted. "Us?"

He swallowed. Took a chance. "If you'd like there to be an us."

She stared out the stable door. Why did waiting for her response make him so nervous? He'd stared down ruthless executives, not a wave of fear making him back down as he pursued a deal. Yet this admirable woman had him tied up in knots.

"How about we see how the show goes and then decide."

Not what he wanted to hear, but it was better than no.

"Deal."

CHAPTER NINE

LATE MONDAY MORNING, Gayle Ann sat across from Harry in Smitty's Pub, hoping to clear the air before the lunch crowd arrived.

"What did you wish to talk about?" he asked, his silver hair and mustache expertly groomed, his clothing neat as a pin.

She hesitated, suddenly nervous. Today she was taking a big step. "I invited Logan and Reid to join us today."

Harry tilted his head. "To what end?"

"To tell them about us."

"I see."

Oh no. Had she waited too long? Harry's lack of inflection scared her.

"It's what you wanted," she reminded him.

"I'm surprised is all. I thought you wanted to wait until the end of summer?"

"I changed my mind. You're too important to put on hold."

When he smiled, her fears melted away. He took her hand in his.

The door opened. Rachel and Alveda charged inside, chatting like old friends.

"Problem ahead," Gayle Ann whispered. Harry glanced over to see what she was talking about.

Before she'd met up with Harry here, she and the women from the Matchmakers Club had come across Rachel while strolling down Main Street. Rachel had stopped to ask directions, not realizing Adam's aunt was part of the group. When she'd inquired about Adam, Bunny told her he was at the office. Wanda Sue countered, saying he was at the lake, which had started an argument over why Adam would be at the lake when he didn't have a boat. Gayle Ann had reined them in and announced he was most likely at city hall getting permits. Clearly, they were not going to tell her where she could find Adam.

Gayle Ann had felt a bit guilty when Rachel lifted her chin and met their gazes, politely thanking them for their time.

Alveda had told Gayle Ann to go on to her meeting with Harry, staying behind to catch up to the young woman. Now they were acting like long-lost buddies. Alveda noticed Gayle Ann and a suspicious grin crossed her lips. She led Rachel to the table.

"Here for lunch?" Gayle Ann asked.

"We are," Alveda said. "Rachel wanted a bite to eat before she left town and I didn't want her to think badly about the folks of Golden."

Gayle Ann's eyebrows lifted. "Have you some place to be, Rachel?"

"Not really."

"Don't much like the sound of that," Alveda said with a frown.

Rachel pulled the purse strap closer to her body. "It's okay. I'll find my place."

Alveda pressed her lips together. "You remind me of someone."

"I do?"

"Yes. It's a long story, but it has a good ending."

Rachel frowned. "Why are you being so nice to me?"

"I made some questionable choices when I was young." Alveda confided. She glanced at Gayle Ann, who nodded in encouragement, then continued. "Lost a good man in the process. Never thought I'd get over it, but I did. I think you will, too."

Bitterness edged Rachel's tone. "You don't know anything about me."

"Maybe not, but I recognize the misery in your eyes. You need to pick yourself up and carve out a life for yourself no matter how hard it is. You'll be much happier if you do."

"And you don't think that life is with Adam?"

"Do you? Truly?"

Something about the young woman's uncertainty softened Gayle Ann's heart. Now she realized why Alveda had reached out to Rachel. The girl needed her, and by extension, the Golden Matchmakers Club.

"Well, putting one foot in front of the other is the way to start," Gayle Ann suggested.

"Would you like to join us?" Harry asked, picking up on Gayle Ann's unspoken change of heart.

Rachel's voice wavered. "Um, if you don't mind, I need a minute." The girl seemed on the verge of tears.

"We'll be here," Gayle Ann told her.

While Rachel moved on, Alveda set her purse on the table and claimed a chair.

"What are you up to?" Harry asked.

"Doing what the matchmakers do best, butting in." Alveda's eyes narrowed. "How about you two?"

"Discussing the future."

Alveda's gaze moved from Gayle Ann to Harry and back.

"Care to explain?"

Gayle Ann found herself at a loss for words. Alveda was her oldest friend and she hadn't confided that Harry's attention made her feel twenty years younger.

"I've asked Gayle Ann to date me," Harry answered.

Silence for a beat, then Alveda said, "Dating? As in falling-in-love dating?"

Gayle Ann's cheeks heated. "Yes."

Alveda slapped her hand on the table. "Well, it's about time."

Gayle Ann was shocked. "You knew?"

"A dead person could sense the sparks between you two."

Harry puffed out his chest.

"Been waiting for you to tell me," Alveda groused.

"You don't think it odd, at our age?"

Alveda shrugged. "No harm in enjoying a second go-around."

Harry grinned, his mustache quivering. "See, I told you she'd be happy for us."

"Only thing I'm miffed about is you keeping this a secret," Alveda huffed.

"Sorry. I wasn't sure how everyone would react." Gayle Ann breathed in relief. "The boys are meeting us, so I can tell them the news."

"Oh, this I gotta see." Alveda settled into her chair. "I'm definitely sticking around."

Harry chuckled, no offense evident in his merry laugh.

The door to the kitchen swung open. Jamey stopped short behind the bar when his gaze fell on Rachel.

Alveda lowered her voice. "Ooh, this should be good."

They watched as Rachel quickly swiped at her eyes. "Hi."

"Would you like something to drink?" Jamey asked.

"Water with lemon, please."

He grabbed a glass to fill her order.

"Rough day?"

"Kind of."

He took a lemon from the bar setup. "You're new in town, right?"

"Yes. I came to see a friend."

"How's that going?"

"Not good."

He set the glass in front of her. "Sorry to hear that." Then he went back to the kitchen.

"Should we be eavesdropping?" Harry asked.

"It's not eavesdropping," Gayle Ann corrected. "It's acquiring intel, and as members of the group, it's in our purview to protect the mission, namely Carrie and Adam."

"Or start our new mission," Alveda cut in.

Harry mumbled, "I really must insist—"

As Jamey returned, whisking a mixture in a bowl, Gayle Ann and Alveda hushed Harry at the same time.

"I'm Jamey, by the way."

"Rachel."

He put down the bowl to grab a spoon. Rachel peeked inside.

"Rémoulade sauce?"

Surprise crossed his features. "Good eye."

She shrugged. "I like to cook."

"Yeah?" He slid the bowl toward her and handed her the spoon. "Give it a try."

She dipped the tip of the spoon into the sauce, then dabbed it on her tongue. After a moment she said, "Needs more hot sauce."

He grabbed another spoon and tried. "You're right."

"It's no fun if there's no kick."

He grinned. "I agree."

"I do wish we had some popcorn," Alveda stage-whispered.

"How'd you learn to pick out missing spices?" Jamey asked.

Rachel had a sip of her water. "I went to culinary school."

"Oh yeah? Where?"

"In New York."

"Fancy."

"Not really. It was a community college."

"So," he asked. "Do you own a restaurant?"

She shook her head. "No. I couldn't do that."

"Why not?"

"I just don't think I have it in me."

He chuckled. "Take me for example. I never went to cooking school and I own a pub where I create my own dishes. If I can do it, anybody can."

Her shoulders slumped. "I wish I had your confidence."

He considered her for a long moment, then said, "Come with me."

She slid off the stool and followed him into the kitchen.

"Oh, this is disappointing," Alveda said. "We can't hear them now."

"Maybe not, but did you notice the interest between those two?" Gayle Ann nodded.

"I did. Do you think…?"

Gayle Ann grinned. "I do."

Harry frowned. "Did I miss something? I thought Rachel wanted to reunite with Adam?"

Gayle Ann patted his hand. "Plans change."

Jamey poked his head out the swinging doors. "Would you folks mind judging a cooking test? It'll only take a few minutes."

The three glanced at each other, then nodded eagerly at Jamey.

"I'll bring the food out when it's ready."

"Or," Gayle Ann countered, "we can watch the entire process."

"Even better."

They all filed into the clean, high-tech kitchen to see Jamey scrounging about in the huge commercial refrigerator. He dropped an armful of items on the central prep table and said, "You've got twenty minutes. Go."

"What?" Rachel squeaked.

"Show me what you've got." He pointed to the trio. "They'll be the judges."

Rachel stared at two hearts of romaine, whole garlic, cooked chicken breast and a block of parmesan cheese. She glanced at Alveda, who nodded in encouragement, then went to the sink to wash her hands. Jamey grabbed an apron from a hook on the wall and came over to loop it over her neck, tie it at her waist from behind, then twirled her around.

"Can't have you messing up that pretty dress."

"Oh my," Gayle Ann gushed, not missing the spark between the two.

Rachel gaped at Jamey, then cleared her throat and took a step back. Jamey waved his hand to signal she should get working.

She grabbed the chicken and diced it, then set it aside. Chopped up the garlic and romaine.

Found a pan and set it on the stove cooktop, then took a bottle of olive oil to spread in the pan before adding the ingredients.

"I always watch those cooking competitions on television where they have to whip up a meal in a specified time," she said to the group watching her. "I never thought I'd participate in one."

Jamey never took his gaze from her, his big arms crossed over his chest.

As the pan heated, Rachel found the spice rack and took oregano and basil to add additional flavor to her concoction.

"Five minutes," Jamey's deep voice bellowed.

With time to spare, Rachel placed it all on the dishes Jamey had pulled from the shelf. Like she'd worked in a commercial kitchen for years, she found the grater and added cheese on top in a finishing flourish.

"Time's up."

She lowered the grater and wiped her hands on the apron. Jamey passed out the dishes for the group to taste her concoction. They ate in silence.

Rachel bit her lower lip.

After a few bites, Jamey smiled at her. "This is really good."

"I have to agree," Gayle Ann added.

"You could outdo me in the kitchen and that's saying a lot," Alveda complimented.

"I'd hire you any time to cook for me," Harry said as he finished his portion.

Rachel's smile burst with happiness.

"I don't care what you think," Jamey told her. "You could make a go of your own restaurant."

"Thanks, Jamey. That was fun."

She started gathering the utensils she'd used to carry them to the sink, but Jamey insisted he'd clean up, since she'd cooked.

"We need to get back out to the dining room. My grandsons will be here any minute." Gayle Ann's comment hung in the air. Jamey and Rachel were already solely focused on each other.

When they returned to the table, Gayle Ann asked, "Well?"

"Jamey couldn't take his eyes off Rachel, and not because she was cooking up a most excellent meal," Harry said.

Alveda grinned. "I can't wait to tell Bunny."

"Tell her what?" Harry sputtered. "Adam still has a problem with—"

"Didn't you detect the heat in the kitchen that had nothing to do with the stove?" Alveda demanded.

"Well, I suppose."

Gayle Ann grinned at Alveda. "Are you thinking what I'm thinking?"

"Most definitely."

"What did I miss?" Harry asked, throwing up his hands.

Before Gayle Ann could tell him, the swinging doors from the kitchen burst open, with Rachel holding up Jamey's arm wrapped in a kitchen towel, hurrying him across the room. Gayle Ann gasped when she noticed blood blooming on the cloth.

"Oh my goodness, what happened?"

Rachel grimaced. "We went for a knife at the same time."

"I know better than to be distracted in my own kitchen," Jamey muttered under his breath.

"My car is in the parking lot," Rachel told him, leading him to the door. He called to one of the waitstaff who'd just arrived that he'd be back soon.

"Do you think you'll need stitches?" Harry called after him.

Jamey's face turned white. "Feels like it."

"I'm so sorry," Rachel said, tears in her eyes.

"It wasn't your fault, but you are going to make it up to me."

"I am?"

"Yep. Since I'm going to be out of the

kitchen for a while, you're in for the duration."

With that they left, and the three at the table sat in stunned silence.

"I didn't see that coming," Alveda said.

"And from the sounds of it," Gayle Ann concluded, "Rachel will be in Golden for longer than we thought."

"THAT'S IT," ADAM CROONED.

Carrie could barely make out his words as he walked the black horse around the paddock. Ty had ridden Juniper this morning during archery practice but had commitments, so Adam had volunteered to groom the animal once he cooled down.

Tired after a late night at the office preparing for a meeting Shelia bailed on, Carrie hadn't known what to expect when she rolled out of bed. The sun was just starting to rise, so she'd dressed quickly in jeans and a light yellow T-shirt, heading to the farm to watch Adam and Ty practice their stunts.

The Tuesday morning dew dissipated, leaving behind a rich earthy scent mixed with hay straw, leather cleaner and animal. She was surprised at the appeal of nature compared to the noise and smells she'd considered normal back home. Birds chirped in the distance, so cheery instead of a background of car horns that had been the music she'd listened to as she walked to work each day in the city.

Adam placed his hand on the animal's neck, said a few more quiet words and led Juniper to where Carrie stood just outside the paddock. Ty had taken the saddle into the barn, leaving Adam to take care of the beautiful animal.

Adam's strong shoulder muscles flexed as he guided the horse to the grooming area, his long legs encased in denim, striding to keep the horse moving. His heavy boots trudged through the dirt and all Carrie could think was that this Adam was just as attractive as the Adam who dressed all button-down for the office. There were more layers to him than she suspected and she couldn't wait to peel back more. Man of mystery, indeed.

He rubbed his hand down Juniper's neck, then came over to her.

"We can get to work now," he told her with a wink as they all moved toward the stable, Juniper's hooves clomping as they went.

"We?"

"No one shows up here at the crack of dawn and ends up not pitching in."

"Fine. You convinced me."

He chuckled, securing the lead rope to a post.

"Sure you're up for this?"

No. She wasn't.

"Just try and stop me."

"I like the enthusiasm. Especially since it wasn't long ago that you didn't want to get close enough to Maggie to give her a snack."

She shrugged. "I've grown since then."

And had become curious. Once some of her fear had subsided, she was interested in learning everything horse-related before the Eureka Games. Seems she'd picked the perfect person to instruct her on the care of a horse.

He gathered up brushes, handing her one. "This is what we call a currycomb."

She nodded.

"Watch me, then you can try."

He slipped on the brush strap, then rubbed in a circular motion from the animal's neck down toward its body. "We start from the top down." He glanced at her. "Want to give it a go?"

"Sure." She stepped close, a little shaky. When she placed her brush against Juniper's body, Adam put his hand over hers.

"Slowly at first, until you get the feel."

She nearly held her breath, not wanting to make a mistake.

"Don't worry, you won't hurt him."

They moved again and Juniper sidestepped,

causing Carrie to jump backward. She landed against Adam, then stepped aside once she got her footing, afraid of her toes being stomped. When Juniper settled, she released a puff of air.

"Sometimes they like to move around."

"Noted," she said in a tight voice.

Adam moved away, taking the sandalwood scent of his cologne with him. He motioned for her to take over. Tentatively at first, she did as instructed, starting at the neck and moving to chest, shoulders and over the back. Soon she found the steady movement calming, even with Adam watching her.

"Great job," Adam said when she was finished. "I'll get the belly and haunches now."

"You're giving up on me?"

He sent her a wry glance. "You want to brush his back end?"

She held up her hands in surrender. "No. I reverse my position. Carry on."

Shaking his head, he smiled in amusement, then walked to the other side of the horse.

"I had no idea what to expect this morning, but I was impressed by how you and Ty work together."

"After practicing on my own, it was easier to get into the rhythm of the act in the arena." He looked over Juniper's back at her. "I hate to admit it was like getting back on a bike because I know there'll be no living with you, but you were right."

She tried not to gloat. "Honestly, I said those things to get you motivated. It worked!"

"We should be ready once the games roll around."

Four weeks and counting.

Rubbing Juniper's neck, Adam came back to her side to place the brush down and picked up another. He followed the process again.

"We just did that."

"Yes, but like before, we'll use a stiff brush to dissipate the dirt, then we'll finish with a soft cloth to remove the remaining dust." He went through the motions, then handed the brush to her. "Like before, only this time use short strokes."

Feeling more comfortable now, she finished the job as Adam kept an eye on her, arms folded over his broad chest. How she wished she had brought her camera to capture a snapshot of him, so comfortable in this setting.

"This is weird."

He tipped his head. "What is?"

"Us, spending time together in a stable."

"Why?"

"If anything, I could picture us running

into each other at some kind of business seminar. Seems more natural."

He dropped his arms and tucked his fingers in his front jeans pockets. "Carrie, there's more to me than numbers."

She caught his gaze. "So I'm finding out."

His shoulders went stiff. "And?"

She smiled. "Fishing for a compliment?"

"I'm only human."

At his uncertainty, she cut him some slack. "Then you'll be pleased to know I like what I see."

His crooked grin and dimples were all the reward she needed.

Once she finished, he took the brush and ran it down Juniper's legs. Satisfied, he took a cloth and wiped the horse one final time. Carrie smiled at the shine in Juniper's coat.

Lastly, Adam ran a brush through Juniper's mane and tail, then used a pick to clean his hooves. The horse shook his head and huffed, but still remained docile.

"It's amazing that he allowed you to clean him off."

Adam ran a hand down Juniper's neck again. "He's a good horse. Ty's had him for a long time, so we tend to spoil him."

"Do you ever ride him?"

"No. If I take a horse out, it's usually Big Tom."

Her eyes went wide. "That huge horse in the stall next to Maggie?"

"That's the one."

She shivered.

"He's as gentle as they come."

"I'll take your word for it."

"Why don't you give it a try?"

Her brow puckered in confusion. "Give what a try?"

"Getting on a horse."

She burst out laughing. "Me?"

His lips twitched. "Why not? You mastered offering snacks."

"I know nothing about riding."

"You could learn."

Could she? She'd never given the idea any thought. Since coming to Golden she'd been doing new things, so why not consider it?

"You'd be good at it," he insisted.

"How can you possibly know that?"

His gaze pierced hers. "Because you have determination."

"Determination doesn't always signify success."

"Maybe not, but I know you'd master it like everything you do."

She tried not to gape at him. She'd only

been around the animals a few times, yet he was encouraging her. Unlike her father who needed proof of her blood, sweat and tears, and then he'd nitpick the results. She hadn't attempted climbing on a horse, yet Adam assumed she could ride without seeing any tangible evidence.

Her heart squeezed. Adam had faith in her abilities. She didn't have to prove herself to him—he simply believed, which had her runaway emotions careening down a path she wasn't sure she wanted to veer from.

She followed him to the outdoor sink where they washed their hands. Then he took the lead from the post and walked with Juniper to his stall. Once the horse was inside, Adam leaned back against the closed door.

"So? What do you think?" he asked.

"That there's this entire world I'd never considered. Ty is an amazing rider and I can tell he cares about his animals."

"He always has."

She brushed stray hairs that had escaped her ponytail. "When you guys started the routine, I was mesmerized. My heart was in my throat when you let the first arrow go and Ty rode toward it. You'll have the crowd eating out of the palm of your hands."

"That's the idea."

"Is he always so fearless? The other day he was hanging off Juniper's side while they raced around the arena. Is that even safe?"

Adam chuckled. "Trust me. He knows trick riding front and back. Plus, he's always had a wild streak, which you need if you're going to attempt those feats."

"Grooming Juniper was interesting, but what Ty does? Next level."

He pushed away from the door and leaned in close to her. His warm breath caressed her ear. "And what about my mad skills?"

She moved back an inch to meet his gaze. His eyes were so clear, with a deep gray, hinting that there was so much more to Adam.

"You mean your precision aim?"

He ran a finger down the side of her neck and this time she couldn't hide the quake. He sent her another heated grin and glanced at her lips.

They were alone. She wanted this to play out, so she scooted closer and pointed to her lips. "That's the direction."

He lowered his head and claimed her mouth with gentle persuasion that made her heart soar. She pressed closer so he could angle the kiss more deeply. By their own volition, her hands moved over his solid chest and into his thick hair. His hands held her tight. The kiss went on and in that moment her heart was lost to him.

Just when she thought she'd run out of air, he broke the kiss.

His voice was husky when he said, "This isn't how I envisioned the morning playing out."

She licked her lips. "Are you disappointed?"

He sent her a look heavy with meaning. "What do you think?"

"That you're talking too much."

She pulled him to her and they exchanged another fevered kiss. What had happened to work-conscious Carrie? The woman who lived for the job and the clients? She barely recognized herself when she was with Adam.

The sound of a vehicle door slamming broke them apart. Adam glanced out the other end of the open stable door while Carrie ran a finger over her mouth, trying hard not to break out in giggles over his magical kisses.

Liz, Ty's sister, ambled in and unlocked the door to the office. She smiled when Carrie and Adam came her way.

"Juniper is taken care of," Adam informed her.

"Thanks. Ty called to say you had it under control. It gave me time to sit down with

Colton and discuss the upcoming school year."

"Is he registered at Golden High School yet?"

Liz tossed her dark braid over her shoulder. "Last week. He's nervous and I can't say I blame him. This will be his first year at school full-time, now that we've settled down somewhere permanent."

"Brando'll be his rock. He takes being the head of the family seriously."

"Don't we know it." Liz chuckled, then turned her attention to Carrie. "Actually, I'm glad you're here. I have an idea I'd like to run by you."

"Fire away."

"Since you've been interested in interactive events for the Eureka Games, I remembered a competition we did a few years ago when we swung into my cousin's hometown. They were organizing a fundraiser and came up with the idea of a saddle competition."

"What's that?"

"Anyone in town who wanted to enter would saddle a wooden sawhorse in a timed event to see who could get the saddle on correctly the fastest." Liz's excitement was contagious. "It was lots of fun and the raffle brought in money for a clinic meeting the needs of people with disabilities in their community. The money we raise can be donated to a good cause. It's also a chance to remind local kids and their parents that we're offering horseback riding lessons soon."

Carrie thought it over. It sounded like fun and something that would get the town involved, as well as raise funds to benefit those who could use them.

"What if a person has no idea what to do with a saddle?"

Adam chuckled. "Sounds like we have our first contestant."

Carrie playfully whacked his arm.

Liz laughed. "If a person has never done it, we'd give detailed lessons beforehand. Some folks who know how to saddle a horse might just do it for fun."

"And who could use the donation?" Carrie asked. "Any group in Golden you want to support?"

"We always give to the multiple sclerosis society."

"That's a good idea."

Liz spoke frankly. "My brother has the disease. It's progressed so that he's in an assisted living facility."

"Liz, I'm sorry. Is he in Golden?"

"No, but we hope to move him closer when we get ourselves established."

"Then I'm all for supporting a local facility."

"Thanks."

Adam's phone rang. He glanced at the screen and frowned. "I need to take this. I'll be right back."

He walked outside, leaving the women in the breezeway. Another idea occurred to Carrie and she decided to go for it.

"Liz, can I ask a favor?"

"Sure."

"So, being around horses is new to me, but I've been watching Ty and Adam around them, and this morning, I got to help groom Juniper."

"What did you think?"

She waved her hand in the general direction of the stalls. "I really enjoyed it. I was wondering if I could hire you."

"For?"

Was Carrie ready for this? She watched Adam pace at the far end of the stable and decided, yes.

"I'm interested in taking horseback riding lessons. I'm assuming I'd learn all about placing a saddle correctly, but I'd like to actually ride a real horse."

"I'd love to. Your promotion idea for the town is going to draw a crowd to the farm. It's the publicity and business we need to really make a go of this place. I'm offering riding lessons to start, then we're going to make the farm interactive. Open it to the public." She motioned to the office. "Why don't we check my calendar to see when we can start."

They moved into the cool confines of the office. After targeting a few different dates, Carrie set an appointment for next week.

"You're going to love it," Liz said.

"We'll see."

Liz patted her shoulder. "You will."

Carrie nodded in agreement. As they were leaving the office, Carrie stopped Liz.

"One more thing. Would you mind if we kept this a secret?"

Liz furrowed her brow.

"I want to surprise Adam."

A grin crossed her face. "No problem. Your secret is safe with me."

"Thanks."

Adam caught up to them outside the stable, a frown line deep between his eyebrows. "I need to take off."

Carrie glanced at her watch. "And I need to go home to change and get to the office."

"I'll walk you to your car," he offered.

Carrie held out her hand to Liz. "Thanks for everything."

Liz shook. "My pleasure."

The warm sun beat down on them. The deep blue sky loomed overhead. From the stable came the sound of a whinny. Carrie had a tough time keeping up with Adam. She was appreciating the beautiful surroundings that she probably would have overlooked in her old life.

"Hold your horses." She realized what she'd said and stopped, smacking her palm to her forehead.

Adam halted. Her response lightened his expression.

"Are you okay?" she asked. "What's going on?"

He paused, then said, "There's been a development."

"At Deep North?"

"No. With Rachel."

His words rattled her. "I thought she left town."

"Apparently not."

Unease slithered over Carrie. "What does that mean?"

"That the Rachel saga is not over."

CHAPTER TEN

THE PHONE CALL from Aunt Bunny had thrown Adam off. He was sure Rachel had accepted his decision and would be on her way back to the Big Apple. Instead, she'd been spotted at Smitty's two days in a row.

He tugged open the door to the pub, letting it slam behind him. It took a moment for his eyes to adjust to the dim lighting. The familiar scents of hickory smoke and beer greeted him, but today he was too tense to appreciate the atmosphere. Sure enough, Rachel was here, standing behind the bar.

Wait. Behind the bar?

He strode over, silently commanding himself to keep his cool. "Rachel, what's going on?"

She glanced at the kitchen door. "I'm helping Jamey," she stage-whispered.

"Helping him do what?" he stage-whispered back.

"Right now? Pick out the daily specials."

He frowned.

"There's been a change in my plans." She smiled. It was genuine, he noted right away.

"We agreed you were leaving."

"No, we didn't. You agreed without hearing me out."

It wasn't defiance he read on her face; more like she'd made a firm decision and was sticking to it.

Frustration bloomed in his chest. "Why are you making this so difficult?"

"I'm not. I like Golden and have decided to stick around for a while." She shrugged. "It's not like I have anything waiting for me back home."

"What do your parents think about this?"

She looked away. "I haven't told them."

"Sounds like a pattern."

Hurt glistened in her eyes. "That was uncalled for."

"But true."

She hesitated, but then blurted, "They cut me off financially. I need a job and Jamey offered me one. End of story."

Surprise washed over him. "I didn't realize it was so bad."

"Now you do." Hurt laced her tone as she set down the pen in her hand with a little heat. "I'm sorry about what happened, Adam. I was wrong and selfish. Is that what you want to hear? Because that's what everyone else says."

"Your last-minute decision to end our engagement has left me second-guessing everything for a year now. How did you expect me to feel when you arrived unannounced, informing me that you wanted us to get back together? You don't get to show up and act like taking off right before the wedding didn't affect me."

After a drawn-out moment, she said, "I had to leave, Adam."

"But you could have talked to me about it. At least given me a heads-up."

"Oh? I'd just call you and say…" She put her hand, thumb and pinky near her ear as if she was holding a phone, "By the way, honey, I've decided to call off the wedding. Just giving you a heads-up. Ciao."

His jaw clenched.

"You're right. I could have. But it was complicated." She held her hands up as if she was surrendering. "That's not a good excuse, I know, but it's the truth." She stared at him. "Honestly, I'm not sure how well we really knew each other."

It felt like she'd stabbed his chest.

"What's that supposed to mean? We were engaged. Planning a life together."

She crossed her arms over her chest. "What was one of my favorite things to do?"

"Shop?"

She rolled her eyes. "No. Cook."

Where was she going with this? "I knew you liked to throw dinner parties."

Her face went red. "It was more than dinner parties, Adam. I wanted to make a career as a chef."

"You never said."

"You never listened."

Silence settled over them as Adam digested what she'd just told him.

"I thought it was a hobby."

She threw up her hands. "Well, you, and everyone else, were wrong."

How had he missed this? Apparently this was important to Rachel and he hadn't a clue. And if he missed this, what else didn't he have an inkling about?

"I don't expect you to understand," she went on. "You always had your eyes on numbers and investments. The few times I brought up the idea of working at a restaurant, it didn't go over well."

"Because you made it sound like you were going to hang out with your friends, not that you wanted to be a chef."

Her expression grew stony. "Be honest.

Would you have been okay with me working as a chef?"

"Of course. But that's a rhetorical question because you never brought it up. I had no idea that becoming a chef was important to you."

A flash of sadness crossed her face. "There's so much we don't know about each other and I want to find out what went wrong."

"And you're going to accomplish this by staying in Golden?"

"I can't make amends if I'm far away."

He stepped back. "Amends…"

"I used the excuse of wanting to get back together so you'd at least give me a chance to speak to you. I wasn't sure how to broach the topic, but it doesn't matter, because you wouldn't have a serious conversation with me."

He'd finally started moving on after the heartache, taking that giant step to see if he was capable of romance again. How would Rachel's plan to stick around affect what he had with Carrie? It was new and precious, and he wanted to see where it might lead. Would Rachel's decision cause Carrie to turn around and run?

"This isn't going to work," he insisted.

"It won't if you don't try."

"There's nothing to try."

She lifted her chin. "I'm not leaving."

"I don't remember you being this stubborn."

"Maybe I'm trying to learn who I am."

"I thought that was why you ran the first time."

"Well, I'm not running now." She raised her shoulders. "I'll be cooking."

"Jamey never lets anyone in his kitchen."

"There's a first time for everything."

The doors to the kitchen swung open, revealing Jamey. Had he been listening to their conversation? Adam was about to ask for an explanation when he noticed his friend's hand wrapped with a thick bandage.

"What happened?"

"Kitchen accident."

"Are you okay?"

Jamey held up his hand. "Twelve stitches. Won't be able to help out at the Eureka Games."

"I can see."

"Finished with the specials?" Jamey asked Rachel.

"Yes. I have a few suggestions."

"You're *cooking*?" Adam couldn't curtail the shock.

"Jamey needs another chef."

His friend nodded. "I do. And she's an amazing cook."

What was happening?

Rachel picked up the pen and pointed it at Adam. "I'm not leaving, Adam. Jamey needs me. And as much as our broken engagement was my fault, I can't go until we make things right."

"We?"

Jamey's eyebrows rose and he turned tail back into the kitchen.

"Yes. I'm not in this alone. If you search deep down, you'll see we were both at fault. We should never have gotten engaged."

She spun on her heel and disappeared into the kitchen.

He stood there for a moment, reeling. Had he used the hurt of her leaving as a way to shut out the problems that were lurking beneath the surface?

If Adam was wrong about his relationship with Rachel, what else was he wrong about?

On the drive to Deep North, he processed Rachel's news. She was staying in Golden. He still wondered about her motives—then *and* now. He didn't trust her and now she'd be hanging around town.

You never listened.

Was she right? If so, he couldn't place all the blame on her, which didn't sit well with him. He'd always made sound decisions, doing the research, posing the pros and cons. Could he have been that off base?

He pulled into the parking lot at Deep North Adventures and noticed an RV in the vacant lot next door. Concern washed over him as he hurried inside. Crossing the gathering area, he nodded to the few folks waiting for their tour, before stopping short as he faced the couple standing behind the counter. "Mom. Dad. What are you doing here?"

His father stepped out from behind the counter to tug Adam into a tight embrace.

"We cut our trip short."

"Why?"

His mother joined them and after a quick hug, said, "We need to be in Golden."

"No, you need to be enjoying your retirement."

His parents exchanged glances, which didn't put him at ease, especially when his mother pointed down the hallway. "Let's talk in your office."

His father stayed put.

"Are you coming?" he asked his dad.

"No. I'll stay out here and make sure Brea doesn't add another color to that rainbow head of hers."

"I heard that," Brea yelled back.

As his dad and employee started a heated

discussion about the merits of multicolored hair, Adam went to his office. He closed the door behind him. His mother had already taken a seat on the opposite side of the desk.

"What's going on, Mom?"

"Mr. Fletcher. You told me that he's insisting we make a decision or he'll move on."

Adam rubbed his temple. "He did. We spoke only once, but we've emailed."

Adam thought back to his conversation with the man. "When I pressed Fletcher, he said he had connections in Golden and was eager to move here, but when I asked who, he changed the subject."

His mother looked confused. "Why the secrecy?"

"I don't know." He lifted a file from his desk and removed the contents. "I read through all the paperwork."

"No red flags?"

"The offer is good, Mom. I sent it to our attorney to get his input."

He'd been looking for a reason not to sell because he didn't want to take the next step. But he couldn't lie to his parents and brother just so he didn't have to face his hazy future.

"I did my due diligence and checked into every possible scenario about the company. Fletcher has a strong plan and could be an asset to Golden by bringing what could become a national chain."

"So now we have to decide as a family what we're going to do? Is that what you're saying?"

"Yes."

He couldn't read his mother at this moment, knowing that the gears in her mind were spinning. Much like his own. If his three family members decided it was time to move on, Adam truly had to face what his future would look like.

Carrie coming into his life had added a dimension he hadn't expected, but it made him happier. Happier than when he was at the height of his career on Wall Street. They had the same outlook on life, enjoyed the business world. She'd drawn him into the events surrounding Golden's future, not that it took much arm-twisting when she'd persuaded him with that savvy style he couldn't resist. Maybe selling the business would help him find the fire he'd lost in New York.

"I have some other news," his mother said.

"Which is?"

Her expression grew wary. "Carter is under negotiation to sell the vacant lot next door."

He shook his head. Ever since their falling-out in high school, Carter had held it against

Adam by refusing to sell the plot of land next to them so they could expand Deep North.

"So he finally got an offer he accepted?"

"Yes." She bit her lip, then blurted, "From Mr. Fletcher."

Adam winced. "Carter is Fletcher's connection to Golden?"

"Seems that way."

"Now it makes sense why Fletcher wanted to deal with you and Dad. I should have known."

"How could you?"

"Because Carter has always been about number one. And this sounds like petty revenge to me."

His mother frowned. "I've never understood the mutual dislike."

Because Adam had never told her how Carter had cheated by using Adam to get better grades in school. "It really doesn't matter. The point is, you can sell and be set for retirement."

"I thought you'd be more reluctant."

"It's a good deal, Mom," he reasserted. "You can do your own thing and not keep tabs on Deep North. Dad can get more involved in his new hobbies. You can travel as often and as far as you want."

Even though he ran the company now, this

had always been his mother's baby. It had been a long time since he'd put himself out there, in either business or love. He was a smart guy. He could figure something out.

"This is why I insisted we come home. I want us to work together and I can't be as involved if I'm hundreds of miles away."

His chest went tight. "I hate that you cut your trip short."

"It's fine. Your father wanted to come home and show off the photos he's taken. And honestly, from the first day Mr. Fletcher called, I've been antsy to make a decision."

He understood. Deep North Adventures had been a lifelong endeavor for his mother. Deciding whether or not to sell was a big move.

She tucked her hands beneath her chin and leaned her elbows on the desk in front of her. "Now, what's all this I hear about Rachel showing up in Golden?"

"What, no segue, Mom?"

He really didn't want to talk about Rachel, but knew his mother wouldn't let up.

"You can't fault me for being curious."

"She claims we need time together." He ran a hand through his hair. "To understand where we went wrong. To fix us."

"Fix what *she* broke?" A flush spread

across his mother's face. "You told her no, didn't you?"

"Apparently she's developed a stubborn streak. Or it was there before and I never saw it."

Now that Adam thought about it, there were a lot of things he and Rachel had missed in each other. Could her insistence on making amends have merit?

Indignant now, his mother sputtered, "Why couldn't she run out of Golden like she ran before your wedding?"

"Like I told Colin, there's more going on here."

"And I suppose you feel the need to ferret it out?"

"As long as she's in town, this will be uncomfortable, but yes, I want to get to the bottom of what happened between us, like she said, so it never happens again."

"Hmm."

He recognized that tone. "Don't get any ideas."

"Like what?"

Pure innocence stared back at him. He wasn't buying the act.

"No confronting Rachel."

She waved off his concern. "I'm just looking out for my son."

"Who is more than capable of taking care of the situation." He sent her a stern glance. "Stay out of it, Mom. Please."

"I don't like it, but I will unless you tell me otherwise."

"Thank you."

His phone rang. He answered while his mother gathered the reports on his desk. The call didn't last but a few seconds.

"Who was that?" his mother asked when he ended the call.

"Addie Lane. She needs some advice about opening a new business. She asked if we could meet now."

"It's nice that you help the other merchants."

"I'm fortunate to have the expertise. Might as well share it."

She stood and smoothed her white capri pants. "Now I need to go meet Bunny. She's bringing me up to speed on what's been happening in Golden."

Which meant she was going to root around in his and Colin's business whether they wanted her to or not. He imagined Carrie would also come up in that conversation, which didn't bother him as much as it would have a few months ago.

He pictured Carrie's bright smile and decided, yeah, with her by his side, it wouldn't be so daunting to jump-start his life. But would she wait while he straightened out his past complications?

AFTER PLAYING CATCH-UP at the office all afternoon, Carrie was ready for a break. She'd been delighted to see the prints for the *Discover Golden!* campaign on her desk. She was pleased with the results and hoped Adam would be comfortable signing off on them, too.

She picked up her favorite photo of Adam, the one of him walking along Main Street, and smiled. His intense expression took her breath away. She couldn't deny how attracted she was to him. What had he been like when he worked on Wall Street? Here in Golden, where he was much more casual, he still had that silent strength she was drawn to. Her feelings were about more than attraction now, and that worried her. How would Adam affect her future decisions?

She focused on the picture again, pushing aside her misgivings. They hadn't talked about it, but what if Adam did want to get serious? She couldn't help hoping that the way he looked at her was an indication that he might be ready to move on from his heartbreak. That she was special.

"Stop being silly," she muttered to herself.

"Silly about what?" Lindsey asked as she walked into the office to drop a report on Carrie's desk.

"Nothing," she quickly answered. "Just trying to decide which print to go with."

"Ooh. Are these the pictures of Adam?"

"Yes." Carrie handed her coworker the stack. "What do you think?"

Lindsey slowly studied each one. She grinned. "I think he could easily draw me to Golden if I didn't already live here."

Carrie chuckled as Lindsey handed them back. She slid them, and the print copy she'd written for the final layout, into an oversize envelope. "You're supposed to consider it from a business point of view."

Lindsey sent her an incredulous smirk. "Have you seen him lately?"

Carrie had. Up close and personal. She ducked her head so Lindsey wouldn't notice the heat rising up her neck.

"You have." Lindsey hadn't missed it.

"C'mon. How could anyone not see how handsome Adam is?"

"No one." Her friend tapped her finger against her chin. "But come to think of it, you're the only one Adam's had eyes for since he came home. Interesting."

"Not interesting. We're working together

on Golden projects so it's necessary we bump into each other."

"Necessary, huh?"

Carrie grinned. "Someone has to do it."

Lindsey's laugh filled the room. "You go, girl."

Still chuckling, Carrie rose and placed the envelope with the photos in her briefcase.

"And now it is necessary for me to get Adam's opinion on the pictures. Once I have his feedback, I can finish the campaign and move on to the Eureka Games."

"Which sounds like fun. My niece keeps telling me she can't wait to visit the animals."

"What kid doesn't like a petting zoo? The local 4-H organizers have been amazing and the kids volunteering are too cute for words. They've actually taught me a lot."

"Most people in Golden are willing to chip in for the good of the community."

A common trait Carrie kept noticing. As she worked with everyone, from the seniors to group organizers, the Pendergrass family and Adam, the appeal of this small town took on a life of its own. Not everyone was in a hurry or needed quantity over quality. Could she ever live this way? The question had occurred to her more and more frequently.

Lindsey cut into her thoughts. "Before you leave, do you have a minute to talk?"

"Sure. What's up?"

"Shelia."

Now what? "Is anything wrong?"

"That's what I'd like to know. She's asked you to handle some of her client meetings and just called to cancel a budget meeting we had scheduled. Should we be worried?"

"I don't know." Carrie stopped to think about her latest interactions with the director. "I've tried to talk to her about it a few times, but she always changes the subject."

Lindsey worried her lower lip. "Should we say something to Carter?"

"I hate going behind her back in case she has a good reason for being distracted."

"I agree. Maybe we just give her a little more time?"

"Once the Eureka Games are over, I'll have more time to focus on a solution."

Her coworker puffed out a breath. "Thanks."

After saying goodbye to Lindsey, Carrie stopped at Blue Ridge Cottage to tell Serena she'd be late for the wedding planning they'd scheduled for later that afternoon.

Serena greeted her at the door. "I'm glad you're here. I've got news," she said, yanking Carrie to the back room.

"Don't tell me you're going to bow out of the saddle competition? You promised to do it with me."

"No. That's not it."

Serena's pause made Carrie nervous.

"Rachel is still in town."

Carrie's stomach dropped. "I was with Adam when he got a call about her, but he didn't say much."

"It gets worse."

Carrie raised an eyebrow. "How could it get worse?"

"She's working at Smitty's Pub."

She held up a hand. "What? Why would Jamey hire a stranger? Did she even have waitressing experience?"

"Mrs. M. says she's a talented chef."

"Mrs. M.?" Carrie pinched the bridge of her nose. "Wait. She's going to be working in the kitchen? Serena, could you please make more sense?"

"Sorry. Mrs. M. and her pals were at Smitty's for lunch when Rachel was there. Somehow they ended up judging an impromptu cooking test that showcased Rachel's culinary skills. Then, Jamey cut himself and needed stitches, so she's filling in for him."

"Wow. That's a lot to unpack." She stared

at her friend. "Bottom line, the ex is staying in Golden?"

"Yes. How do you feel about that?"

Carrie wasn't sure. It didn't sound like Adam had encouraged her to stay, which was good. But there was always the possibility that the longer Rachel hung out in Golden, the better she could convince Adam that they deserved a second chance. And after experiencing his kisses, Carrie wanted more time to see where this was going. Could it go deeper? With time, Carrie hoped the answer was yes.

But you're leaving.

Yeah, there was that, too.

Stupid inner voice.

"If Rachel is working," Carrie reasoned, "she won't have time to go after Adam. And knowing how Jamey feels about the pub's reputation, he'll be watching her like a hawk."

"So… Bright side?"

"I guess that remains to be seen." Carrie bit at her lower lip.

"Haven't you talked to him?" Serena asked.

"Not since this morning. However, I do have Chamber business to discuss with him."

Serena took her by the shoulders, turned her around and marched Carrie to the door, then gave her a little push.

"Go find him."

Carrie twirled on her friend. "That was my plan!"

"Then why did you stop into the store?"

"To let you know I might be late for the wedding planning."

Serena placed her hands on her hips. "You have a suitable excuse."

"Gee, thanks."

"Go." Serena made a get-out-of-here motion with her hands.

Carrie stood on the sidewalk in the bright sunshine. Was Rachel going to be a problem? Sure seemed like it. So, what was Carrie going to do about it?

She took a few steps when Bunny appeared before her.

"What're you doing standing out here all alone?"

Carrie shook off her musings. "I was actually going to drive over to Deep North."

"To see Adam?" Bunny beamed. "I bet he'd like that, but he's not there."

"Oh."

"But I do know where you can find him."

Carrie didn't miss the cagey expression in the older woman's eyes.

"Are you going to tell me?"

"Only if you promise not to break my nephew's heart."

"I think Adam is safe from me."

Although, with the way she was falling for Adam, it was highly possible he might hurt her.

Bunny nodded. "Remember that evening you went hiking with us?"

"Yes."

"He's up at the lookout. Likes to go there when he's got some heavy-duty thinkin' to do."

That didn't sound good.

"But he won't mind you crashing his sanctuary. After the day he's had, I think you'd be a pleasant surprise." Bunny angled her head. "Go on now."

Why was everyone so bossy today?

Carrie detoured to the apartment to change into shorts, a tank top and the boots Adam had given her. Then she made sure she had a water bottle and the prints for Adam to approve and drove to the parking lot at the base of Bailey's Point.

Climbing the trail under the late-afternoon heat wasn't any easier than the twilight hike, but she reached her destination sooner than she'd expected. Sure enough, Adam was at the far side of the clearing. He'd laid out a blanket and sat staring at the scenery below. He had one leg stretched out before him, the other bent, a hand draped over his knee. His hair was mussed and she had to fight the urge to run her fingers through the thickness and tame the waves.

Twigs snapping under her feet caught his attention. He looked at her, his eyes hidden behind sunglasses. When he recognized her, his slow smile made her feel special. He started to rise.

"Don't get up," she told him. "I'll join you."

"What's up?"

He moved over and she dropped down beside him. "The proofs came in."

"And you couldn't wait to show me?"

"Just because we aren't in the office doesn't mean I can't be efficient."

His gaze ran over her. "I must admit, I'm impressed you dressed for a meeting in the forest."

"Someone insisted I wear the right clothes for a trek in the woods."

"Smart guy."

"He is."

She handed him the envelope. "I do need you to check these over before I finish the campaign."

He took the photos, his fingers brushing hers. She didn't move, waiting to see what he would do next. He ran his thumb over her palm, then removed his hand in order to sift through the photos. As always, his touch made her heart race .

She definitely had it bad for Adam.

After a few minutes he said, "Let me guess, you've decided?"

"I've got a couple of favorites, yes." She selected the one with Adam striding up Main Street and another with him on the steps of City Hall. "I think these capture the image I was going for."

He nodded.

"That's it? No discussion?"

"I trust you to decide what's best for the campaign."

He handed her the stack, but this time his touch didn't linger. Carrie swallowed her disappointment because this was a beautiful place for them to further their romance. Was he too preoccupied to notice how much she wanted to kiss him again?

She handed him the print copy she'd written. After reading it, he said, "Looks good."

"Then I'll send the promotion to the graphic artist tomorrow for a mock-up."

"Ever diligent. Before long you'll have your pick of high-profile jobs."

She looked at him warily. Did he want her to leave Golden? "I don't know about that."

"Why wouldn't you? You work way more

than you have fun." He sent her a serious glance. "Don't you ever miss taking a day off just to do nothing?"

"You don't get ahead that way." She frowned. "Have you forgotten the pressures of working that stressful corporate job now that you handle your family's business?"

"Not one bit."

"Then why are you…" She put the photos away. "What's wrong?"

He ran a hand through his hair. "You want a list?"

"That bad?"

He turned to face her. "My parents came home early from their trip."

"I thought they were going cross-country?"

"We've had an offer to buy Deep North, so Mom wanted to be here."

No wonder he was out of sorts. She sensed she needed to approach the topic with a soft touch.

"I didn't know it was for sale."

"It isn't. The offer came out of the blue."

"Is there anything I can do to help?"

He blew out a breath. "No. I just need to start considering next steps."

"Personal or business?"

His lips tipped into a rueful grin. "Both."

The gesture shouldn't have made her heart lurch, but it did just the same.

Get back on track here.

"If you don't work for the family business, does that mean you'll go it alone?"

"It's tricky."

"When I first met you, it seemed like you kept to yourself. Not really a loner, but more like you observed and then reacted."

He chuckled. "Yeah, that sounds like me."

"Was it like that when you worked at the financial firm?"

"The partners let me cultivate my own clients. Because I brought in a lot of revenue, they pretty much let me keep to myself."

"So you've always been reserved?"

"I suppose." He gave her a sidelong glance. "What are you getting at?"

"Just putting it all together. You help the merchants in Golden, yet keep up your guard. You're not the definition of a team player, yet you've been all in with the Eureka Games. I haven't had to twist your arm once."

"You mean like suggesting I volunteer to do the work, so it'll highlight Deep North when actually it benefits the Chamber projects?"

"No, more like we help each other." She placed her hands palms down behind her and leaned back. "I was like you when I was focused on my clients' promotions. When I did work with a team, I tended to take over."

"I can't imagine."

At his wry tone, she reached over and playfully slapped his shoulder.

"But since coming to Golden, I see that everyone chips in for the good of the community. It really does lessen the load. I get more work done knowing that I can ask you, or Mrs. M. or any number of people, to help me."

"Which makes Golden special."

"And easy to promote." She angled her head, noticing the sun sifting through the tree limbs. "Remember that day in the park—"

"With the binder?"

"—and I was stumped? We had a nice chat and I got an idea for what to do next."

"I didn't give you any advice."

"We just talked."

"Yet you came up with a concept."

"That's right."

He grinned and she grinned back.

"What can I say? Just think what would have happened if I'd given you actual advice."

"I'm not gonna lie, I like that about you."

Their eyes met and held. Would he kiss her again? Her heart picked up pace. She had to stop wishing for his lips on hers every time they were alone. He so easily took her breath away that it made her forget about her goals.

He nudged her. "So, what are you saying?"

"Whether your family sells or not, you'll land on your feet."

He stared over the vista before them, the glistening lake below, the lush treetops swaying in the welcome breeze. If this could be her view from the corner office, she'd take it any day.

"Do I listen to you?" he asked out of the blue.

She turned, feeling her ponytail bounce against her shoulder. "What do you mean?"

"Rachel accused me of not listening. That when the wedding preparations were too much, I wasn't in tune with her. She implied that I should have backed her up so she didn't have to run."

She didn't really want to talk about Rachel, but she knew this was important to him. "So far, yes, you've listened."

They fell into silence again.

"Rachel isn't leaving."

"I heard." She chanced a glance at him. "Are you okay with that?"

His gaze met hers and held.

"Are you?" he asked.

"It isn't my dilemma."

"True, but what you think is important to me."

Carrie ran that through her mind. "I'd

rather she got her life together elsewhere, but I understand."

He considered that.

"Is she still convinced you two belong together?" Carrie asked.

"It's more complicated."

"More complicated than your ex wanting you back?"

The long pause made her nervous.

"I talked to her this morning."

"And?"

He looked like he was having a hard time saying the next part. "She has some good reasons for staying."

Carrie's stomach dropped like a lead weight.

"Do you want to get back together with her?"

"No, but I think we both need to work some things out."

She definitely didn't like the direction of this conversation. "Is that why you asked me if you listen?"

"Yes. Rachel thinks otherwise and she may have a valid point."

She hated to ask, could barely get the words out. "So you're going to spend time with Rachel?"

After the last couple of days, Carrie thought she was becoming important to Adam. Could she have been wrong?

"I need to figure things out, too," he added.

Who was she to tell him not to settle things with his ex?

"Then do that, Adam." Ignoring the tightness in her chest, she grabbed the photos and copy, and rose. "I have to run. Serena is expecting me at home."

He jumped up. "I have to see this through, Carrie."

Adam was the type of person to consider all the facts, going over all the contingencies, before making a decision. That was one of the traits she found appealing about him. And besides, she'd spent the bulk of her time when she arrived in Golden searching for the best course for her future. How could she argue with his need to find answers?

"It's your life, Adam. If figuring out your relationship with Rachel is important—"

He reached out and took hold of her hand. "I don't want a romantic relationship with Rachel. I like spending time with you."

"But?"

"But if we're going to be successful together, I need to know where I went wrong in my last serious relationship, so I don't make the same mistakes."

"And Rachel can help you with that?"

"She can."

Carrie took a step back and pulled her hand from his. "Then I wish you luck."

She forced a smile, then started down the trail, her heart pounding in her ears. She felt so foolish. She got that everyone had a past. She was working on her own issues, too. But did he have to team up with his ex to work on his?

Although she tried not to allow her imagination to go overboard, Adam's insistence that he tackle the issues without her hurt. Why did she have to start falling for a guy who so tightly guarded his heart?

Maybe this was for the best. It wasn't like she'd come to Golden to fall in love. She still had her hopes set on the corner office, not getting her heart trampled on. If she stayed in Golden for very long, she was afraid she might be headed in that very direction.

CHAPTER ELEVEN

"YOU'RE DOING MUCH BETTER."

Later that evening, Carrie sat astride Tri, her boots secure in the stirrups, her hands gripping the reins. It was her second lesson and she was still nervous.

"That's easy for you to say. You have your feet firmly planted on the ground."

Liz chuckled as she leaned against the weathered fence. "You passed your first lesson with flying colors. This should be much easier."

Okay, today when she'd climbed the mounting block beside the horse, her heart hadn't been in her throat. Liz had spoken gently to the horse—or her— Carrie wasn't quite sure.

"Relax."

"Coming from the pro," Carrie groused.

"If you take a deep breath and move with the horse's motion, you'll be fine."

Carrie snorted.

"Attitude."

Liz was right. Taking a deep breath, Carrie

slowly let the tension ease from her muscles. She sat straight in the saddle as Liz reviewed the basics of steering the animal.

She'd been at it for thirty minutes. Dust kicked up as Tri walked around the arena. A light breeze lifted the damp tendrils of hair escaping her helmet.

As Carrie grew more comfortable seated on the paint horse—brown with white patches— she smiled. She loved the animal with the tricolor mane that looked as if it had been dyed specifically in blond, copper and brown sections. To her amazement, the horse had walked right up to her at the first lesson and put her nose in Carrie's hand.

"Nudge him a little faster," Liz said.

Carrie swallowed hard, expecting the horse to take off. Tri merely carried on as if nothing had changed. When she realized she was in control, Carrie eased into the rhythm. Actually, she enjoyed herself.

"That's it," Liz called out. 'You're doing great."

Surprisingly, she was. Her fear of the large animal started to diminish. If she embraced the challenge, much like she did with everything in life, she just might surprise herself, and Adam, with her new skills.

"Good. Sink your heels into the stirrups and make sure your feet are angled upward."

Carrie corrected the position.

"Now stop Tri."

"What?"

"Like I showed you. I want to make sure you have the commands down."

Carrie pulled back on the reins and said, "Ho." Tri slowed to a stop.

"Now go forward."

Squeezing the horse's sides with both of her legs, she loosened the reins and gently tapped the horse with her heels. Tri started walking again. They circled the arena three times before stopping by Liz.

"You're getting the hang of it."

"Really?"

"I would never give you false confidence. It's dangerous and doesn't help you." She pointed to the gate leading to the paddock. "Time to dismount."

Carrie led Tri to the gate. She removed her right foot from the stirrup. With the reins in her left hand, she grasped the saddle horn, then swung her right leg over Tri's hindquarters, her muscles screaming at the movement. Flush up against the horse, she removed her left foot from the stirrup and slowly slid down to the ground.

"Wow. That was much better than last time."

"You mean when I almost landed on my rear end."

Liz chuckled. "You're a fast learner."

Carrie rubbed her sore thighs. "Plus, I'm not into pain."

"You'll feel fine in a few days."

Carrie would have to take Liz's word for it.

As she took hold of the lead to bring Tri into the stable so she could groom him, she asked, "Do you think I'll be able to ride successfully in time for the Eureka Games?"

"It's only the second lesson, but you're catching on quickly. I think so."

Pleasure coursed through Carrie.

"Adam will be impressed."

Would he? She rubbed Tri's neck, forcing away her doubts. Yes, the conversation with Adam on the mountainside hadn't been what she'd expected, but it was better to know the truth now rather than to be surprised later. Once in a lifetime was enough.

"MISS CARRIE! COME SEE my rabbit."

Unable to ignore the little boy's excitement, Carrie joined the group of local children and campers from the 4-H program who had brought their animals to the farm. They were making sure all the enclosures Colin and Ty had built would safely house each one. Rabbits, chickens and guinea pigs would delight other children when they strolled through the farm on the day of the games.

The Saturday sky had been a hazy blue in the morning, but had gradually shifted to a slate gray. Dark clouds were now rolling in and the humidity was building. Rainy days had been few and far between at the start of the summer, but afternoon storms were now a frequent occurrence.

Less than a week had passed since Carrie met Adam at the mountainside. Since then, she'd kept busy and tried not to dwell on their last conversation. Instead, she continued to work at the farm, attended practices and made sure the visiting groups understood their responsibilities prior to the upcoming event. On the sly, she took horseback riding lessons with Liz, not sure what the outcome of the lessons would be, but enjoying every minute. She was still sore, but gaining confidence every time she mounted Tri.

She gave Adam his space. They ran into each other on the farm and still met up in the coffee line each morning. For his part, he acted like nothing earth-shattering had happened. He teased her about entering the saddle competition, and she trash-talked, assuring him she would crush the other newbies. It seemed easier to fall back into the comfortable banter they'd indulged in before kissing each other than to worry over her tangled emotional state. She hated to admit it, but she wanted to see a proud gleam in his eyes when she won the competition. Which confused Carrie. He had that same warm regard when they were in each other's company. That spark that made her wonder if he wanted to kiss her again. So, why was he so adamant about working things out with his ex?

In silent agreement, they never mentioned Rachel. Carrie knew she was employed at Smitty's, but kept mum. What would she ask him anyway? *Have you and your ex found a way to move forward? Together? Separate?*

A hollow ache squeezed her chest. If he wanted to confide in Carrie, he would. If he didn't, there was nothing she could do about it. It wasn't like they'd professed undying love for each other, even though she was falling more and more for him every time they were together.

"Miss Carrie?"

She shook off her melancholy. "Sorry, Eli. Please, show me your rabbit."

The eight-year-old tugged her wrist to lead

Carrie to the hutch, surrounded by a half dozen kids in varying ages.

The petting zoo had grown in size. The local kids like Eli, who went to day camp at the facility, and some of the overnight 4-H campers would oversee the pen during the day of the event. Somehow in the past weeks, Carrie had become enchanted with these kids. She'd never been around children much, but she found them passionate and funny. And after years of not going to the park after her mother left the family, she was totally enraptured with the outdoors. It was like one Carrie had arrived in Golden to rethink next steps, but now a different Carrie woke up each day, an integral part of the heartbeat of Golden.

Between the children, the townspeople, merchants and Adam—mostly Adam—leaving Golden was going to be much harder than she'd anticipated. She still needed to get her résumé out there, but found her interest lagging.

After the Eureka Games.

Then she'd hold herself to it.

But right now, she'd let these little cuties captivate her.

"Miss Carrie," Amy said, "Were you riding Tri this morning?"

She placed a finger over her lips, then said, "That's our secret."

Amy giggled.

Eli frowned. "Why is it a secret?"

"I want to surprise a friend."

"When?"

"The day of the Eureka Games."

He thought about it and nodded. "Makes sense."

"I thought so," she told him.

The lessons had given her more confidence around the big animals. She was growing comfortable in the saddle, but still needed time to get the hang of controlling her horse. Liz was an excellent teacher. The Pendergrass family had a way with horses that put Carrie at ease. She was at the point where the idea of riding out at the end of the acts along with the other performers to thank the crowd for attending the games didn't totally scare her.

More children called her name. Before long she was learning the names of each animal and which children owned them. If their excitement today shone through at the event, what a success it would be. She mentally crossed her fingers that the animated children would entertain visitors as much as the horse acts.

In her peripheral vision, she noticed a tall,

broad-shouldered man walking her way. Adam. Her stomach flipped and a ready smile automatically formed on her lips.

"Hey, campers," he called out as he came closer. "The van is ready to return to the campground since the forecast is calling for rain."

Carrie faced the group. "Thank you so much for all your help. I couldn't do this without each and every one of you."

As the kids took off toward the parking lot, Eli lingered. "Are you sure you don't need me to watch over the animals if it rains?"

"We'll be fine," Carrie assured the little boy.

"Besides," Adam added, "Ty has another space near the barn ready in case the weather gets bad."

"Okay." Eli waved and picked up the pace so he didn't miss his ride back to the camp.

Adam watched Eli's progress, then turned to Carrie, grinning. "Your helpers?"

"The best ones I've got."

"I'll try not to take that personally."

She hid a smile.

"You do have a talent for drawing people into your projects," he observed.

"It's the wonderful folks of Golden who make it easy."

The wind picked up, sending the scent of

Adam's cologne in her direction. Why did he have to smell so good? And why did her fingers itch to touch him? She kept herself from moving closer and doing something she might regret later.

"Ty really needs the games to be a success," he said.

"Liz filled me in. This is a good way to draw attention to their future plans for the farm."

They stood for a moment, Carrie feeling awkward at the pause in conversation. Adam ran a hand through his thick hair. She shifted from foot to foot. They both spoke at the same time.

"I didn't think—"

"I sent the campaign out—"

Adam held out a hand. "You first."

"I sent *Discover Golden!* to the main audience we want to reach. It hasn't been long, but I've heard a buzz of interest already. Now we'll see if it actually helps Golden." She brushed straw from her T-shirt and stuffed her fingers in the rear pockets of her jeans. "You?"

"I thought maybe we could talk."

"About?"

"What's happening with Rachel."

She bit her tongue.

"We haven't been able to settle anything. She's been working all of Jamey's hours at the pub and hasn't put me on the schedule."

They hadn't seen each other? Her spirits lifted. "So, what does that mean?"

"I'm not sure, and that's the problem." His voice was thick when he said, "I told you that when I came back to Golden I wasn't in the right headspace. Now, with Rachel's suggestion that we do a deep dive into what went wrong, I've been considering two things— why I've been holding on to the past and where I belong going forward." A long, charged moment passed between them. His gaze never left hers. "Where you and I belong in the bigger picture."

Oh my.

"Are you free for dinner?"

His uncertainty made her feel extra tender toward him.

"I suppose I could eat."

He chuckled.

"I still have some things to finalize," she said.

"I told Colin I'd help him out by the barn. I'll come find you when we're finished. Does that work?"

She wanted to spend time with him, had missed him this past week while they'd both been busy. Maybe this Rachel thing would resolve itself after all.

"Yes," she said, in a firm tone. If she wanted to move to the next stage with this man, they needed to come together. She'd make sure they hashed out all her concerns tonight.

As Adam walked away, Carrie went to the stable office to check in with Liz. Ty was there, so they went over the order of events for the opening day and addressed a few logistical problems that had popped up. By five, dense, dark clouds had filled the sky, making it feel later in the day. Moisture hung in the air. When Adam found her, they drove to town in separate vehicles. After she parked her car near the apartment, she slid onto the leather seat of his sedan.

"Any suggestions?" he asked as she buckled her seat belt.

"Anywhere but Smitty's."

"Jamey will be heartbroken," came Adam's wry reply.

"He'll survive."

"In that case, let's head over to Clarkston. They have a good steak restaurant there."

Her stomach growled. "Lead the way."

Carrie decided this was a good idea as they drove the ten miles to the next town. Let them get out of Golden for a few hours and focus on each other, not all the busyness and people who required their attention. She'd make sure Adam knew that this wasn't just a nice friendship; for her it was turning into more. In recent days, when she studied herself in the mirror, she wasn't surprised to see the same infatuated expression that were permanent fixtures on her friend's faces since they'd fallen in love. A combination of astonishment and happiness that radiated from the core.

She'd never envied others their relationships before now. She looked over at Adam. His strong hands gripped the wheel, his intelligent eyes steady on the road. He turned just then, caught her gaze and sent her a dazzling smile. She wanted to remember this moment. He was everything she never knew she wanted.

It floored her to realize she'd never once in her life felt such a deep connection to a man.

The revelation shouldn't have shocked her, but somehow Adam had gotten under her skin and her emotions had become involved. This wasn't part of her plan. The question was, what did she do about it?

They hadn't gone more than a mile when Adam's cell phone rang. He hit the Bluetooth button. "Adam Wright."

"Adam, it's Chief Maloney. We have a missing child."

"I can be at the firehouse in five."

"The others on search and rescue duty are gathering as we speak."

He ended the call. "Sorry, but I need to go."

"Of course. We can reschedule."

"Let me drop you off at your apartment before it starts to rain."

"No, go to the station. I can walk home from there."

"Are you sure?"

"Positive."

She was curious about what a search and rescue entailed and about the volunteers who put themselves in harm's way, dropping everything to assist in a time of need. Another aspect of the townspeople that made her proud to live in Golden. She hoped the lost child was all right.

When they pulled up to the brightly lit firehouse, pickup trucks and cars crowded the parking lot. Adam removed his backpack from the trunk and Carrie followed him, careful to stay out of the way.

Police Chief Brady Davis nodded at them, and then addressed the group.

"We're all here now. The missing child

took off from the 4-H camp. His name is Eli Smith."

Carrie gripped Adam's arm.

The chief pointed to a map on the wall. "We'll head to sectors near the campground and lake. Grab a two-way radio on the way out and keep in constant communication."

Adam went to the shelf, took a handset and checked to make sure the battery was live. As he started back to his car, he stopped short when Carrie stepped into his path.

"I'm going with you," she announced.

HAVING CARRIE ALONG wasn't his first choice, but she was unyielding. He tried to dissuade her with the fact that she didn't have training, but since the missing child was one of the kids helping at the farm, she refused to take no for an answer. Thankfully, she had on sturdy sneakers. Once they got to the search area, she'd be hiking again.

"You need to stay with me and listen to instructions," he told her.

"I promise, I won't make searching for Eli any harder than it has to be."

He hadn't told the police chief that Carrie was going to search with him, but there was no way he'd leave her behind. The concern on her face made him realize just how worried she was for the little boy. This was personal for her, and she was smart. She'd be an asset.

"What are the odds of finding a lost child in the forest?"

He shot her a glance. "I don't consider the odds when I'm called to a search and rescue. I can't. Otherwise I get sidetracked."

She licked her lips as she stared out the window. Thunder rumbled in the distance.

"That can't be good," she muttered.

No. It wasn't.

He felt her gaze on him. "How did you get involved with the team?"

"My dad worked in forest management. He started the original search and rescue emergency response team with the local police and fire chief. Both Colin and I are trained and certified."

Her voice was wobbly when she said, "Good to know."

"Are you sure you're up for this?"

When he turned to her, tears shone in her eyes.

"Yes." She swiped her cheeks and straightened her shoulders. Carrie was determined to find the little boy. Adam couldn't love her more.

He blinked. Love? No, it was too soon. He was still figuring out how Rachel walking away without a word had changed him. Broken and reshaped him into the man he was today. But there was no denying that Carrie had slipped through the cracks in the armor protecting his heart.

The radio crackled. "Adam? Location status."

The sky grew darker with the approaching storm. Thankfully, he knew the area well.

"Coming up to Marker 52."

"The boy may have headed that way."

"10-4." The turnoff was up ahead. No time to dwell on personal revelations when they needed to find Eli.

Carrie's soft voice calmed the building tension. "Marker 52?"

"An access road we're coming up to…" He slowed down and turned, the car headlights falling on the dirt road entrance. "Now."

"Are we near the camp?"

"Closer to the lake access. The camp is about a half mile east."

"Why would Eli leave, especially with bad weather in sight?"

"We'll find out when we ask him."

The car jerked and bumped down the dirt and gravel road leading to a clearing. He parked and they exited the car. Adam secured his backpack and handed Carrie a flashlight.

"Stay close."

She nodded.

For the next hour they walked a trail adjacent to the lake. Adam checked in periodically and updates came over the radio, but no one had found the little boy. Adam was just about to make the decision to turn back and try another area when Carrie tugged on his shirtsleeve.

"Did you hear that?"

Over the wind and rustling leaves, he heard crying. They made their way toward the sound. A large limb had fallen across the path. Adam stepped over it and discovered Eli huddled against the tree trunk.

"Hey, buddy," he said as he knelt beside the boy.

Eli swiped the tears trailing down his face. "It hurts."

"What hurts?"

"My ankle."

Adam gingerly inspected his foot. The boy's hiss told him the injury was significant, but not life-threatening. He radioed the team to say he'd located Eli, who was injured but safe, and went to work. Grabbing his backpack, he nodded at Carrie. She sat down next to Eli and took hold of his hand.

The boy calmed when he saw her. "Miss Carrie, what are you doing here?"

"Searching for you. You didn't think we'd let you roam around this forest alone, did you?"

"I didn't think anyone would come."

She hugged him close. Over the boy's head she sent Adam a relieved smile. She'd never looked so beautiful.

Adam rolled out a length of compressive bandage to wrap around the boy's ankle. If it was a sprain, at least the bandage would reduce the swelling for now.

"Do you hurt anywhere else, Eli?" he asked as he did a visual examination.

"No. I tripped and fell and when I tried to walk it hurt, so I sat by the tree until I felt better."

"You'll be fine, buddy. You did the right thing by staying put so we could find you."

The wind picked up and Carrie angled herself to shield the boy.

"Eli, what are you doing out here all by yourself?" she asked.

"I heard one of the counselors talking about the storm and I got worried about the rabbits. I wanted to go back to the farm to make sure they were safe."

"You know Mr. Ty would never let anything happen to the animals."

"But it's my job."

Carrie brushed Eli's bangs from his eyes. "Your job is to listen to the counselors and tell them if you have concerns, not take off without telling anyone."

He dropped his head, wincing as Adam wrapped the bandage.

"Sorry," came his quiet reply.

Carrie hugged Eli again. "Next time you'll ask for help, right?"

"I will."

"Good boy."

Adam's chest went tight at the sight of Carrie reassuring Eli. She may be a force of nature when on the job, but she had a soft side, too. He'd seen it the way she'd worked with the merchants in town, the way she'd gotten the Eureka Games together on short notice, giving orders and expecting success, always with a smile on her face and a tone of encouragement. Golden was better for her being here. *He* was better.

He cleared his throat as he finished up. "What do you say we get you back to the camp?"

"Am I gonna get in trouble?"

Adam stood. "Probably."

Eli frowned. "Aw."

Carrie's lips quivered. She glanced at Adam. "What can I do?"

"You take my backpack and I'll carry Eli to the car."

"Got it."

They hiked back to the vehicle. The sky turned completely black and the wind buffeted them. Leaves scattered in a frenzy. As the first raindrops fell, Adam picked up the pace. They arrived at the clearing just as the sky opened up and the rain fell in sheets. He got Eli settled in the back seat, pulling a blanket over the little boy, then dashed to the trunk for a towel he kept with his supplies and jumped behind the wheel.

Carrie shook out her hair, releasing the fragrance he couldn't get enough of.

Adam reached over and brushed the stray hair stuck to her wet cheek. "You okay?"

"Yes, now that we found Eli."

She turned to look over her shoulder to find the boy curled up under the blanket.

It took only a few minutes to drive to the camp. The staff was waiting and swooped in as soon as the car stopped. Both he and Carrie stepped out of the car, the rain pelting them. Carrie took Eli's arm and went with the others.

"Thanks," said a young man as he shook Adam's hand and led him to a building overhang where they could be relatively dry.

"I wrapped Eli's ankle, but you should have it examined by a doctor."

"We will. The police chief is on the way, but in the meantime, we'll check Eli over and take him to the clinic in Golden."

Having done all he could, Adam watched the man run to the building where Eli and Carrie had disappeared. He sent an update on the radio. He'd just finished when Carrie joined him and they ran back to his car.

"Wow," she said, resting her head back against the rest. "That was intense."

"Calls like that usually are."

"Afterward you must feel drained."

"If the rescue is a success, yes."

The rain battered the roof of the car. Leaves swirled and flew in all directions in the heavy wind, some sticking to the windshield. Airborne twigs banged the side of the car.

She rolled her head on the rest toward him. "I see why you came back to Golden."

His chest went tight. "You know why I had to."

The inside of the car was quiet, but no less tense. This was as good a time as any to talk, since he wasn't driving in this storm.

He stared out the window. "I think I handled the Rachel situation wrong."

"There was a good way?"

He needed to explain. Hoped she'd understand. It hurt to admit the truth, but he didn't have a choice. Not if he wanted Carrie in his life.

He focused on her. "Bottom line, I didn't want to believe she'd used me."

Carrie straightened and twisted in her seat. "Why would you think that?"

He swallowed. "It's happened before."

She watched him with keen eyes.

He ran a hand through his wet hair, grimaced and wiped his hand on the towel. "I was on the fast track in New York. Brought a lot of business to the firm. They were happy with my performance and I finally settled into what I thought was my place in life."

"And then Rachel canceled the wedding."

The memory that had made him so angry now blurred at the edges. "Her dad was the one who introduced us, since I didn't know many people when I first moved to New York.

"We went to social activities together. Her father had the name, but I had the skill to move the firm to the next level. I guess I didn't notice that Richard Harrington had intentionally eased Rachel into my orbit not just as a friend, but to cultivate potential clients. Rachel and I liked each other, and before I knew it, one thing led to another and we were engaged."

"You sound like you didn't have a choice."

"Of course I did. But I was caught up in the hype. I'd have a father-in-law who respected my work and our life would be perfect." He stopped. Shook his head. "Until it wasn't."

"You really think she used you?"

"In a way, but not maliciously. She always had a hard time living up to her parents' expectations. I suppose being with me made her life easier." Now that he'd examined both their motivations, it was clear he'd played a part in the mess as well. "Thankfully, she saw through the facade when I didn't. In her way, Rachel saved us from heartache down the road, even if it didn't feel like it at the time."

"And that's why it's been so important to rehash what happened with Rachel? For the future?"

"Yes."

"Makes sense, I suppose, but Adam, you don't need her to discover what to do next."

She didn't know what really kept him awake at night.

"That's the problem." Did he dare speak

his fear out loud? If he acknowledged it, he had to act on it and he didn't know if he was ready, but he plowed ahead anyway. "I don't know what comes next."

"For us?"

"For everything. If the family agrees to the sale of Deep North, what are my next steps? I came back to Golden to lick my wounds. What do I have if I don't go to the office every day?"

"Wow. Okay."

He could almost see her brain at work.

"Adam, you're a really smart guy. There must be plenty of business opportunities that would interest you." She paused for a moment and then her face lit up. "We could work together to find the right fit. You don't have to go back to the city. You already advise the merchants here in Golden. It's a start."

"I suppose." He paused. "I sort of…stalled after New York. Everything that happened kind of derailed me. Working for the family business was a positive step to get past what happened." And now he could finally confess what he hadn't told another person. "But I haven't been able to regroup."

A blast of wind shook the car. Exactly how Adam felt, blown off his moorings and unable to get back to solid ground.

"Who else used you, Adam?"

Did he really want to go down this road? If Carrie were to understand, he'd have to. "Carter."

"More of that history between you two. Are you going to fill me in?"

"It's dumb. Kid stuff really."

"But obviously it had an impact on you."

He blew out a breath and ran a hand though his damp hair again.

"Carter and I were friends in high school. At least I thought we were."

The memories he'd thought had faded returned like the tempest outside.

"We worked together on class projects where I did the bulk of the assignment, or if we were studying for a test, I'd calculate the formulas or mathematical equations, thinking Carter appreciated my work. Being smart set me apart from the kids in school. Either they'd ask me to do the work they didn't understand or joked about me being a nerd. I never really knew if people liked me for me. But Carter's friendship seemed real. Then, in our junior year of high school, he asked me to take his college prep test for him."

Her eyes went wide. "He wanted you to cheat?"

He nodded. "When I learned that Carter

only needed me to get into the prestigious college his family expected him to attend, it hit me hard. Colin had tried to warn me but I didn't think my friend would use me. I was wrong."

"What did you do?"

"I said no. But I was so ticked, I refused to study with Carter for finals, which he tanked. Ultimately he didn't have the grades to get into his first-choice schools. Ever since then, he's had it out for me."

She stared into the night. The rain had hit its zenith and was now slowing. The wind had tapered off.

"So, when it seemed like Rachel had used you to keep her parents happy, it was like high school all over again?"

She'd connected the dots far faster than he had. Leave it to her to get straight to the heart of the matter.

"Yes. I wondered if she'd ever wanted to get married in the first place. Wondered if we'd truly loved each other. I didn't consider New York home enough to put up with the emotional roller coaster, so I came back to Golden."

"It explains a lot."

"It seems ridiculous at thirty-two to be figuring out my life from here, but it's the truth.

I retreated into myself when I came back to Golden." He caught her gaze and held it. "You brought me back out."

She blinked. "By gently persuading you to be involved in the Golden campaign?"

"And by involving me in the Eureka Games."

A small smile formed on her lips. "Well, my job here is done."

"Not by a long shot."

She reached out and cradled his hand in hers. "I get it. I'm an overachiever because I've always wanted my dad's approval. We only had each other when I was growing up. He had pretty high standards. I always felt I needed to exceed them."

"Explains why you work so hard for others."

Her forehead crinkled. "I do that?"

"You do. It's one of the things I really like about you."

Her tone turned sassy. "Only one?"

Unable to resist, he wrapped a hand around the back of her neck and pulled her in for a much-needed kiss. The air around them grew warm and sultry. In this cocoon, they could hide from the world. Just the two of them.

The two of them.

He liked that idea.

Carrie reached up to stroke his cheek and the kiss went deeper. A tide of emotions swept over him. She listened and didn't judge, instead encouraging him to pursue a new direction. How had he gotten so lucky as to find her?

She broke the kiss. There was just enough light to see the determination in her expression. Coming from Carrie, it was heady, indeed.

"So, after the Eureka Games," she said as she put inches between them, "we'll work on your dilemma."

A huge weight lifted from his chest, replaced by hope. "I'm a project now?"

She leaned in and whispered against his lips, "You know how good I am with projects," then kissed him.

After a long moment, he ended the kiss, catching his breath. Stared at her precious face. For the first time in a long time he couldn't wait for tomorrow and the challenge it would bring. He'd make it plain to Rachel that all was forgiven and no amends were needed. She was on her own path of discovery, but they'd needed each other to kickstart the change. Once Adam explained, how could Rachel not agree?

"It'll be okay. We'll be okay," Carrie whispered.

Would they? He'd have to work overtime to convince Carrie, but he would, no matter the obstacles.

He was finally ready to open his cautious heart.

CHAPTER TWELVE

"STATUS REPORT?" GAYLE ANN asked the match-makers who were gathered on the wide front porch of Masterson House on the Monday morning following the storm. They were sipping sweet iced tea and enjoying the breeze from the ceiling fans. Gayle Ann and Harry shared a bench seat while Alveda, Bunny and Wanda Sue commandeered the rocking chairs. The summer heat and humidity still held Golden in its grip, but after the storm, the mornings were a touch cooler.

"Rachel is still working at Smitty's," Bunny grumped.

Alveda stared down her friend. "This is good for Rachel. She needs to prove that she can be productive."

"To Adam?"

"No. To herself." Alveda rocked her chair harder. "Rachel finding herself will be good for her and Adam."

Wanda Sue nearly choked on her tea. "There's a her and Adam?"

"No," Alveda rushed to say. "I mean that whatever they decide, Rachel is taking a stand on her own two feet. That's important for her, and important for everyone."

Gayle Ann glanced at Alveda. "I'm glad you've spent time with her."

Alveda smiled. "I drop in every few days to see how she's holding up. My, that girl makes my kitchen skills seem amateur."

"But that doesn't solve what's not going on between Adam and Carrie," Bunny countered.

"What is going on?" Gayle Ann asked.

"Nothing," Alveda, Bunny and Wanda Sue said in unison.

"Oh dear." She'd been so sidetracked by Harry that she, the leader of the group, hadn't been on top of matters. "I thought for sure that working together on the Eureka Games would bring them closer."

"After the search and rescue call, when Carrie tagged along, I thought it would be a turning point for them. But for some reason Adam is more quiet than usual and that doesn't bode well for romance."

"But they found the boy safe and sound," Gayle Ann said. "Did I miss something?"

Bunny nodded. "They worked together to bring the little boy back to camp."

"Myrna at the coffee shop said they still drop in every morning," Wanda Sue informed them.

"So, what is the problem?"

"I'm not sure." Bunny swirled the amber liquid in her glass. "Something is going on at Deep North, but Sandy and Beck have been tightlipped about it. Usually I can crack them for information, but not this time. It could be what's got Adam distracted from wooing Carrie."

"Then we need to put our thinking caps on."

The group went silent. Birds sang in the distance, creating a soothing atmosphere for them to come up with ideas. Gayle Ann inhaled the scent of her blooming flowers, pleased by this year's colorful bounty. Harry's shoulder brushed hers and she couldn't hold back a smile.

Wanda Sue finally broke the silence. "Maybe we're going about this the wrong way. Carrie could be the key."

"In what way?"

"She's been able to get Adam to commit to her projects. What if she had a reason to stay in Golden, besides falling in love with Adam?"

"She can't still be thinking of leaving," Bunny protested. "Not after all the good she's done here."

"I have heard a rumor…" Harry said.

Alveda stopped rocking. "Spill."

"I ran into Don Baxter at the golf course. He mentioned that since he retired earlier this year, he and Shelia are thinking of moving away from Golden."

Gayle Ann straightened. "Which means that the director position at the Chamber would need to be filled. And who better to take over the job than Carrie, who has practically been running the place as it is."

Bunny grinned. "If Shelia retires and Carrie takes her job, that'll give us more time to work on the romance problem."

"But how can we be sure this happens in our time frame?" Wanda Sue's eyebrows furrowed. "What if Carrie stumbles upon a job she'd leave Golden to take?"

"Then we make sure that doesn't happen." Gayle Ann turned to Harry. "Any way we can speed up the time line?"

"I do have access to Carter through the club. Perhaps I can make a few veiled suggestions? Get him to agree that Carrie is an asset to Golden and could be promoted."

Bunny pointed a finger at him. "And make him think it's his idea."

"Please," came Harry's reply. "This isn't my first go-around."

Gayle Ann grinned. The judge had been known for some very creative rulings during his time in court. "I get the impression that Carrie is enjoying her job. What better way to keep her interested in remaining in Golden than to offer her a new position? In case you haven't noticed, the girl loves a challenge."

"Then we help push along the retirement, get Carter on board, and make sure Carrie gets promoted?" Bunny asked.

Wanda Sue held up her hand. "Aren't we overstepping? Maybe Shelia needs her job. Although, when I talked to her last, she didn't seem happy there."

"And I heard she's been missing meetings," Bunny added. "Maybe they need a fresh start."

"According to Don, he received a very attractive bonus for early retirement, so it sounds like they're flush." Harry frowned. "The last couple of times I saw Don, he seemed a little under the weather. Perhaps there is more going on with the Baxters than we realize."

The group glanced at one other, concern on their faces.

"Then we proceed with caution. We don't want to be insensitive to any health issues or other problems." Gayle Ann clasped her hands together. "Harry will talk to Don and Carter. Wanda Sue, you know Shelia. Gently try to find out what it'll take to get her to retire early. I remember hearing she loves a certain lake located in New Hampshire. Perhaps talk about how romantic it would be to get away with her husband. After all, we're all getting older. We should enjoy life while we still can."

Wanda Sue gasped. "Gayle Ann!"

She shrugged. "It is the truth. We all know how that feels."

"Speak for yourself," Alveda said, her eyes squinty.

"This from the woman who was complaining about her achy knees this morning?"

"Just because we're older doesn't mean we have to embrace it."

"Our weekly hikes have done me a world of good," Bunny chimed in.

Gayle Ann grinned as the matchmakers fussed and argued, but still banded together when the stakes were important.

"Now, then, do we all agree on our tasks?" Harry asked.

Leave it to the judge to get them back on track.

"And if this doesn't work?" Bunny asked.

"Then we pull out all the stops at the Eureka Games," Gayle Ann said. "Are we ready to move forward?"

"Final question," Wanda Sue said, crossing her arms over her chest. "What's going on with you and Harry?"

"Uh-oh," Alveda muttered under her breath.

Drat if Gayle Ann didn't feel her cheeks heating. She cleared her throat. "We're... dating."

"About time," Bunny said.

Gayle Ann's tension fled. "You suspected?"

"Yep. Thought we were going to have to use our skills on you two. At least you both came to your senses."

Harry sent Gayle Ann an amused glance. "I told you they'd read between the lines."

Bunny rolled her eyes. "How could we not, with the way you two are goo-goo-eyed over each other."

Gayle Ann's hand flew to her heart. "It's that obvious?"

"Only since we started working on this match," Alveda assured her.

"Personally, I think you should tell the world," Wanda Sue encouraged.

"Yeah," Bunny said, pointing to Alveda and Wanda Sue. "Then maybe the three of us will get lucky."

"You never know when the stars will align," Harry said, taking Gayle Ann's hand in his.

"I HAVE AN IDEA," Carrie said as she marched into Adam's office at Deep North Adventures two days later.

Adam looked up from the paperwork on his desk, holding back a grin. "Good morning to you, too."

"You weren't at the coffee shop, so I had to come here."

"Sorry. The family is going to vote on the sale later today, so I needed to get all the financials in order."

"Then my timing is perfect."

He tossed his pen on the desk, leaned back in his chair and clasped his hands behind his neck.

Carrie was dressed in business mode: fitted blouse, skirt and pumps. He kind of missed her more casual attire, but either way, she was stunning.

"You remember the other night in your car?"

The night they'd shared kisses and confidences? Oh yeah, he remembered. Her soft lips burned in his memory.

She squared her shoulders, blushing. "We

talked about Deep North. Why not hold on to it and start your own regional company?"

He dropped his arms. "Sorry, what?"

"Expand Deep North yourselves."

"Expand?"

"Hear me out." She pulled papers from her briefcase and handed them to Adam. He rolled up his shirtsleeves before taking them. "I researched adventure companies in this region. There are a few, mainly in larger metropolitan locations, but nothing with as many options as Deep North. Either they only offer one kind of trip or don't sell clothing and other amenities. You've managed to do both and do it well in the process."

He blinked. "You spent your time off researching all this?"

"Why not?" She tapped a finger against her head. "Problem solver, remember?"

His chest went mushy. She'd seen how unsure he was about the future and tried to come up with solutions for him. He was well and truly lost to this woman.

"Here, have a look."

He picked up the papers to read through. She'd hit good points, mostly from a marketing perspective. He'd have to crunch the numbers on his own. If he was interested.

Oh, you're interested.

For the first time since coming home, he was getting his mojo back.

"You haven't given an answer to the potential buyer yet, so you still have time to pivot to a regional model."

Be still, my heart.

"Anyway, it's one path forward." She pulled out her phone. "I also found a few stores for sale. I'll email you the links."

"Regional, huh? What if Fletcher, the CEO we're dealing with, buys another company in this area? He wants us as a way to step into the market here. I'd face stiff competition."

Carrie tapped her chin while she paced. She stopped, turned on her heel, her eyes alight.

"Adam, if you build regionally or buy an already existing chain to integrate with Deep North, it would be yours. You can buy out your folks so they can continue their travel plans. And Colin? If he wants to keep working here, hire him as a guide. That'll give him the flexibility to do what he wants with his woodworking business."

He stared at Carrie. They were so in sync, but the possibility of her going back to her old life created a hollow feeling in his chest.

"You could go from a single store owner to a CEO, which is up your alley anyway."

"It's like you're reading my mind."

She chuckled. "I can see where you don't want to influence your family's decision, but Adam, it's an open door for you."

There was no denying that truth. And they'd be on board if this was what he wanted.

"And when Fletcher eventually learns that you're going to expand, that may dissuade him from coming East."

He rose and came to the front of the desk, sitting on the edge. "You seem pretty invested in this."

"After spending time with you, I could tell you were in a rut. But it seems like now is the time to climb out and get back to the work you love."

"Without the New York distractions?"

She paused. "Yes."

Her terse reply told him she wasn't thrilled with Rachel still in town.

"Adam you could go anywhere and be successful, but you chose Golden as your home. Make that love work for you and this town." She grinned. "My idea has merit and you know it."

"I'll think about it."

His mind was already spinning. It was as if he'd needed someone to give him permission to pack up the past and start anew. When he was around Carrie, the past was forgotten. Would she consider walking into the future with him or was she still planning on leaving Golden?

She gently tapped his temple with a finger. "Got your wheels turning, didn't I?"

He pushed from the desk and closed the distance between them. "In so many ways."

He leaned in, inhaling her unique scent and covered her lips with his. Her soft sigh had him tugging her closer. For him, past and future didn't compare to the present reality of Carrie in his arms.

After a few moments he let her go.

"What about you?" he asked.

"Me?"

He needed to know. "Still holding out for the fancy job?"

"That goal hasn't changed, though I do like living here."

"Would you consider staying?"

"If I had the right offer."

"Which consists of?"

She counted off on her fingers. "A roomy office space. Unlimited resources from my superiors. Free creative agency with my clients."

He crossed his arms over his chest. "Seems you've been thinking about your future, too."

She shrugged.

"So, why haven't you left?"

"With all I have going on?"

"You've talked about it."

"I have, but I can't look for another position right now. The Eureka Games await."

So she was going to leave eventually? But until then…

"Does that mean you're also invested in us?"

Her eyes turned troubled. "You have to ask?"

"Carrie, I—"

"I know you said you needed time to figure things out with Rachel. But that can't be going well if you can kiss me with so much… zeal."

He forced back a smile. "You're right. I like kissing you."

"So give me a reason to stay in Golden."

He went still. "Please tell me you aren't kidding."

"Not about this, Adam." She placed a hand on his chest. "I know you were reeling when you left New York. I was, too. And I know you don't open your heart easily. But you and I… We have a connection. I get the feeling you've shared parts of yourself with me that you wouldn't reveal to anyone else. Didn't we both come up with the same idea for your business? There's something to pursue here,

Adam. I'm willing to give it a chance if you are."

"I have things to work out, but yes, I want to see what happens beyond today."

"We both have decisions to make, so after the Eureka Games, we'll sit down and truly consider what we want out of this relationship."

"Just give me a date and time."

She grabbed her briefcase, then went up on her toes to kiss him. With a sassy grin, she said, "I'll have my people get in touch with your people."

"You know you're a dream come true, right?"

"Sweet talker." Then she sauntered out the door.

It didn't take a full minute later for Brea to pop her head in the room.

"Have you okayed my increase in budget?"

Adam shook his head. "Your what?"

Brea stepped into the room. "My food budget."

"Oh, right. Give me a few minutes to read it through."

"I knew you'd forget all about my budget when Carrie walked through the door."

"You did?"

She started laughing. "You've got it bad."

He didn't hold back his smile. "I do, indeed."

CARRIE COULDN'T BELIEVE she'd been so bold. She hadn't meant to be, but the time had been right to tell Adam what she was feeling. If they were to become a couple, they needed to put everything on the table. Her going after a dream job. Adam settling things once and for all with Rachel. Until they were on the same page, they didn't have a chance of lasting. But Carrie was willing to do what she had to. She wanted Adam in her life.

After the drive back to town, Carrie parked behind Blue Ridge Cottage and hurried on foot to the Chamber for her next team meeting. Lindsey had managed to lock Shelia into a time and date, so Carrie didn't want to be late. Maybe their boss would finally tell them why she'd been so unfocused this summer.

She'd just made the turn onto Main Street when she collided with a woman carrying multiple bags. The bags scattered across the sidewalk, a large shoebox skidding to a stop by Carrie's feet. When she steadied herself, Carrie realized it was Rachel, wearing another designer dress and to-die-for heels.

"I'm sorry, I wasn't paying…" Rachel's voice trailed off when she recognized Carrie.

Carrie cleared her suddenly tight voice. "Are you okay?"

"Yes. Silly me, thinking instead of paying

attention." Rachel stuffed the box in a bag and picked up the others. "You're Adam's friend. I remember we met at the pub."

"Yes. And you're his ex-fiancée."

Rachel's eyes shadowed for a split second. "Afraid so."

They stood in awkward silence as cars passed by, visitors went in and out of stores and the minutes ticked away.

"I'm sure Adam has told you that we're working things out."

"He has."

Rachel's brows angled together. "I really want us to get to the bottom of what went wrong."

What did she say to the woman who was a part of Adam's past? Even when they were trying to untangle that past.

"Adam has made it clear he wants that, too."

With sadness in her eyes, Rachel nodded.

A truck passed by, with the Crestview Farm logo on the side, the horn blaring. Carrie glanced over to see Ty waving at her and returned the greeting. When she turned back, Rachel pointed at the vehicle.

"Isn't that where the end-of-summer event is taking place?"

"That's right." Surprised, Carrie said, "You've heard about it?"

"Are you kidding? The entire town is talking about it."

Good to know the news was out.

"And you're the one in charge of the farm thingy going on?"

"The Eureka Games?"

"Right, I was told I should talk to you."

Carrie's eyes went wide. "About?"

"The saddle game."

"The saddle competition?"

Rachel nodded. "I want to join."

"Do you know anything about it?"

"I know it's for a good cause. I can't tell you how many benefits I've been part of back home."

"Are you aware of the details?"

"Something about a sawhorse and mounting a saddle on it. Whoever does it fastest wins."

"That's about it."

"Can I sign up?"

Carrie pulled out her phone, found the Eureka Games folder and tapped the saddle competition page. "Rachel Harrington, correct?"

At Rachel's nod, Carrie added the name. "There are ten other people entered."

A full smile bloomed on Rachel's lips. "Then it should be fun."

"You're all set."

"Thank you." Rachel tilted her head. "I feel like we got off on the wrong foot. You were working with Adam and I interrupted your lunch, but I didn't realize until later that Adam is interested in you."

"It's fine." What more could she say?

"Good." Rachel glanced at her watch. "I should get going."

"Me, too."

Rachel nodded and started her trek, then stopped. She toyed with her purse strap, then blurted, "I'm really not a bad person."

Her admission caught Carrie off guard.

Before she could come up with a coherent answer, Rachel moved on. Shaking off the odd encounter, Carrie picked up her pace. She'd just gotten through the Chamber door when Lindsey met her.

"Did I miss anything?" Carrie asked as she hustled to her office to drop off her belongings.

"No. Shelia has been here all morning, locked in her office."

"Is she planning on coming out?"

Lindsey lowered her voice. "I could have sworn I heard her crying."

"Oh dear."

Lindsey bit a fingernail. "What should we do?"

"Knock on her door and see if she still wants the meeting?"

"Okay. You knock."

"Why me?"

"Because it was your idea."

Containing an eye roll, Carrie smoothed her skirt and marched to Shelia's door. She lifted her hand in a fist, ready to knock…

"Do it," Lindsey said in too loud a voice.

Rolling her shoulders, Carrie knocked.

"Yes?" came a muffled voice.

"Shelia, are you ready for the meeting?"

"I'll meet you in the boardroom."

Carrie hurried to push Lindsey down the hallway. "Let's get ready."

They rounded up their notebooks and pens and each took a seat. The minutes clicked by.

Lindsey glanced at the door. "Where is she?"

"She should be—"

Shelia strode into the room. "My apologies, ladies. I had an important call to finish."

"Of course. We're ready whenever you are," Carrie told her.

The next hour was spent catching up on future projects and events involving the Chamber. Lindsey made sure to get her budget requests in, which Shelia okayed. In contrast to the woman who'd been missing in action the last few weeks, the director was clear and on the mark.

Finally, she asked, "Anything else we need to discuss?"

Carrie met Lindsey's gaze. She gave Carrie a slight nod. When had Carrie been voted the office spokesperson? Before she could ask if their boss was feeling all right, Shelia stood.

"Thank you, both."

Then in a cloud of perfume, she left the room.

"Why didn't you ask her what's going on?" Lindsey huffed.

"Why didn't you?"

"It doesn't matter now. We lost our opening."

Carrie tapped her finger on the table. "The good news is she's just as on-target as when I first started working here."

Lindsey stood. "I was able to get my budget proposal approved, so I'm set for a while."

Carrie gathered up her pen and notebook. "I don't give another report until after we get data from my two latest projects." She glanced at the empty doorway. "Think things will be normal from now on?"

"We'll find out."

As Carrie went back to her office, she decided that nothing was normal these days. She'd just run into Adam's ex, the man Carrie definitely had strong feelings for, right on the heels of said man wanting to test next steps in their own relationship. But Rachel was still in Golden. What did that mean for any kind of romantic progress? Carrie did not want to be blindsided like she had been in New York.

And speaking of New York, why hadn't she updated her résumé? Months had passed. She'd had ample opportunities. Had Adam, and Golden, truly captured her heat?

She dropped into her chair. So much for coming to Golden to reboot her future. If anything, she was more unsure of next steps than when she'd arrived.

CHAPTER THIRTEEN

FIVE DAYS UNTIL the Eureka Games, and Carrie was laser focused. She pored over her last-minute lists, checked details and kept everyone on task.

She'd been approached by a number of local merchants who wanted to feature their products during the event. This meant more logistics, more tables and booths and headaches. She'd also decided to start the games two days earlier than she'd promoted, to build up the excitement. Not that it mattered; word of mouth spread quickly in Golden so there would be a turnout no matter how many days the event lasted.

Carter wanted a summer splash. From the petting zoo to the live acts, to locals bringing fresh produce or homemade products to sell, along with games and crafts, he was certainly getting his wish.

She rose from her desk and stretched her arms over her head. Maybe getting out of the office for a bit would help. She could walk to the park, drink in the scenery and still be back before lunch.

Her thighs were sore after yesterday's horseback riding lesson, but Liz had been pleased with her progress. Carrie would have no trouble trotting out behind the performers after the main acts ended, to thank their guests for supporting the games.

She changed from pumps into the sneakers she now kept in the office in case she needed a fresh air fix. They didn't exactly go with the sleeveless black dress, but at least they matched the white piping along the hem and neckline.

She'd become more comfortable wearing casual work clothing. Over time, it became less strange to duck out of the office during work hours. The walks actually boosted her creativity. She waved to townspeople who had become her friends and supported her efforts to profile Golden. Maybe going back to New York was unnecessary. She liked her position at the Chamber and could see being here down the road. Maybe a year could roll into two or three. She was still adding to her work portfolio, so it wasn't like time spent in Golden was a hindrance to her career.

She popped her head into Lindsey's office.

"Going for a walk. Want anything while I'm out?"

"No," her coworker said with a shake of her head.

"I'll be back for lunch."

"Right," came Lindsey's response as she lowered her head and concentrated on numbers.

Carrie tossed her hair over her shoulders, breathing in the warm mountain air. The sun shone; the deep blue sky held few clouds. A perfect day to be thankful for all she had, Adam topping the list. It was amazing how he made her feel, giddy and special and important, all rolled into one. As she turned toward the park, caught up in her daydreaming, a man in a suit approached.

She slowed. Stared. "Dad?"

"Hi, Carrie."

"What are you doing here? Is something wrong?"

He chuckled, the sun shining on his dark hair shot through with gray. His topaz eyes, so much like hers, smiled back at her. "Can't a father visit his daughter?"

After the way they'd left things between them?

"On a work day?" She took in his light gray suit. "And you hardly ever leave Manhattan."

"Since you don't live there any longer, I decided to come see where you've planted yourself."

"It's been months."

"Sorry I didn't get here sooner."

Now that the shock had worn off, she ran over to hug him. He wrapped his arms around her and time slipped back to when she was a child, after her mother left, when he'd tried to put her first, if only for a short time.

He held her out at arm's length to inspect her. "Your hair is lighter than I remember."

"I've been out in the sun a lot."

"I see." His forehead creased. "Sneakers on a work day?"

He seemed to forget that even in New York, women wore comfortable shoes to the office and changed to heels later.

"Golden is more easygoing than the city, Dad. I'm actually overdressed."

"Hmm." He dropped his hands. "Then it's a good thing I arrived before you got too caught up in this trend."

"So, why are you here?"

"We need to talk. Is there someplace we can sit?"

"I was headed to the park. It's very peaceful there and the benches are spaced out, so we can have some privacy."

He frowned. "I recall you disliked the park."

"Things change, Dad," She linked her arm through his. "It's beautiful."

"If you say so."

During the walk, Carrie found herself on pins and needles. It was not like her father to show up out of the blue. He meticulously planned every minute of his day.

As they passed under the stone arch into the park, she pointed to a nearby bench shaded by a leafy oak tree. They sat and she couldn't take it any longer.

"Dad, you've got me worried. What's going on?"

"Like I said, I wanted to see you."

After she'd been fired, the strain had been heavy between them. They didn't talk anywhere near as much as when she'd lived in the city.

"I also miss our dinners. My friends ask about you."

"How sweet." She hesitated. "You know I needed a change."

"I do. I'm glad Serena was there for you."

"She's been awesome. And she got engaged."

"Hopefully I'll be able to see her and congratulate her while I'm in town." His phone beeped but he didn't make a move to remove it from his pocket. "And her business? It's doing well?"

"Yes. Locals and tourists alike love her sketches. I've helped her with her online marketing, and both the store and her website are a success."

"Of course. I wouldn't expect anything less from my hardworking daughter."

Warmth spread through her chest. "Speaking of working hard, this summer has gone by in a blur. I had two really important projects to tackle." She crossed her feet at her ankles to keep from fidgeting. "In fact, you're just in time for the end-of-summer blast I put together. It's going to be so much fun."

"When is it?"

"Officially Saturday, but we've got some earlier events."

"I'm not sure I can take that much time away from the office."

She tried not to let her disappointment ruin their visit. Really, she would have been shocked if he stayed. "Of course."

"I'm flying back tomorrow."

She nodded.

He shifted. "In the meantime, I have good news. Your work here in Golden has not gone without notice."

Puzzled, she asked, "What do you mean?"

"The campaign you did with Adam Wright."

She frowned. "You've seen it?"

"It was brought to my attention by Bradford Wheeler. You remember him?"

"Yes."

Wheeler had opened an agency about six months before she left Manhattan. It was rumored that he was becoming a rival of Paul Craigerson, her old boss. Why would he care about *Discover Golden!*?

"I don't understand."

"When a man as talented as Adam Wright goes missing, it leaves a vacuum in the financial world. When he resurfaces, people take notice."

"What has that got to do with Mr. Wheeler?"

"He found out you were the one to lure Adam out of hiding. He was impressed."

"I… Adam wasn't in hiding. Not exactly."

"He disappeared after that wedding debacle."

"Wouldn't you if your private life had become public?"

Her father cleared his throat. "My point is, Brad is interested in the campaign, despite the circumstances of you leaving New York."

After all this time, he still couldn't utter the word fired.

"The misunderstanding was unfortunate, but now it might play into your favor."

"What's changed?"

"Adam Wright. I know our conversations have been few, but you did lead me to believe you two were seeing each other."

"We are." She rubbed the side of her nose. "And I get it. He's a big deal."

"As I said, your project with him was noticed. I ran into Brad and he mentioned that he's starting a new division at his marketing firm. I told him you'd be interested in sending your résumé."

Her eyes went wide. "His company would consider hiring me?"

"It's not a certainty, but I played up your experience and the work you've done so far. He was impressed."

"Over a project I did here in Golden?"

"A project that is getting some buzz." Her father was warming up to the subject. "Brad wants to start a small-town division to reach beyond the usual clients. That's how he came across *Discover Golden!*"

She couldn't help herself and asked, "Do you have any idea what the job entails? Or what the compensation package or perks would be?"

"I imagine the same type of work you're

already doing, just for more small towns. I dug around and found out that he's offering the going rate for an executive position, which this would be, plus additional bonuses once you start to manage the branch. There will be travel, and of course you'd move back to New York so you can lead a team at the office. He said something about a corner office and creative discretion."

Her mind spun. This was everything she'd wanted. All because of Adam.

"I don't know what to say."

"Say that you'll go after the position. Second chances like this don't always happen in a career."

True, but did she want to go back? Just this morning she'd been thinking about future projects for the Chamber. Did she want to leave that behind?

Her father pulled his cell phone from his pocket. "I can get Brad on the phone right now and tell him your résumé is on the way."

A résumé that needed updating.

"Hold on, Dad. I have no idea what my answer is."

Lines stretched across his face. "Carrie, this is a chance of a lifetime. You'd be foolish not to get in the running."

"This is so sudden, Dad. I need to think about it."

"What's to think about?"

"I like my job. I have friends here."

Adam was here. Her father may have thought her only connection to the man was that they'd worked together and were seeing each other, but he didn't know that she'd lost her heart as well. Could she leave Adam before they'd had a chance to see where their relationship would lead them?

"I have commitments."

"Your future is where the big players are, not in this small mountain town, as nice as it seems. And, you never know, if your relationship with Adam grows more serious, you can persuade him to return to Manhattan. Knowing that Adam is back in the city will certainly be a boon."

For whom? Was this why her father was really here?

"I can't speak for Adam, Dad."

She had always known that one day she would have to choose her ultimate path. Not looking into the new opportunity would disappoint her father, whose approval had been so important to her before coming to Golden.

But Golden had accepted her for herself. The merchants were happy with the exposure she'd gotten them, but even if she hadn't done that, they liked her anyway. She didn't have to prove herself to anyone, not like she would under constant pressure if she took this job with Mr. Wheeler.

And there was Adam. She couldn't leave him, could she? Perhaps they'd try a long-distance relationship. Would that work? Or would she let her job consume her as it had before?

She massaged her temples. "Dad, you just dropped this in my lap. Can you give me a little time?"

"Fine. But the clock is ticking, Carrie."

Yes, she felt the reverberations down to her soul.

He rose. "I have a reservation and should check in."

She stood beside him. "Where are you staying?"

"A bed-and-breakfast. Nugget, I think?"

She managed a tepid grin. "Golden has a theme."

"How about we meet for dinner?"

She nodded, her head awhirl.

"I'll call you." He leaned over to kiss her cheek. The sweet action flooded her with memories. She closed her eyes against the onslaught.

"This is good," he said, patting her shoulder.

She opened her eyes, hoping she came off as calm and collected, which he'd expect. He'd laid out the facts and like he always used to tell her, *now is the time to make an informed decision.*

"Thanks, Dad."

He turned on the heel of his highly shined shoes, already on his phone. Just because he'd come to lure her back to New York didn't mean he'd slow down to investigate the town she'd become a part of.

She started back to the office, her stomach in knots.

She needed to see Adam. He'd understand why she wanted to excel at her career, because he'd been that way once upon a time. She'd finally found a guy who didn't crab about her work ethic, but would she lose him if she took her dream job?

"RACHEL, YOU'VE BEEN giving me the runaround. Enough is enough."

After the last conversation with Carrie in his office, Adam had decided to clear the air once and for all with Rachel. He didn't want Carrie to think she wasn't important to him. Rachel needed to understand that they were finished. If Rachel wanted to stay in Golden, that was on her, but Adam needed a clean break.

It seemed like every time he'd tried to track her down, Rachel was either working or hiding out. She'd checked out of the B and B, so he had no clue where she was living. He'd given her plenty of time to realize her scheme wasn't going to work, and now he needed to make sure they were on the same page before the Eureka Games. So he'd shown up at Smitty's Pub, ready to throw down the gauntlet.

Wiping her hands on a towel, Rachel faced him from behind the bar. It was weird seeing her in a chef's jacket and jeans. Where were her stylish outfits?

"I apologize for not being available, but Jamey is just now able to get back to the kitchen."

He rested an elbow against the shiny wood. "Can you spare me five minutes?"

"After all we've been through, only five?"

Most people would think Rachel was flirting, but he read the hesitation in her eyes.

"I'd give you as much time as we need, but I'm afraid you'd slip away. This is important."

Jamey strolled up beside Adam. He sported a bandage, but wasn't wrapped up as heavily as the last time Adam had seen him.

"Hassling my star chef, Adam?"

"No, I just need a few minutes with Rachel."

Jamey nodded her way. "It's okay, Rach. Take all the time you need."

Rach?

She hesitated.

"Go," Jamey said.

As she rounded the bar, he stopped her with a touch on her arm and said, "You can do this."

At her half smile, Adam couldn't help but wonder what was going on here.

It was after the lunch crowd had thinned, and they took a seat in a quiet corner. He pulled out a chair for her and after she plopped down, he pulled out one for himself.

"Rach?"

"I guess it's my nickname." She grinned at him. "I've never had one before."

"I can see that makes you happy."

"It does. Everyone at the restaurant is so nice. I fit right in and that's never happened before."

"Golden is vastly different than the world you grew up in."

"Isn't it? I still can't get used to the whole town knowing who I am and saying hello whenever I walk to work. The regulars call me Rach, too."

"That makes your stay here sound permanent."

"It could be."

"Then stay if it's for the right reasons. What happened between us is in the past, Rachel. We have to move on."

"But you were mad."

Given the chance to think things through, he'd realized what she'd said was true. He had put work first, and if there was time left over, it went to Rachel. She'd accepted that, but she deserved better. Thankfully, she'd seen what her future would entail and had escaped.

So, yeah, he wasn't upset with her any longer. She'd actually done the right thing. And when Carrie walked into his life, he'd been able to fully give himself to her, even if it took a while for him to get in the best headspace.

Rachel picked at her cuticle. "Are you sure? Because I don't entirely forgive myself."

"I see now that we were both swept up in the ride but neither of us was truly in control. I liked the idea of you by my side and you wanted to please your folks. I don't think love was ever the motivating factor."

Tears glistened in her eyes. "I did love you, Adam. In my own way."

"And I loved you, too." He paused. Ran a hand over his chin. "I think it's safe to say we were never *in* love with each other."

A sad expression crossed her face. "You were a good friend."

Yes, he realized that now. They would only ever be friends.

"But not husband material?"

"For me, no."

"Then what's going on?"

She sighed. "I did come to Golden hoping to win you back. Expecting you to bail me out of my predicament. You were right to make it clear we were over, but I was scared. I thought with time, I could wear you down."

"Okay…"

She glanced at Jamey standing behind the bar, drying a glass. "Things changed the day Jamey cut himself in the kitchen. He didn't bat an eye when he told me I was going to fill in for him. He just knew I could do it."

"And you?"

"I was a nervous wreck. But cooking calms me and once I started, there was no going back."

"Is this your dream, to work in a pub?"

"To work in this pub, yes. Jamey gave me

my dream job. He doesn't think I'm going to screw up or lose interest. And look." She lifted her foot, showing off the ugliest pair of pink, nondescript shoes he'd ever seen. "He bought me nonslip shoes to keep me safe in the kitchen. It's the most thoughtful gift anyone has ever given me."

"Ouch."

She laughed.

"Are your parents aware of your decision?"

"No. And to be honest, I'm not ready to face them until I can prove to them that I've made the right decision for my life. They'll think this is just another fad. I need to prove them wrong."

"I have no doubt you will."

Relief crossed her face.

"Do you think we can be friends?" she asked in a tiny voice.

"I'd be disappointed if we weren't."

A full smile broke out on her face. "Thank you. I don't want things to be weird when I see you around town."

He shot a glance at his friend who was still behind the bar, polishing the same glass.

"What's the story with you two?"

A pretty blush covered Rachel's cheeks. "I'm not one hundred percent sure, but since the day he challenged me in the kitchen, we've been inseparable."

"That was...fast."

"We just clicked. Like lightning striking, but in a good way."

"So, one day at a time?"

"That's what we've decided."

The door opened and closed as the last of the lunch guests left.

She sent him a curious grin. "And you? I've noticed you around town with Carrie."

"We're also working on it. I needed to get things settled with you before I could truly commit to her."

"I'm sorry if I caused problems." She wrinkled her nose. "Even your aunt thinks I'm a bother."

"Don't worry about Aunt Bunny."

Rachel leaned forward. "So, you and Carrie?"

"I'm hoping. And this time, I can say it's the real deal."

Rachel beamed at him. "I'm happy for you, Adam. You deserve the love of your life."

And that was exactly what Carrie was. Now he had to let her know it.

"Thanks for letting me get my act together," Rachel said. "I know I was unwelcome at first."

"And thank you for being honest with me. You coming here seemed misguided at first—"

"Hey!"

"—but brave."

"I've never been known to make good choices." She glanced at the bar, her smile genuine when she sent it to Jamey. "Until now."

The door opened, the sun casting light along the scarred floor.

Adam grinned. "If we had glasses with something to drink, I'd say let's toast to new beginnings."

Rachel rose and hauled him up. She threw herself in his arms. Caught off guard, his arms circled her waist to keep himself and Rachel upright. She kissed his cheek and said, "You're the best."

The sound of someone clearing their throat drew them apart. They looked at Jamey, who jerked his head to the door. Carrie stood there, her eyes wide.

"What's going on?"

CHAPTER FOURTEEN

TAKING IN ADAM'S SURPRISE, then moving her gaze to Rachel's grin, Carrie realized she'd walked in on something significant. Just what that was, she didn't know.

"Carrie." Adam took her by the elbow and led her out the door.

Was this going to be like New York all over again? Betrayed by the actions of her coworker and bosses? Or her father, for not loving her for herself? Once they were outside, she stabbed his chest with a finger. "Are you going to tell me that all the time you've spent figuring out things with Rachel was so you two could get back together?"

"No. You've got it all wrong."

She crossed her arms over her chest. To protect her heart? "Then please explain it to me."

His eyebrows drew together. He stepped toward her and she moved back. He sighed.

"Could we at least go to the park where we won't have an audience?"

She glanced around. A few people she knew were headed into Smitty's, questions on their faces.

"I have a feeling the park won't be private enough."

"No, but it's close by and we can take a seat where no one will bother us."

"Fine."

"Fine."

She spun around and before she knew it, they were in the quiet park. Her nerves were frayed, but she needed to hear what Adam had to say. He waited until she dropped down on the bench beside him. And didn't his presence grab hold of her senses so that she wanted to throw caution to the wind and kiss him, no matter his excuses?

Adam didn't waste any time launching into his explanation. "Rachel and I are not together."

"That's not what it looked like to me."

"We finally found closure. She apologized for showing up unannounced and we both agreed we should move on."

"Oh."

Now she felt foolish, but she wouldn't let it show.

"It sure didn't look like that."

"Without subtext, it wouldn't."

"You don't have to be so logical," she said, pouting.

"And you shouldn't jump to conclusions."

She dropped her arms, her hands resting in her lap. "I'm painfully aware."

The air between them was static. Neither said a word for a long moment.

A muscle jumped in Adam's jaw. "We had to get to the point where we could forgive each other before we could move on to any kind of a meaningful relationship with other people. Rachel being here helped me see that the past was just that, the past. I had given it too much power. Now I want to go forward. With you, Carrie."

Could it really be this simple?

He must have read the skepticism on her face.

"I came back to Golden with a chip on my shoulder. I had to admit my mistakes with Rachel so I didn't relive them with you."

She wanted to hope… "So that was a 'we're okay' hug?"

"Yes. Trust me, she's not interested in reuniting with me any longer."

Carrie brushed her hair from her face and gathered it back with both hands as she blew out a breath. "Sorry for overreacting."

"Your timing was pretty stellar."

She smoothed her hands through her hair before lowering them.

"But I kind of like the jealousy thing going on," he said in a teasing tone.

She rolled her eyes.

"Seriously, I only want to be with you, Carrie. Every moment we spend together makes me happy. All because you showed up in my coffee line."

Her frustration slowly ebbed. "You're calling this fate?"

"What name would you give it?"

She thought that over for a moment. Smiled. "Fate."

"Then we're on the same page."

They were, in so many ways. From day one. It had taken both of them time to realize it.

"So, now what?"

He took her hand in his and all her fears melted away. The heat in his eyes as she met his gaze made her toes curl.

"We continue getting to know each other. See where our feelings lead us."

She squeezed his hands. "That's a good plan."

"We're a good team."

"When I'm not jumping to conclusions?" she teased.

"Water under the bridge." He leaned back. "The Eureka Games are right around the corner. After that, we do some serious dating."

All at once, the promise of a new job flashed to the forefront of her mind. The disaster she thought was going on with Adam had been resolved, but this news? There was going to be a different kind of tension between them.

"There's something I need to tell you first."

He frowned. "Not sure I like the tone of your voice."

"My dad is in town."

"You didn't mention he was coming for a visit."

"Because I didn't know. He came to see me. With the hope of a job offer."

Adam went still. "Your dad wants to hire you?"

"No, he was bringing me up to speed about a new agency looking for a marketing executive. They're opening a small-town division inside the firm. The owner saw the *Discover Golden!* campaign and my dad thinks this is my opportunity for a second chance."

Adam stared out over the park. Carrie couldn't read his eyes, so she followed the line of his gaze. Toddlers were in the play area, their parents chatting nearby. The children's laugher filled the air, along with the sound of traffic along Main Street. Would she miss these picture-perfect moments if she moved back to the busy city?

Adam turned to her. "So, what have you decided?"

"That's the thing, I haven't. That's why I wanted to talk to you. I need your input."

"Carrie, ultimately it's your decision."

"Yes, but I have no one to talk to except my dad, who is pushing for me to go back. No one who will consider it from a strictly business point of view. My friends here will just tell me to stay in Golden, no matter the raise and perks that come with the job."

"Maybe I'll tell you the same thing."

She shook her head. "No, you weigh things out. Rationally. Fairly. Like you have with your own family business. I know you'd do the same for me."

"Tell me more about it."

She repeated the terms her father had told her. "I have to send in my résumé, so really, this is all conjecture right now."

"Then it all boils down to what works best for you. Going back to your career in New York or staying in Golden, where you've been doing a great job."

"That simple, huh?"

He shook his head. "Far from it."

His uneasy expression made her chest ache. "Talking about not simple, what has your family decided about selling Deep North?"

"We aren't."

She leaned back. "What happened?"

"I took your advice. After looking at the links you sent me, I approached a couple of the sporting goods chains to see if we could merge or come up with a buyout deal. You're right, I really want to be my own CEO, and purchasing companies in this area makes sense. I'll be traveling to check out the new acquisitions, but my base will be here."

"How did Fletcher react?"

"He wasn't surprised." His lips thinned before saying, "It seems Carter was behind the sudden offer."

"Carter? Why?"

"Just another way of messing with me. Apparently, they met at a business networking conference and Carter mentioned that Deep North might be a good addition to Fletcher's group of stores. Carter got Fletcher thinking about expanding East."

"But what was in it for Carter?"

"A well-recognized name setting up shop in Golden. As we've said, Carter is all about exposure for our town."

"Is Fletcher going to look for another business in this area?"

"No. He's decided to go in another direction. Which means I can focus on my plans."

Wow. Things were moving so fast.

"It's what I do, or used to do. Buy and sell businesses. Only this time I'm going to purchase the stores and run them under one umbrella."

She clasped her hands together. "Your family is okay with this?"

"Yes. They're happy to see me interested in a project again." He grinned. "And they're happy to take my money when I buy them out."

Which meant he wouldn't leave Golden.

"I always thought you'd make a good CEO."

"We'll find out."

She would if she stayed in Golden. But would he be too busy building his empire to have time for her? Before now, he'd had the flexibility to focus on her. When he managed a chain of stores, things might change. She had to factor that into her decision, because if she turned down the job and then became second in Adam's life, she'd resent it.

"So, what does your gut say about taking the job?" Adam asked, turning the conversation back to her.

"I don't know. Ever since you kissed me, my gut hasn't been very dependable."

He sent her a self-satisfied grin.

"But you've given me lots to think about."

Too much, actually.

"Can I say one final thing?"

"Please."

Adam seemed to consider his words. "Golden has a lot to keep you here. Maybe not the energy of the big city, but a different kind of ambience. Life is slower. You can live it instead of watching it streak by. When I was in New York, I missed the quiet moments. And since you've lived here, you see how the town works together, how we unite for a cause. I'm not saying you won't have that if you leave, but your support group will be different. No Serena or Heidi or Lindsey. No Mrs. M. or your other friends. Those are important aspects to consider."

"You certainly don't fight fair."

He shrugged. "How do you think I got my reputation in business?"

He was being honest. So should she.

"I do want to see what happens between us, Adam, but what if I don't say yes to the job? Am I always going to wonder what if?"

"I can't answer that question, but you're

right. No matter what decision you make, you will always wonder."

The breeze lifted a strand of her hair. She had to make a decision, and soon. Usually she had a plan and went with it, but this was more than just a job decision. Would she be happy without Adam in her life every day? Was a career worth it, or was a life with Adam more important?

She shook off her doubts. "Are you busy tonight?"

He cast her a curious glance. "No."

"Would you mind coming to dinner with me and my dad?"

"Social or business?"

"A little of both. Since I told him we're… involved, I'd like you to meet him. Plus, you might have questions I've missed because I'm so surprised by this latest turn of events."

"Sure." His gaze pierced hers. "Do you have to give your dad an answer right now?"

"He'd like me to say I'm getting on a plane to New York with him tomorrow, but no."

"So you need a buffer?"

"Yes."

He leaned over and kissed her. "Then I'll be there."

With relief, she returned his kiss, bitter-sweet under the circumstances. He was making it hard to truly consider the timing in her career.

After a few moments they stood.

"I need to get back to Deep North."

"I'm sure you have a lot going on there."

"What time tonight?"

"I'll text you after we pick a restaurant."

"I'll see you then." He kissed her again, lingering a touch too long, before he strode away, taking a piece of her heart with him. This decision was not going to be easy.

Shaking off that thought, she called her father.

"Hey, Dad. I wanted you to know there will be three for dinner tonight."

"Three?"

"I invited Adam Wright."

A pause. Excitement infused his voice. "You did? I have to admit, I'd like to meet him."

"I'll stop by the B and B and we'll decide where to eat."

"I'll be here."

AT SEVEN, ADAM opened the door to Roma's, a new Italian restaurant in Golden, dressed business casual since he was meeting Carrie's father for the first time. He shouldn't be nervous, but meeting the parent was a huge step. Especially since he'd fallen hard for her.

The idea of her leaving physically hurt, but he would never hold her back. She had her dreams. But before she left, he had to find out if he was part of those dreams. Long-distance relationships were not ideal, but for her, he'd make it work. He could only hope she'd do the same for him.

The hostess led him to the table where Carrie and her father were seated. Mr. Mitchell rose and shook his hand.

"Meeting the famous Adam Wright. I have to say, I didn't expect the pleasure when I came here to visit my daughter."

"Nice to meet you, sir."

"Please, call me Trent."

Adam nodded, then smiled at Carrie, dressed in a dark green lacy dress. "You look nice tonight."

"Thanks." She blushed.

He took a seat and ordered a drink when the server stopped by the table.

"So," Trent said, amusement on his face. "Carrie tells me you've taken to small-town living."

He made it sound like a bad thing.

"I grew up here."

"Nothing wrong with being around the

great outdoors. Other than the times Carrie and I went sailing, I'm afraid I don't leave the city much."

"What do you think of Golden?"

"It's quaint." He smiled at Carrie. "My daughter has spoken highly of it, so I thought I should check it out for myself."

"If you came here more often, Dad, we could sail on Golden Lake. It's really beautiful."

"With you so busy? Don't you have an event coming up?"

"The Eureka Games."

"Will you be able to attend?" Adam asked Trent, watching Carrie's reaction.

"I'm afraid not. I have to get back to work."

Trent took a sip of his drink. Carrie glanced across the room.

Unaware of, or ignoring the tension at the table, Trent asked, "Did Carrie tell you about the job opportunity?"

"She did."

Trent sent Carrie a wry glance. "If you move back, sailing on Golden Lake won't be an issue."

"It was just a thought."

Adam didn't like the hurt reflected in Carrie's eyes.

"Maybe after the games you and I can rent

a boat," he suggested. "I'll let you take the helm."

"Giving up control?" she teased, her face softening at his obvious attempt to put her at ease.

"I know the forest like the back of my hand, but I'm a little fuzzy on boats."

Carrie chuckled. "Somehow I doubt that."

Not to be left out of the conversation, Trent spoke. "So, do you miss Wall Street?"

"No. I keep busy here."

The server came to take their orders.

"Running the family business must be rewarding, but are you open to other opportunities?" Trent asked.

Adam decided he needed to be cautious here. This was Carrie's dad and he wanted the dinner to go well, but he recognized the gleam in the other man's eye.

"It depends."

"If you were presented—"

"Dad, I didn't invite Adam to dinner so you could grill him. I thought you might like to know more about Golden."

Her father looked her way, then back to Adam.

"Of course. Golden." Trent took another drink from his glass. "Are there many ways to increase business here?"

"Thanks to Carrie, yes. Her initiatives have been a real asset to the merchants in town."

"The upcoming event will bring out the community," she said, her eyes sparkling as she talked. "There are so many wonderful people here and if we build up tourist travel in the area, there's no stopping future growth. New businesses. More housing. You name it."

Trent nodded. "Tourist travel. Seems rather seasonal."

"It can be," Adam added, "but the weather here is great, and more and more folks want to escape the city for an adventure. Golden might be considered a small town, but it's growing."

"That's right. Your family owns a sporting goods store?"

"More like outfitting. We sell merchandise, but focus on featuring trips for people who want to try, say, zip-lining or river tubing."

Trent's expression telegraphed that he couldn't understand the allure. "It doesn't bother you to not to be involved in multi-million-dollar deals?"

"Not at all. There are many other ways to be fulfilled in business."

Adam glanced at Carrie, who half smiled at his remark. Had she made her decision yet?

"Then let me tell you about a new company

I'm investing in. There will be good dividends after this startup hits it big. I thought we could—"

"Dad, what are you doing?"

"Letting Adam in on the ground floor of what I see as a very promising investment."

"But he's here tonight to visit, not make deals."

"Why should tonight be any different? It's like the old days, sitting around the table talking numbers, stock prices, you name it."

She glanced at Adam and mouthed, *I'm sorry.*

"Trent, I appreciate you thinking of me, but I'm pretty involved with my own deals at the moment."

"But this is different." He turned to his daughter. "Carrie, we talked about this. The financial world needs a man like Adam. Don't you want him to come with you when you go back to New York?"

Adam gripped the fork in front of him. So she'd made her decision? "Back to New York?"

Carrie's face turned red. "He just threw out the idea of you going back if I did. Not that I'd mind."

Her cell phone rang. She read the screen

and said, "It's Ty. About the games. I need to take this."

She said hello and hurried to the foyer.

Adam turned to Trent. "And what would my role in this new startup be?"

"We need a healthy influx of capital. I thought you could invest, we'd make money and then you would sell the business for top dollar."

"Which means more money."

"I knew you'd see it my way. If we decide to do this deal, you can come back to New York and work at my offices during the transition." Trent chuckled. "When I saw Carrie's campaign and realized she'd sought out Adam Wright, I knew it was time to come down here and speak with you. I never thought coming to this place would mean doing business with you, but your friendship with my daughter has turned out to be the best thing that could happen in this town."

Adam removed the napkin from his lap, slowly folded it and placed it on the table.

"And what about Carrie?"

Trent frowned. "What about her?"

"What if she decides to stay here?"

"How could she? Not when she was so excited by the possibility of a new position. It's as much as a done deal."

It was? Carrie hadn't mentioned that fact.

Adam rose just as Carrie returned to the table. Her eyes were wide, as if she knew her father had overstepped but didn't know to what extent.

"Adam," Trent said. "Is something wrong?"

"I'm afraid we got our signals crossed. I thought perhaps we were going to talk about why Carrie should stay in a town where everyone loves her. I guess you both had other ideas."

Carrie moved closer. "What are you talking about?"

"Moving back to New York. To work with your father."

"What?" She glanced at her dad.

He turned to Trent. "Did you consider my relationship with your daughter a means of access to me?"

Trent frowned, realizing something was off. "My daughter is the one who is stepping back into the corporate world. I assumed tonight's dinner was her introducing us so we could forge a business alliance. Carrie knows how these dinners work."

He glanced at Carrie, her mouth open as if to say…what? That Adam belonged in New York with them?

"I'm sorry, but you were wrong. About me, at least."

He stepped from the table and calmly pushed in his chair, despite the pressure building inside him. He headed to the exit, his chest aching and his steps heavy. He thought Carrie had understood him, that she knew he was going in a different direction than what he'd done on Wall Street. That he didn't want to be used as a business connection. That he didn't want to be used at all.

He'd just entered the restaurant foyer when Carrie called his name.

"Adam! Please, wait."

He stopped. Carrie caught up with him.

"Was it your intention all along to invite me to dinner with your father where he could ambush me? Was asking me for advice on your career just a ploy to get me to invest with your father?"

Her face took on a stunned expression. "Now it's your turn to jump to conclusions. I never suggested my father talk to you about a startup opportunity or moving to New York."

"Yet he felt the freedom to do so."

"My dad lives and breathes business deals. That's all this was, I promise."

"Well, all you've talked about was waiting for your dream job and moving into the corner office. Maybe this was the plan all along? Ask me about your job opportunity in hopes that I'd want to go back to my old life? Please your dad by hoping I'd go into business with him? I won't be used again, Carrie."

She gasped. "You think I'm using you?"

"I'm not sure."

"Not everyone has an ulterior motive, Adam."

"But if I agreed with your father and said I'd go back to New York, you'd be on the first plane out."

"That's not fair."

"No, but it's probably the truth." His whole body hurt when he said, "I think you should pursue the job, Carrie. Go back to New York. It's what you've always wanted."

"But…"

Her voice trailed off as he opened the door and walked into the quiet evening. His ears were ringing and his heart stung. Of all the people in his life, he never thought Carrie would use him, but he shouldn't be surprised. She'd talked him into the ad campaign and helping at the Eureka Games. If he kept giving in, what more would she ask of him? She'd never come right out and said she didn't want the new job, so how could he trust that she hadn't just been waiting it out until a better offer outside of Golden materialized?

Not everyone has ulterior motives.

Her words echoed in his ears. He'd thought Rachel leaving him before the wedding was the worst thing that could happen. But with Carrie?

He stopped, drawing air through his tight throat.

With Carrie, he'd been all in. Heart and soul. And she'd used their relationship so her father could make a deal.

It didn't matter. He couldn't live with that, no matter how much he loved her. No matter how much his heart throbbed with pain. He'd been played by the woman he loved.

STUNNED AND CONFUSED by what had just happened, Carrie made her way back to the table.

"Everything all right?" her father asked as she took her seat. Their meals had been delivered to the table. The zesty aroma should have been mouthwatering, but instead made her stomach turn.

"Dad, what did you say to Adam?"

"I offered him the use of my New York offices to work with me. A man as accomplished as Adam, a man who made a name on Wall Street, doesn't just walk away. He needed an incentive."

Pain lanced her chest. "Me?"

Her father's eyes grew wide. "Why wouldn't he want to follow you?"

Carrie pressed fingers against her eyelids. When she looked at her father again, confusion was written on his face.

"Carrie, be reasonable. If Adam wants a future with you he'll move. You may have to wait a few months, but I'm sure he'll join you in the city. Then he'll need to work. I just thought I'd speed up the process while I was here."

"Dad, I haven't decided if I'm taking the job."

"Don't be ridiculous."

Disappointed Dad was back.

"This chance won't come around again. You have to consider your future. If you want Adam in it, you need to convince him that New York is the place for him to be."

He cut into his chicken parmesan, not looking at her.

"What's in it for you, Dad?"

Her father slowly laid down his utensils as if a man at the end of his patience. "When you called to say we were all having dinner tonight, I reached out to a few contacts to let them know I was meeting Adam. They were excited. You can't imagine the deals I'll be included in now."

Her heart dropped.

"So this had nothing to do with you being proud of me?" She paused, numb. "Wait. When you spoke to Mr. Wheeler, did you throw in the fact that I'd worked with Adam to pave the way for me?"

"I might have mentioned that you worked closely with Adam."

How was this happening?

"Which means all this talk, during my entire life, about working hard and keeping my nose to the grindstone and giving all for the job was just a story?"

He reared back as if offended. "Not at all."

"It sounds like it to me. Coming here to see me had nothing to do with my abilities and everything to do with using me for a deal. You know how it is in business. As you've always told me, we do what we have to do to get ahead."

But not Adam. Never Adam. He had made the hard choice, the right choice for him. And it involved Golden.

She closed her eyes, appalled. Was this how Adam had felt? Destroyed, because he was being used by someone he cared about?

"Carrie, I meant everything I taught you. You put the job first, do the hard work, and if you're lucky, an opportunity falls in your lap."

Wow. She couldn't believe her ears.

"So, what, I'm an asset?"

"You're my daughter and I brought you up understanding the business world."

Carrie took her small purse from the table and stood. "Not the business world, Dad. Your business world."

How could she have been so naive?

"You did teach me. I see now that my hard work really isn't important. Just make a deal by using your daughter and all is well. You know what? That's not good enough for me. I don't want to live in that world."

She walked away, hot tears welling in her eyes. When she got outside, she gulped in the fresh air.

Adam had known all along that he needed time to work things out with his ex to make sure he was truly ready for a serious relationship with Carrie, and over one dinner with her father, it had all blown up. But how could Adam think she'd use him to impress her father, when she understood how badly he'd been hurt in the past? Just as she had when she'd been betrayed at her old job. That's what made Adam's rejection hurt all the more.

As she walked aimlessly, her heart ached. Why had she willfully ignored what her heart already knew? That she was hopelessly in love with Adam. He was the only man for her. And there was no going back from this mess. Not in his eyes.

If she hadn't been so consumed with returning to her old life, she might have admitted her feelings sooner. Or else used her work ethic as an excuse to avoid getting hurt. She was safe by putting the job first. Safe, but alone.

She walked on, finding the streets eerily silent.

She'd learned so much from the wonderful people of Golden. Learned that proving herself to someone didn't equal love.

It had taken a little time, but folks here had welcomed her and her ideas with open arms. They had shown her more respect than any person she'd worked with before. And while she'd tried to convince herself that all along Golden was only a stop on her journey to the corner office, she'd thrown herself into her work and her life here, and she'd reaped the benefits.

Most importantly, she'd discovered that her heart belonged to Adam. In Golden, New York, or anywhere in the world.

So now she had to decide whether she should stay and fight for Adam and a life here or do as her father asked and go back to the familiar business world where she might not have love, but she could be successful.

Tonight had been a disaster. Was there any good choice to be made now? It didn't matter, because she didn't think her heart would stop hurting long enough to decide.

CHAPTER FIFTEEN

ADAM PULLED BACK the bowstring. Aimed. Waited for Ty, astride Juniper, to get into position, then released. The arrow sailed through the air, through the hoop Ty held over his head, and met the target. The crowd cheered at the display.

Ty trotted up to him. "This time hold back when I make the turn at the other end of the arena. I want to be almost on top of you when you shoot."

"You're crazy."

"Nah. I trust you."

Adam shook his head as Ty galloped away. This would be the final trick and he'd be done with the games. He could change out of this itchy period costume and into his regular clothes.

As Ty rounded the arena, charging up the crowd and leading them in a chant, Adam pulled another arrow out of his quiver and took his stance. Ty gave him a salute, picked up speed and headed Adam's way. He waited,

waited, then let the arrow fly. Claps and shouting filled the air while Ty stood in the saddle and took a bow. Rolling his eyes, Adam gathered his belongings and headed to the stable.

Saturday had dawned sunny, not a cloud in the sky. All day, he'd only seen Carrie at a distance. Not that he was avoiding her, but she was busy and he'd pitched in where needed. Then the afternoon wore on to the second to last act of the day, the archery show. He'd escaped just before to a quiet spot to collect his thoughts and get a clear mind, then walked to the arena for his event. Now that it was over, he had plenty of time to think.

The day after the dinner with Carrie and her father, Adam had driven to the neighboring state to talk to the owners of the stores he hoped to buy. In the ensuing days, he'd hammered out equitable deals to build his small empire. It felt like old times.

He'd returned home the day before the Eureka Games and gotten in one final practice with Ty. His parents had decided to hit the road after the end-of-summer bash, now that Deep North was all Adam's to control. Colin was happy for him, agreeing to stay as an adventure guide. And while Adam should have been excited at the idea of plunging into a new venture after being in a rut for so long, his heart was holding back.

He'd made a lot of money over the course of his life through investments and high-profile positions. He could secure his future with this new business model. But what was it worth without Carrie?

She'd called and texted him multiple times while he was out of town, but he hadn't answered. Hadn't been sure what he'd say, so he'd erred on the side of caution. The thing was, with distance and time to calm down, he'd realized that Carrie would never have hurt him intentionally. That she was just as surprised by her father's offer as he was. He wanted to go to her as soon as he got back to town, but knew she'd be preoccupied with the last-minute details for the games.

Now he had to wait it out until he could catch her later.

The silence was broken when three women entered the stable.

"Adam, you should go cheer Carrie on. The saddle competition is coming up next."

Mrs. M., Alveda and Aunt Bunny, dressed in jeans, fringe vests and cowboy hats, stood together. Good to see some folks were getting in the spirit of the day.

Thankfully, no one commented specifically on his black mood, especially Carter, who had stayed out of his path all day.

"She'll be fine without me there. I need to take care of the horses."

"But she has news," Mrs. M. insisted, tipping back her black hat.

"Yes, she took the job—"

Mrs. M. poked Bunny's arm. "It's her news to tell, not yours."

"Sorry."

So she'd decided to pursue the New York job. Today was probably her last hurrah before she left town. More reason not to watch the saddle competition.

But what if he could convince her not to leave? Was he too late to make a pitch for her heart?

"Please, Adam," Mrs. M. pleaded. "She's put so much work into making the final summer event a smash. You saw the people in the stands. The number far exceeded what we expected. And everyone's been having a great time."

He had to admit, Carrie had reached enough people to make the Eureka Games an annual rousing event. The crowd from town and people from the whole mountain area had come out in force. Too bad she wouldn't be around to see it grow.

The women stared him down.

He stared back. "You're not leaving until I say yes, are you?"

Mrs. M. drew closer. "I heard you two had a…misunderstanding."

That was the problem. He hadn't told Carrie he loved her. He hadn't wanted to influence her decision about the position in New York. He regretted that now.

Did she love him? They'd talked about job opportunities and businesses, but not the most important topic, love.

If he wanted to win her back, he'd need to make sure his negotiating skills were at their finest. He didn't like losing, and he'd hate it if Carrie walked away because he'd been too stubborn to try.

If he wanted to keep Carrie in his life, he'd need the last of the guardrails around his heart to come down.

"You ladies seem convinced that Carrie and I have a shot."

The three women nodded.

"Have you talked to Carrie?"

They exchanged glances, then Mrs. M. said, "Have we ever steered you wrong, young man?"

"No ma'am, not that I can recall."

His aunt moved beside Mrs. M. and placed

a hand on his arm. "Then don't doubt us now, Adam."

"You want a happy future in Golden?" Alveda asked as she joined the others.

"I do."

"Then what're you waiting for? Tell Carrie how you feel. Whatever is coming between you two can be fixed, trust us. We've been around and seen a few things."

"You're playing the age card?"

Alveda grinned. "Is it working?"

He didn't have the heart to tell them he was ready to lay it all on the line, good or bad.

"I think you ladies may be on to something."

Aunt Bunny beamed at her friends. "See, I told you he could be reasonable."

He chuckled. "Should I be offended?"

"Not if you do the right thing."

If it wasn't too late.

So far Carrie hadn't run into Adam. The saddle contest was about to begin and she couldn't pick him out in the crowd. He'd shown up for his part of the archery act, but he'd disappeared after the show. Was he still on the farm?

She'd tried contacting him several times after the horrible night with her father, but he hadn't answered. Hadn't been at Deep North, either, when she stopped by there.

Not that she blamed him for refusing to see her. He thought she'd set him up. Far from the truth, but his silence spoke volumes. He believed the worst and she was afraid nothing she said would change his mind.

She'd hated the pity on Adam's mother's face when Carrie showed up at Deep North looking for him. She had great news she wanted to share with Adam, but the difficult man was making it next to impossible.

"Carrie?"

She shook her head and turned to her friend. "Did you say something?"

Serena laughed. "It's time."

"Right."

The contestants were lined up and raring to go. Mostly women, plus one brave man grinning ear to ear. By the look of it, they all had their heads in the game. Carrie, not so much.

"Hey," Serena said. "You talked me into this. The least you can do is act excited."

Carrie pasted a smile on her face, smoothing her damp palms over her jeans.

"Get in the spirit. This'll be fun," Serena told her, rolling her shoulders before the race started.

Liz stood ten feet in front of them at the

sawhorses. She held a microphone, talking to the audience.

"As you can see, folks, the saddles are on the ground next to our competitors. Some very nicely decorated."

Carrie glanced three people down the row to Rachel, wearing pink boots and a Western outfit, beaming at her festive saddle decked out with paper flowers and streamers.

"We've strapped large bags filled with sand under each sawhorse to simulate the width of a horse. On the count of three, each of you contestants will carry your equipment to the sawhorse and correctly mount it."

Cheers came from the crowd.

"Before we begin, a shout-out to everyone who donated toward this event. My family thanks you."

The crowd clapped and hollered.

"Okay, down to business. Ladies and gentleman, three, two, one." Liz blew a whistle.

Inhaling, Carrie tossed a saddle pad over one arm, then lifted the Western-style saddle, making sure to hold the cinch securely. She was comfortable with the weight of the saddle since she'd been taking horseback riding lessons, and kept a steady pace to the sawhorse. She went through the steps, digging her boots into the ground for balance and trying to ignore the cheering going on behind her. In her peripheral vision, she saw one contestant drop the cinch, stopping to awkwardly retrieve it. Another woman slowed when the padding drifted down to trip her. Serena was five steps behind, laughing as her fiancé, Logan, cheered her on. Carrie picked up her pace, determined to win.

"Show-off!" Serena yelled.

Once at the sawhorse, Carrie lowered the saddle to the ground and placed the padding on top. Then she hefted the saddle, wincing when the stirrup clunked her knee. She fed the cinch into the buckle on one side of the saddle, brought it underneath the bag and then made sure the cinch was snug before tightening it like a belt.

She'd just made sure the saddle was balanced when Liz blew the whistle again. Everyone stopped. Carrie's gaze fell on Rachel, who was doing a victory dance. Rachel, with her cute decorations, had beaten Carrie?

"Well, that was fun," Serena said, her breathing labored.

Carrie pointed out the obvious. "I lost."

"Sorry," Serena offered with a grin. "At least we lost together."

Then, just when Carrie didn't think she could be any more flabbergasted, Jamey ran in Rachel's direction. With a whoop, she jumped into his open arms, her cowboy boots swinging in the air as he twirled her around.

She glanced at Serena. "What's going on?"

"Apparently they're a couple."

Carrie's mouth fell open.

Serena laughed. "You didn't know?"

"How would I? I'm not besties with Rachel."

"Logan told me," Serena said. "We may not have won the contest, but I had some juicy gossip before you, my friend."

Carrie didn't care about the gossip. She still didn't see Adam. If he missed this event, would he also miss seeing her once she got on a horse to close the show? She hoped not. She'd taken the lessons because he'd encouraged her. She wanted him to know what that meant to her.

Carrie congratulated Rachel, then made her way to the stable to find Tri already saddled for her. She donned her helmet and took the reins from one of the many helpers, mounted the block and slid a foot in the stirrup to swing up and onto the horse. She patted Tri's neck and crooned, "Good horse. Let's go make a statement."

She trotted to the arena, her heart pounding. Ty was already on his horse and waiting for her, while Liz rode over on her chestnut horse from the paddock. Ty held up his hands to quiet the crowd.

Carter stood beside them, holding the microphone.

"Well, folks, we've come to the end of the Eureka Games. The town of Golden sure knows how to end the summer in a spectacular way."

The crowd clapped and cheered.

From the corner of her eye, Carrie saw Adam exit the stable. Her heart froze, then started thumping again.

He leaned against the building, arms crossed over his broad chest. How had she missed him in there?

Her horse danced about and Carrie spoke softly to soothe him. When she straightened in the saddle, she saw Adam gazing directly at her, surprise etched on his face.

So far her plan was working.

"We have one final announcement," Carter said, shooting Carrie a grin. "We'd like to thank Carrie Mitchell, manager of business development and marketing at the Chamber of Commerce, for spearheading this event. We hope her recent promotion to director means she'll be here for many years, and events to come!"

Carrie kept her gaze pinned on Adam. He didn't move an inch at the news, but she could tell by the way his fingers tapped his crossed arms that he hadn't seen this coming. Good. She'd needed a big gesture to show him what he, and by extension, Golden, meant to her.

Ty leaned over. "I think the crowd wants you to say a word or two."

She gripped the reins tighter as the horse grew antsy. Carter handed her the mic.

"Thanks, everyone. I'm thrilled that I'll be continuing to work to make Golden the go-to vacation spot. I appreciate everyone coming out today and I hope we see each other again in the future." She glanced at Adam, her nerves jangling. "Seems you're stuck with me, folks."

A slow grin spread over his lips, revealing his dimples. Her heart leaped.

"Thanks to all of you for coming," she addressed the crowd. "We'll see you next time."

As the crowd dispersed, she led Tri to Adam. He stared up at her, shaking his head. In disbelief or anger?

She dismounted, then met Adam's gaze. One of the volunteers came over to take her helmet and lead Tri away.

Nervous, she swept her arms out at her

sides. "Surprise! I've been taking riding lessons."

Confusion crossed Adam's face. "Why?"

"Because you said I could do it and I believed you."

He paused for a long drawn-out moment, then yanked her to him and kissed her. Hard. She grabbed hold of his shirt with her fists and returned the kiss, needing the feel of him when she was so convinced she'd lost him forever.

When the kiss ended, he rested his forehead against hers. "I'm sorry."

She swallowed hard. "So am I."

"So you're not leaving Golden?"

"Nope."

Relief crossed his dear face. "Then *you're* stuck with *me* now."

She ran her hands up to his shoulders. "So you aren't upset at me?" She cleared the lump of emotion in her throat. "You don't believe I set out to use you?"

"Not once I really thought about it. If I'd been more logical, I would have realized immediately that using people isn't how you operate. You keep at it until you come up with a solution. You don't put it off on others. And you've worked tirelessly for the town merchants. I was too surprised by the conversation to put it all together at the time. And once I did, I realized that I'd hurt you, too."

"Thank you," she whispered.

His throat moved as he swallowed. "I thought you were leaving Golden for good."

Her voice quivered. "We really have to stop jumping to conclusions."

He stared at her for a long moment, a wealth of emotions running across his face.

"I'm in love with you, Carrie, and I'm not going to apologize for it."

Her legs went wobbly again. She held on to him and smiled. "Then it's a good thing I'm staying in Golden, because I love you, too."

"Are you sure? If you want to go to New York, we'll make it work."

"No." She shook her head. "After dinner the other night, I thought I'd lost you, and if that was the case, I wasn't sure how, or if, I could win you back." She blinked against the heat welling in her eyes. "Then I was offered Shelia's job and the answer fell into my lap."

"How did that happen?"

"Shelia had been absent from the office a lot, but I was truly surprised when she announced her retirement. I guess her husband's health isn't good and they want to spend more quality time together." She ran a finger over his beloved face. "You know what the funny thing is?"

"Tell me."

"I didn't have to think twice. When Carter asked if I'd fill the position, I said yes immediately. No debating the issue. No pros and cons. It meant staying here in Golden. How could I say no?"

"You couldn't."

He kissed her as if they had all the time in the world.

When she could breathe again, she smiled at him. "Turns out I don't need to go back to New York to be happy. Everything I need is right here in Golden."

"That sounds like a promise."

"One I mean to keep."

Adam linked his hand in hers. With no regrets, Carrie walked into a future with the man she loved.

A WEEK LATER the Golden Matchmakers Club held its usual meeting outside Sit A Spell Coffee Shop, the location where their latest love story had begun. The cool morning held little humidity, and the leaves bristled in the breeze. A perfect morning for a recap.

"Another fine match," Gayle Ann announced.

Bunny cupped her coffee cup in the palms

of her hands. "It was touch-and-go there at the end."

"You can't fight true love," Wanda Sue said, then sighed.

"I must say, this never gets old," Harry added, smiling at Gayle Ann. She grinned his way, happy that they'd told their friends about their relationship.

"We had us a two for one," Alveda said, with a feisty grin as she patted herself on the shoulder. "Not only did Carrie and Adam realize they were meant for each other, but Rachel and Jamey are going gangbusters as well."

"That girl can cook," Bunny acknowledged. "Even if she's not one of my favorite people."

"You can't hold a grudge forever, Bunny, especially since Adam forgave her."

"I know." Her acquiescence didn't sound sincere. "I'll admit, it was wonderful to see Adam and his gang of friends at Smitty's last night, all celebrating the end of the summer."

"I heard the group was celebrating Adam's new business venture," Wanda Sue said.

"That, too. He's keeping Deep North and is going to expand locally. Start his own chain. Even though Carrie has the Chamber job, she's going to help him with marketing. It's perfect for both of them."

"I heard about that," Gayle Ann said. "Also, something about giving her a corner office?"

"Don't know about all that," Bunny continued, "but Carrie and Adam have teamed up to start a new initiative for the merchants in town. Adam will be on the advisory board while Carrie creates new programs."

"I always thought Adam had a knack for helping out the business owners in town," Harry said. "I'm glad to see him continue with that."

"Their first project is Brea," Bunny told them. "She wants to expand the snack bar at Deep North, but Adam thinks she should have a larger vision. She's nervous but excited that Adam is supporting her."

"At any rate, Carrie and Adam are happy." Gayle Ann opened the club notebook. "Now we move on."

"Any suggestions?" Wanda Sue asked.

"How about one of the Lane sisters?" Alveda suggested.

"I'm not sure. We'd have to do more research," Gayle Ann said.

"What about the Harper brother?" Harry asked.

Gayle Ann thought it over. "I'm not sure he's ready to settle down."

The group grew silent as they each racked their brains for their newest match.

A few moments later, Brando Pendergrass sidled up the sidewalk. Instead of going into the coffee shop, he stopped at their table. "Mind if I join y'all?"

"Sure," Alveda welcomed him. "Grab a chair."

He glanced around, then took a chair from the empty table nearby and brought it over.

Gayle Ann noticed the serious expression on the man's weathered face. "Something on your mind, Brando?"

He glanced at Alveda. "She always this direct?"

Alveda shrugged. "You get used to it."

He turned his gaze to Gayle Ann. "In that case, yes. I need your help."

"And what help would that be?" she asked sweetly.

Clearing his throat, he blurted, "Heard you folks have a way of guiding couples together."

The group exchanged amused glances.

"We've been known to assist a match or two," Gayle Ann admitted.

"Then I want to hire you."

"We're not a business."

"Then I'd like to ask you to consider helping me."

"Are you looking for love?" Alveda asked, eyes wide.

"Me?" He snorted. "No. I'm concerned about my son, Ty. I'd like him to find a fine woman and settle down. Since we're in Golden for good now, he needs to plant some roots." He ran a work-roughened hand over the back of his neck. "Kept my family on the road for far too long. Ty's worked real hard and now I need to make sure he has a family of his own."

Gayle Ann met the gaze of each member, receiving a nod from each one in return.

"Well, Brando, this is your lucky day. We can help."

"Good." He nodded, his expression relieved. "Good."

Harry glanced at Gayle Ann. "You know, it wouldn't hurt to have another male perspective in the group."

Gayle Ann grinned. "Why, Harry, that's an excellent point." She turned to the newcomer. "Brando, any interest in being part of the Golden Matchmakers Club?"

His brow wrinkled. "Do I have to do anything special?"

"Be sneaky," Alveda said.

Bunny winked. "Interfere in your son's life."

"Pretend you have no idea when we have a plan," Wanda Sue added.

After a blank expression, a slow grin crossed his rugged face. "Sounds like a group I can get behind."

"Then you're in." Gayle Ann held up her coffee cup. "Here's to another match."

The group raised their cups.

"Let's get started. I think I have just the woman in mind for Ty."

* * * * *

For more Golden, Georgia, romances from acclaimed author Tara Randel and Harlequin Heartwarming, visit www.Harlequin.com today!

Get 4 FREE REWARDS!

We'll send you 2 FREE Books <u>plus</u> 2 FREE Mystery Gifts.

FREE
Value Over
$20

Both the **Harlequin® Special Edition** and **Harlequin® Heartwarming™** series feature compelling novels filled with stories of love and strength where the bonds of friendship, family and community unite.

YES! Please send me 2 FREE novels from the Harlequin Special Edition or Harlequin Heartwarming series and my 2 FREE gifts (gifts are worth about $10 retail). After receiving them, if I don't wish to receive any more books, I can return the shipping statement marked "cancel." If I don't cancel, I will receive 6 brand-new Harlequin Special Edition books every month and be billed just $5.24 each in the U.S. or $5.99 each in Canada, a savings of at least 13% off the cover price or 4 brand-new Harlequin Heartwarming Larger-Print books every month and be billed just $5.99 each in the U.S. or $6.49 each in Canada, a savings of at least 20% off the cover price. It's quite a bargain! Shipping and handling is just 50¢ per book in the U.S. and $1.25 per book in Canada.* I understand that accepting the 2 free books and gifts places me under no obligation to buy anything. I can always return a shipment and cancel at any time by calling the number below. The free books and gifts are mine to keep no matter what I decide.

Choose one: ☐ **Harlequin Special Edition** ☐ **Harlequin Heartwarming**
　　　　　　　(235/335 HDN GRCQ) 　　　**Larger-Print**
　　　　　　　　　　　　　　　　　　　　　(161/361 HDN GRC3)

Name (please print)

Address　　　　　　　　　　　　　　　　　　　　　　　　　　　　　　　　Apt. #

City　　　　　　　　　　　　State/Province　　　　　　　　　　　Zip/Postal Code

Email: Please check this box ☐ if you would like to receive newsletters and promotional emails from Harlequin Enterprises ULC and its affiliates. You can unsubscribe anytime.

Mail to the **Harlequin Reader Service:**
IN U.S.A.: P.O. Box 1341, Buffalo, NY 14240-8531
IN CANADA: P.O. Box 603, Fort Erie, Ontario L2A 5X3

Want to try 2 free books from another series! Call 1-800-873-8635 or visit www.ReaderService.com.

*Terms and prices subject to change without notice. Prices do not include sales taxes, which will be charged (if applicable) based on your state or country of residence. Canadian residents will be charged applicable taxes. Offer not valid in Quebec. This offer is limited to one order per household. Books received may not be as shown. Not valid for current subscribers to the Harlequin Special Edition or Harlequin Heartwarming series. All orders subject to approval. Credit or debit balances in a customer's account(s) may be offset by any other outstanding balance owed by or to the customer. Please allow 4 to 6 weeks for delivery. Offer available while quantities last.

Your Privacy—Your information is being collected by Harlequin Enterprises ULC, operating as Harlequin Reader Service. For a complete summary of the information we collect, how we use this information and to whom it is disclosed, please visit our privacy notice located at corporate.harlequin.com/privacy-notice. From time to time we may also exchange your personal information with reputable third parties. If you wish to opt out of this sharing of your personal information, please visit readerservice.com/consumerschoice or call 1-800-873-8635. **Notice to California Residents**—Under California law, you have specific rights to control and access your data. For more information on these rights and how to exercise them, visit corporate.harlequin.com/california-privacy.

HSEHW22R2

COUNTRY LEGACY COLLECTION

19 FREE BOOKS IN ALL!

Cowboys, adventure and romance await you in this new collection! Enjoy superb reading all year long with books by bestselling authors like Diana Palmer, Sasha Summers and Marie Ferrarella!

Get 4 FREE REWARDS!

We'll send you 2 FREE Books plus 2 FREE Mystery Gifts.

FREE
Value Over
$20

Both the **Romance** and **Suspense** collections feature compelling novels written by many of today's bestselling authors.

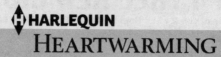
#439 WYOMING RODEO RESCUE
The Blackwells of Eagle Springs • by Carol Ross

Equestrian Summer Davies's life is on the verge of scandal, so an invitation to host a rodeo comes at the perfect time. But with event organizer Levi Blackwell, opposites do *not* attract! Has she traded one problem for another?

#440 THE FIREFIGHTER'S CHRISTMAS PROMISE
Smoky Mountain First Responders • by Tanya Agler

Coach Becks Porter is devastated when a fire destroys her soccer complex, and firefighter Carlos Ramirez, her ex, is injured. Their past is complicated, but an unexpected misfortune might lead to a most fortunate reunion this holiday season.

#441 SNOWBOUND WITH THE RANCHER
Truly Texas • by Kit Hawthorne

Rancher Dirk Hager doesn't have time for Christmas...or his new neighbor, city girl Macy Reinalda. But when they're trapped in a snowstorm, Dirk warms up to Macy and decides he might just have time for his neighbor after all...

#442 HIS DAUGHTER'S MISTLETOE MOM
Little Lake Roseley • by Elizabeth Mowers

Dylan Metzger moved home with his young daughter to renovate a historic dance hall in time for Christmas. When Caroline Waterson reconnects with a business proposal he can't refuse, Dylan finds himself making allowances—in his business and his heart.